Trip

SUSANNE O'LEARY

The Road Trip

Bookouture

Published by Bookouture in 2018

An imprint of StoryFire Ltd.

Carmelite House
50 Victoria Embankment
London EC4Y 0DZ

www.bookouture.com

ISBN: 978-1-78681-507-1
eBook ISBN: 978-1-78681-506-4

For my sister Lena
The best travel companion on a mad road trip!

Chapter One

Who would have believed it? It had to be a crazy dream. Maddy checked her phone again. The text message still showed on the screen: *We won! 200k each! Will call as soon as I've collected the cheques. Love and hugs, Leanne.*

Dazed, Maddy put the phone on the table and stared blindly out of the window at the small garden where a blackbird was pecking at the grass for worms that might have appeared after the recent shower. The washing hung limply on the line, her pink silk blouse beside Tom's Y-fronts and his white shirt she had promised to iron for the golf-club dinner that night. She would normally have run out to rescue them, but her phone had pinged and then there was that text.

She checked it again, her heart thumping. It was true, it really was. Unbelievable. They had won all that money. It had been a bit of a joke, getting together with the whole teaching staff in a syndicate for the week's Lotto draw. Twenty people paying a couple of cents each. And now they had won – she calculated – four million euros altogether. Which meant two hundred thousand euros each. Holy shit.

Her first instinct was not to tell anyone. Not even Tom. A slow smile spread all over Maddy's face. *My money*, she thought. *All mine to spend on things I've never been able to afford. My ticket to independence.*

Not that she didn't already have her own money, but this was different. This was a sudden windfall that had dropped from the sky like finding the crock o' gold at the end of the rainbow or some fairy godmother granting a wish.

Her knees shaking, Maddy got up from the table and started to tidy up after breakfast, still trying to take in what had just happened. It was insane. One minute she was doing sums in her head to see if she could afford a year's membership at the fancy new gym, the next she had a small fortune dumped in her lap. She looked out at the garden again, her gaze drifting past shrubs and trees to the distant view of Dublin bay and a ship just leaving Dun Laoghaire harbour on its way to England. She watched the ship sail away and suddenly longed to get away from the house, the chores and her job, even Tom and his golfing dinners and Y-fronts. Twenty-two years of marriage, two children and a nice house in the suburbs. Was that really all life had to offer? Not that she was ungrateful; she was just… unfulfilled. She laughed at herself as that thought hit her. Unfulfilled. It seemed like a buzzword middle-aged women used as an excuse to misbehave. But now she could 'fulfil' herself and do something daring for a change.

Maddy dumped the dishes in the sink and lifted her hair off her neck. Maybe she should start by dying her hair? Go blonde? Or maybe dye it red? Light-brown hair was so ordinary. Her whole look was pretty ordinary, come to think of it. It was high time to get a makeover. She would book a day at that spa in Enniskerry, the one she had drooled over on Facebook during her coffee break. A full day of massage, facials, of relaxing and swimming in the beautiful pool overlooking the mountains. Not affordable then. Now, it suddenly was. Tom would be at the golf club dinner and wouldn't be home until late. The kids were away doing their own thing: Sophie having a year off in Australia, Darren working in a hotel in Killarney. She was free to do what she liked at the weekend – had been for a long time. She had never done anything with that freedom apart from joining the garden club and the odd lunch with a friend in town. But now, with all this money…

Maddy jumped as the phone rang.

It was a breathless Leanne. 'Hi. I just talked to the gang. We've all decided to keep the win quiet, so there'll be no photo shoot with us all holding a giant cheque or anything like that. Nobody seems to want to shout it to the rooftops. Do you?'

'Hell, no. I don't want anyone to know.'

'Neither do I.' Leanne giggled. 'You're not even going to tell Tom?'

'Especially not him.'

'Why not?' Leanne paused. 'Oh, yeah, I get it. It's all yours, and you don't want to share or have anyone advising you on the sensible thing to do, like investing in shares or something. Or a new set of golf clubs.'

'You got it.'

'Same here. My mam would have kittens if she knew. God, I think I just want to grab the money and run away from home. Should have done that years ago, I know. Still living with my mother at thirty-two. How pathetic, right?

'Uh, well…' Maddy couldn't think of anything to say. She didn't know Leanne that well. They met when Leanne took the job as substitute science teacher after the Christmas holidays and immediately clicked, despite the age difference. Maddy enjoyed her company enormously. With her boyish platinum-blonde hair, multiple piercings and unconventional way of dressing, Leanne was whacky and fun, someone who said things Maddy had never dared. Leanne wasn't afraid of voicing her opinion, even if it meant raised eyebrows in the staff room. It seemed odd that she was still living with her mother at her age, but it was a difficult situation. Leanne, being an only child, had stayed with her mother after her parents' divorce, and as the years went by, had found it harder and harder to leave, mostly because of the now-impossible price of property. Her mother was the needy type, using emotional blackmail to keep her daughter at home. Leanne's oddball look might have been a kind of passive resistance. But Maddy had felt herself drawn to Leanne because of her looks and courage. And because of her true-blue nature.

'I'm going to move out,' Leanne stated. 'This money means I can. Mam will have a fit, but I'll deal with it.'

'Good for you.'

'She'll probably fake a heart attack or something. Anyway, I just called to ask you to send your bank details to Liam, so he can transfer the money. It'll be in your account by early next week.'

After she had hung up, Maddy stared out of the window again, the ship now a tiny speck on the horizon. A thought began to form in her mind. Just the grain of an idea, but it seemed like the beginning of something new: an adventure of sorts. Scary, risky and completely mad. Or was it? Could she go back to a time when she was young and confident and not the disillusioned, drab woman she had become? The memories of her Paris love story had never quite faded. Maddy's heartbeat quickened as she thought of all the money she had won. Maybe this was a chance to finally confront her past.

Chapter Two

They met at the Trinity Ball. At the time, Maddy was nursing a broken heart and still grieving for her mother who had died just after her return from France. The ball had provided a welcome distraction. She hadn't gone there to find a man, just to have fun with a group of friends and forget her sorrows for a while. But there he was, asking her to dance, making her laugh and looking at her with his velvety brown eyes. His name was Tom Quinn, and he had just finished a PhD in Economics. He was popular and fun and she soon found herself swept away by his good looks and sweet, caring nature. He looked so handsome in his tux that first night, but even better naked in the early-morning light in her bedsitter the next morning.

When they started dating, everyone wondered how an extraordinarily glamorous man like Tom could fall for a wholesome girl like Maddy. Little did they know how much Tom adored her. He loved her freckly face, blue eyes and lovely smile. But nobody would believe it. Maddy was the lucky girl who had won the prize. Her pregnancy bump under the wedding dress seven months later proved the point: Tom was doing the honourable thing.

*

No one expected the marriage to last once the baby was born. But instead of a divorce, they had another baby. Once they settled into married bliss with their two children, a house in the suburbs, a car and pensionable jobs, the gossip stopped. Happy families weren't interesting. And they were truly happy, Maddy reflected, both focused on the family and each other. Their life was as idyllic as it could have been, given the stress of full-time jobs and stretching the budget to cover mortgage, school fees, sports equipment and all the extras. The fact that Tom was not what you'd call a hands-on dad was the only fly in the otherwise perfect ointment. You couldn't have everything, Maddy thought.

The years went by, and after the children left home, Maddy and Tom found themselves with more time than they had ever had before. *Our golden years*, Maddy thought. *Now we can do all the things we dreamed of.* She started making plans for weekends away, date nights at the cinema and fancy restaurants. But none of that ever happened.

Instead, Tom took up golf.

'More good news,' Leanne announced as they were having coffee in the staff room with a piece of the chocolate cake someone had brought in to celebrate.

Maddy's spoon stopped halfway to her mouth. 'What? Come on, tell me.'

'They've extended my contract.'

'You mean here? At the school?'

Leanne nodded. 'Yup. You're looking at the new science teacher of St Concepta's secondary school for girls. Well, for another year, anyway. The teacher I'm subbing for has asked for extended leave of absence.'

'Great.' Maddy stuffed the cake into her mouth. 'I'm glad you can stay on for another year.'

'Thanks. Never thought they would ask me to. Not the way I look. But they said that I bridge the generation gap or some crap like that. They've never seen teenage girls ditch their phones and actually pay attention before.'

'That's amazing. How did you do it?'

Leanne shrugged. 'Not that hard. I just said I'd teach them how to make their own cosmetics. Creams with only natural ingredients. I told them it would save them millions. They went for it big time, so we might even start a new line and announce it at The Young Scientists' exhibition next year. I'm quite impressed with them myself. We might even start selling the stuff online after that. Then the girls will earn some money for all their hard work.'

'Don't these things have to be tested on humans before they're sold?'

'They're testing them on each other, so that's covered. If you count teenagers as human, of course.'

Maddy laughed. 'Brilliant. And now you have a job with a good salary for another year.'

Leanne nodded and smiled. 'Yes. So then I really can move out of my mother's house. I've been looking at flats for sale ever since we got the news about the win. With the money, I can put a down payment, and then my salary will pay for the mortgage. My life is finally beginning to take a turn for the better. Don't know how I'll break this to my mam, though. That'll be the worst hurdle. But I'll think of something. What about you? Have you told your husband yet?'

'I told you I wouldn't. Yet. I will share some of it with him, eventually. But I want to do something for me first, something I've been wanting to do for a long time.' She hesitated for a moment, but then the words came out in a torrent she couldn't stop. 'Winning that money is like a breath of fresh air to me, a chance to do something utterly silly and irresponsible. I've earned it, you know, after all these years of running the house and family single-handed ever since the kids were tiny,' she said in a low voice, making sure nobody heard.

'He wasn't there for you and the kids?' Leanne asked, looking appalled. 'One of those male chauvinists, huh?'

'Not quite, but yeah, something like that. Oh yes, he was there from time to time, wanting a medal for occasionally giving the baby a bottle or taking us out for Sunday lunch. But he never went to parents' meetings or school concerts, never helped with housework except for putting out the rubbish bins on Monday nights. I was supposed to put up with it because he had a career – I just had a job.'

'Jesus,' Leanne said. 'What a gobshite.'

'Maybe I exaggerated a little,' Maddy said, regretting her outburst. 'We were happy too, of course. Most of the time. And as a family it all worked.'

'Because of you.'

Maddy shrugged. 'Oh, whatever. I'm sure I'm not alone. Lots of women do the same. Men haven't changed since the middle ages, you know. But now maybe you understand why I feel I have the right to a little me-time.'

'Of course,' Leanne said. 'It's payback. Maybe it will teach him not to take you for granted. So what do you want to do?'

Maddy didn't quite know how to explain what she wanted to do. Would Leanne understand?

'I want to go and find someone,' she finally said. 'Someone who lives abroad.'

Leanne's eyes lit up. 'Really? Where?'

'Somewhere in Paris. I have to do a little research before I go.'

'Sounds mysterious. But hey, you know what? I had this idea last night. I want to buy a car and go on a road trip during the summer holidays. Only two weeks to go and we'll have nearly three months of free time. Why don't you come with me, and then we can drive around and see if we can find – who exactly?'

Maddy glanced around the staff room. 'I can't talk about it right now. What did you say? A car? But I thought you said you wanted to buy a flat.'

'Yeah, yeah, I know,' Leanne said impatiently. 'But I'm only putting down fifty thousand as a down payment for the flat. With my new salary, I'll be able to afford the mortgage. The rest will go towards a car and…' She winked. 'A bit of fun, like a trip somewhere. Could be France, now that you mention it. I've never been to Paris. I want to see it before I get too old to walk around it.'

'You're only thirty-two,' Maddy protested. 'If that's what you call old, what about me?'

Leanne laughed and poked Maddy in the side with her elbow. 'Ah, sure, you're only a young thing, me darlin'.'

'I'm forty-four and you're a nutcase.'

'I know. But whatever. You only live once.' Leanne piled some cake into her mouth. 'Great cake,' she muttered through her mouthful.

Maddy sipped from her mug and shuddered. 'But awful coffee, as usual. Maybe we should invest in an espresso machine now that we're all so rich?'

Leanne laughed and leant closer. 'You think any of them will want to give up even a cent of their win? Look around, will ya. They're all whispering, and trying not to smile so that nobody will find out they're suddenly loaded.'

Maddy looked around the room at the rest of the staff talking in muted tones, darting a glance at the door every time it opened. As they had all taken part in the syndicate, it was odd that they seemed to distrust each other. It was as if there was a silent pact not to talk about their sudden good fortune, except for coy smiles here and there and the odd comment about the great holidays some of them were planning.

Leanne stood up. 'Hey, everybody, what are you all going to do with the wad of cash you got?'

'What are you going to do?' Liam, the maths teacher, asked.

'Well,' Leanne started. 'I have a few plans. I'm just discussing it with Maddy. We're going on a road trip, once we've bought ourselves some wheels.'

'A road trip?' Liam asked. 'To where?'

'Anywhere,' Maddy said with a wink. 'We're buying a campervan and we'll be driving east. To the Czech Republic and on through the Carpathian Mountains. You want to come with us?'

Liam squirmed. 'Er, no. Thanks all the same. I'm going to take the kids to Disney World.'

Leanne giggled. 'The Carpathian Mountains?' she whispered to Maddy when Liam had turned back to the others.

'Yeah, well, France seemed so clichéd somehow,' Maddy whispered back. 'But what about our real plan? You still want to go to France?'

Leanne nodded. 'Of course. No time to lose. The holidays start in two weeks. I'll go and look at cars this afternoon. You could find some hotels on the Internet and draw up a plan for our trip. Book the ferry when I have the car. I want to take that fancy French one that goes from Cork to Brittany.'

'That one takes too long,' Maddy protested. 'Why not take the Rosslare to Pembroke ferry? Then we can do a little touring in England and see the sights. I've always wanted to see Oxford and all those ancient buildings. Then we'll get the ferry to Holland from Harwich. Amsterdam's lovely this time of year, I've heard.'

Leanne's eyes lit up. 'God, yes, you're right. Why not do a grand tour while we're at it? Will you look it all up and draw up a travel plan?'

Maddy nodded, her heart beating faster. It wasn't just talk any more. They were going to do it.

'Four-star hotels at least,' Leanne ordered. 'With pools and Jacuzzis. No skimping. I want to live it up.'

'Gotcha. But… how are you going to break this to your mother?'

Leanne frowned. 'I'm not sure yet. It'll take a bit of fibbing. But I'll think of something to placate her. What about you? What are you going to tell Tom?'

Maddy's mouth suddenly went dry. Tom wouldn't like this one bit. Never mind that he played golf for most of the day during their holidays, he liked to have Maddy there with dinner ready when he arrived home after a long day at the golf course. He hated an empty house.

'I don't know,' she said, her voice shaking slightly. 'Maybe just that we're going away together for a beach holiday somewhere in Ireland? A girls-away thing for a week or two?'

'You big chicken. But okay. I get it. Tell him what he'll believe. The truth might cause him to kick up a fuss. Anything for peace and a quick getaway, right?'

'Exactly.'

'Men, huh? I'm not married, but I've been around enough of 'em to know how tricky they can be.'

'Especially middle-aged men.' Maddy sighed. Tom would be turning fifty at the end of the summer. He was already being moody about it. She steeled herself to stick to her guns when she told him she would be going away for a break. He would throw a hissy fit and then sulk for bit. But a good dinner and some wine usually helped. He would get over it. She hoped.

The lamb cutlets were ready for the grill pan, the potatoes roasting in the oven and the table on the patio laid for two with a bottle of Chianti opened to air, when the front door slammed. Maddy wiped her hands on a towel, her heart racing. He was home. Would it be better to wait until after dinner to tell him? She nodded. Yes. Better to hear the news on a full stomach after a few glasses of wine. It was a beautiful evening, too. He would be in a good mood. She suddenly felt annoyed with herself. Here she was humouring him again. Not because she was afraid of him, but she hated confrontation. Maybe she should just go ahead and tell him as soon as he came home?

Her thoughts were interrupted by Tom marching into the kitchen, beaming at her. 'Hi, sweetheart. Grand evening, isn't it?' He threw his jacket on a chair and loosened his tie. 'Dinner nearly ready?'

'I just have to grill the cutlets. We're eating on the patio as it's so warm. I opened a bottle of wine.'

'Perfect.' He walked to her side and put his arm around her. 'I have something to tell you.'

'Me too,' Maddy said, her stomach doing a little flip. 'But maybe we can wait until after dinner?'

He squeezed her waist. 'Good idea. I'll have a quick shower and then we can eat.' He started to walk to the door but stopped halfway there. 'Just one thing. I have to tell you or I'll burst. You have no idea what just happened.'

Maddy stared at him, taken aback by the unusual excitement in his voice. 'What? You've been promoted?'

'No. Much better. I got a text message an hour ago.'

'About what?' Maddy asked, confused by the look of triumph in his eyes.

He pointed at his chest. 'You're looking at the new captain of St George's golf club.'

'Really?' Maddy suppressed an urge to roll her eyes. Standing there, all aglow with his great news, he looked suddenly like someone she didn't know any more. She felt like throwing the frying pan at him, just to make him react. Instead, faking delight, she rushed to his side and planted a kiss on his cheek. 'That's amazing! Congratulations. Was that what you were going to tell me?'

His eyes sobered. 'No. There's something else. Nothing bad, don't worry. Just something I want to—' He stopped. 'Not now.

Dinner first.' He walked swiftly out of the kitchen, leaving Maddy staring at the door swinging shut, wondering what the 'something else' could be. He had looked slightly guilty just then. Maddy had a sinking feeling he was planning something he knew she'd hate.

Despite the nice weather and the beautiful view of the harbour and the Irish Sea, the birdsong and scent of early summer roses, dinner turned into overcooked lamb chops served on a bed of awkward conversation and stiff smiles. They both poked at their food, darting glances at each other, taking gulps of wine as if trying to get the courage to speak. *Is this what we have become?* Maddy wondered. *We're just going through the motions. Is there really any point in staying together?* She put her knife and fork down with a loud clatter. 'I can't eat until I tell you.'

Tom pushed his plate away. 'Me neither. But please, let me go first.'

'Okay.'

He reached across the table and took her hand. 'Don't say anything until I've finished.'

Maddy nodded. 'Fine. I'm listening.'

He let go of her hand. 'It's about the summer. I've made some plans. Before you start jumping to conclusions, please believe there's nothing strange going on.'

Maddy raised an eyebrow.

'With some other woman, I mean. This is about me and my golf game.'

Maddy smirked. 'What else would it be?' she muttered, despite her promise to let him finish. 'Okay, sorry,' she said when Tom glared at her.

He cleared his throat. 'As I said, it's about golf and the club. I'm taking part in a tournament in Lahinch in County Clare at the beginning of next month. I'll be away two weeks.' He held up a hand. 'I know what you're going to say. A tournament doesn't take up two weeks. But I want to go there to practice. It's a links course and quite a challenging one. I want to do my best for our club, and I... well, it's a huge deal for me. I came to golf quite late, so I have to catch up. I've hired an instructor, who'll help me improve my game and get me a better handicap.' He shot Maddy a pleading look. 'Please say you understand.'

Maddy stared at him. 'Do you expect me to come with you?'

Tom's face reddened. 'Uh, no. It'll be boring for you, and in any case—'

'—you'll be playing eight hours a day when you're not in the bar replaying every single hole with the rest of the members?' Maddy tried her best to sound hurt while she did a happy dance in her head. He was going away and thought she would mind. What a stroke of luck. Hello holiday in France without the guilt or lying about anything. 'You'll be eating, sleeping and playing that fecking game the whole bloody time you're there, right?' she snapped, just to add to his discomfort.

'Well, uh, I suppose.'

'I see.'

'You don't mind?'

She looked at him squarely. 'Mind? Of course I mind. I thought we'd go somewhere nice now that we don't have to worry about what the kids want to do.' She looked at his still-handsome face and wondered what had happened to the spark she used to feel, that dart of joy every time he touched her. She hadn't felt that for a long time. 'It makes me sad,' she mumbled, not thinking about golf. 'I mean, it looks to me that you don't want to spend any time with me any more.'

'Maddy, I'm sorry, but I need to do this,' he said, his voice tense. 'I'll be fifty soon. I want to live a little while I still can. We have the rest of our lives to grow old together.'

'If we stay together,' she said under her breath, picking up a cutlet from her plate and nibbling on it.

'What?'

She shrugged. 'Nothing. Forget I said it. Let's settle this and then enjoy the evening. It's okay. You can go and do the golf tournament. But I might not be here when you get back.'

'What do you mean?'

'I'm planning a little getaway of my own, you see.'

Tom looked shocked. 'You are? Where are you going?'

'I've been asked by a friend to go on a trip. She's planning to drive around Europe for a bit, visit the sites and so on. We haven't booked anything yet. I didn't know how you'd feel about it. But now I can aim for the same time you'll be away and maybe a little longer.' She looked coolly at Tom. 'That okay with you?'

He stared at her. 'Who's the friend you're going with?'

'Leanne. The science teacher at my school.'

'The one with the platinum-blonde hair and a ring in her nose?'

'That's her.'

'Didn't think she'd be the kind of woman you'd hang out with.'

Maddy shrugged. 'I hang out with a lot of people you don't know about. Leanne's great. You'd like her if you bothered to get to know her.'

'I doubt it. How are you going to pay for all of this? From our joint account?'

'How are you paying for yours?' Maddy shot back.

Tom squirmed. 'Well, we had a little bit of a surplus, so…'

Maddy lifted one eyebrow. 'You spent that on the golf outing?' She shrugged. 'Fine. No problem. I got a bit of a windfall recently. I won some money on… a scratch card. Not much, a couple of thousand.' The lie didn't seem so bad now that Tom had spent their money on his own trip. If he knew about the two hundred thousand euros sitting in her private savings account, he would have found things to spend that on, which would mostly be related to golf.

'A scratch card?' he said, looking at her pityingly. 'I never do those things.'

'Well, I did and I won something.'

'Good for you.'

She studied Tom. 'You don't look delighted about my plans.'

'I'm just a bit surprised. I thought maybe you'd be here doing the gardening and going to the gym while I was away.'

'And greet you with open arms and a big welcome-home dinner when you came back?'

'Well, maybe.' He played with the fringe of the tablecloth.

'This isn't the nineteen fifties, you know. We've somehow managed to break off the shackles.'

Maddy's scathing tone made no impression on Tom. 'Yeah, sure. Women have it all these days. Maybe that's why we need our golf games and weekends away.'

'I think we both need a break. From each other.' Maddy grabbed the bottle and poured herself a generous amount. 'Cheers, darling,' she said and downed the wine in one go before she got up from the table. 'You'll clean up, won't you? I have to go and book the trip.'

Without waiting for a reply, she walked away from the table, the view and the beautiful evening to call Leanne and make plans. She felt a dart of excitement. Now that there was a sour taste to her marriage, she longed to get away. To leave all of it behind and get some answers to questions that had been haunting her for over twenty years.

Chapter Three

Maddy stood at the window waiting for Leanne to arrive in her new car. She looked down the street and spotted a shiny, red Mercedes convertible with the top down and Leanne at the wheel, her short hair fluttering in the breeze.

Maddy opened the door and ran down the steps to greet her when the car came to a screeching halt at the gate. 'Wow! Look at that car. I had no idea you were planning to buy a sports car. I thought you'd buy something a little cheaper. Like a Toyota Yaris.'

Leanne peered at Maddy over her Ray-Bans. 'A Toyota Yaris? How old do you think I am? Sixty-five?'

'No, but you must have blown all you had on this thing.'

Leanne laughed. 'Relax, it's a rental.'

'What?'

'I leased this thing for two months. It cost me just a couple of grand. I wanted to know what it felt like to drive around in a sports car with a bit of bling. I'll get something small and sensible when we get back.'

'Oh.' Maddy ran her hand over the shiny red bonnet. 'She's a beauty, I give you that. Not very practical, but gorgeous. Four seats and a tiny boot. Where will I put my bag?'

'In the tiny boot. I told you there wouldn't be much room for luggage. I hope you didn't pack a huge suitcase.'

'No. Just a small one. It'll fit with some space to spare.'

'Great. Go get it, then. We have no time to lose. Love the hair, by the way.'

'Thanks.' Maddy ran her hand over the glossy short bob that had been created at a very expensive hair salon in Dawson Street. It had cost an eye-watering amount, but she had paid with a smile, thinking of the large sum that had just been transferred to her account. She just had to get used to having a lot of money, and spending it all on herself.

'Come on, go get your bag. I want to call into Kildare on the way.'

'Kildare?' Maddy asked. 'What do you want to do in Kildare? That would be a big detour. It's not in our plan.'

'Not Kildare, as in the county. Kildare Village. The fashion outlet place. I want to pick up a few accessories and some shoes. We can cut across from there and go through Blessington to pick up the motorway to Waterford. So we need to get going,' Leanne urged. 'Is your bag packed? And have you said a fond farewell to hubby?'

'Yes to both of those questions.' Maddy started up the steps to the front door. 'I'll just get my bag.'

Leanne nodded. 'We need to be in Rosslare by late afternoon, so we can't afford to hang around.'

'I know.' Maddy ran back into the house and up the stairs to the bedroom. The small suitcase lay on her bed, all packed and ready to go. She picked it up along with her tote and jacket and stopped for a moment. There was something she needed to take with her. She searched in the drawer of her bedside table until her fingers found the edge of the small black-and-white photo, worn ragged by time and touch. She slipped it into her handbag, picked up her luggage and closed the door again, bumping into Tom as he came up the stairs.

'All set to go?' he asked.

'Yup. Leanne's waiting in the car.'

He took her suitcase. 'I'll put this in for you.'

'Thanks.'

Maddy followed Tom down the stairs and out the door, where he stopped dead so suddenly she bumped into him.

'What's that?' he demanded, pointing a shaking finger at the car.

'It's Leanne in her car.'

'You're going to drive around France – in that?'

'Yes,' Maddy chortled. 'Isn't it great?'

'How… I mean, is that her car? Or did she—?'

'—steal it?' Maddy filled in, her voice bubbling with laughter. 'Relax. It's perfectly legal. She leased it.'

'Oh.' Tom continued down the front steps to the car. 'Hi,' he said to Leanne and held out his hand. 'I'm Tom. I think we've met before.'

Leanne shook Tom's hand. 'Yeah, I remember you. How are you?'

'Fine.' Tom hesitated. 'So, where do I put this?'

'In the boot. It's open.'

'Okay.' Tom went to the back of the car and opened the boot. 'Not much room here.'

'It's not exactly a family car,' Leanne remarked. 'But we don't need much, do we, Mads?'

'Certainly not.' Maddy couldn't help laughing at Tom's face and Leanne's attempt at trying to shock him.

Tom stuffed the suitcase into the boot beside Leanne's purple bag and slammed it shut. 'There you go.' He pecked at Maddy's cheek. 'We've already said our goodbyes, but have a good time and don't forget to keep in touch.'

'I will,' Maddy said. 'I mean, like we said, just in an emergency. You have a good time, too. Go kill 'em in Lahinch.'

'I'll do my best. Try not to spend all that money in one go.' Tom stood back while Maddy got into the car. She waved, he waved back. Maddy gave him a stiff smile. Tom smiled back politely as if she was someone he'd just met.

'Bye, sweetheart,' Maddy said to soften her stiffness. 'I'll keep in touch, promise.'

He nodded. 'Good.'

'Okay, let's hit the road.' Leanne started up the engine and took off so fast, Maddy was thrown against the seat.

'Do you have to break the speed limit?' she shouted, her hands on her hair. 'And do we have to have the top down on the motorway? It'll be a little breezy, don't you think?'

Leanne slowed down and came to a stop. 'Yeah, you're right. I'll put the roof back on.' She pressed a button on the dashboard and the roof came up behind them and gently settled over them with a soft whirr. 'Can't have the wind ruffle that new hairdo.'

'Thanks,' Maddy made herself comfortable in the bucket seat and pushed her tote bag under her legs.

Leanne pulled out into the street. 'What was that about not spending all your money? What did you tell him?'

'I said I won two thousand on a scratch card.'

Leanne howled with laughter. 'Priceless. You're a hoot, my dear.'

'What did you say to your mam?'

'I just said I was going on a packet to Ibiza. She didn't see the car. I parked it up the street.'

'Chicken.'

Leanne shrugged. 'Yeah, I know. But I needed to get away quickly without having to call an ambulance. It was bad enough with her telling me I'd be sorry if she dropped dead while I was away. She's perfectly healthy, by the way. Walks for an hour every day and digs and plants in the garden, not to mention DIY in the house. And she works full-time in the pharmacy. Her doctor says she has perfectly normal blood pressure and will outlive us all, which she finds very annoying. But her mother died at ninety-eight, so she has a long way to go yet with those genes.'

'How old is she?' Maddy asked.

'Fifty-seven.'

'That's not old at all.'

Leanne sighed. 'I know. She just gets out the violins to make me feel guilty and to make me stay and look after her. But, shite, I need to get free and live a little.'

'You certainly do,' Maddy said with feeling. She looked at Leanne and noticed she had removed the ring from her nose and some of the many earrings. The blue lipstick and weird eye make-up were also gone, replaced by dark red lips and eyeliner with a tiny flick. Still flamboyant, but now more toned down, Leanne was a lot more feminine and very attractive in an edgy way. 'You've changed your... look. Or something,' she added.

Leanne laughed. 'I've lost the grunge, you mean. All that was just a stunt to annoy my mam. Thought she might get sick of looking at me and throw me out. But no such luck. Got a bit sick of it meself, to be honest. Took a good look in the mirror and realised I needed a makeover. Can't drive through Paris in this kind of car looking like a freak. So I lost the excessive piercings and toned down the whole thing. Whaddya think?'

'Looks great. You still have the hair, but it suits you.'

Leanne shot an amused look at Maddy. 'The hair? It's real, you know. Comes out of my head like this.'

Maddy stared at Leanne's white-blonde hair while the car came to a stop at a red light. 'It's really your own colour?'

'Yup. A legacy from my dad. He's Norwegian, you see. But my dark eyes are my mum's, and the black eyebrows are by Maybelline.'

'Oh,' Maddy said while she digested this. 'Norwegian?'

'Yes. Weird, huh? I mean how many Norwegians do you know?'

'Not many,' Maddy had to admit. 'None, actually. I know a few Swedes, a Dane and a Finnish couple who live in our street but no Norwegians.'

'They keep themselves to themselves.'

'That explains it. So where's your dad now? Back in Norway?

'No. He's living in the south of France. I think,' she added.

'Don't you know?'

'Not really, no. But I think I have a lead.'

Maddy stared at Leanne. 'You're going to have to explain this.'

The lights turned green and the car rolled forward. Leanne changed gears. 'I will when we're on the ferry. Tonight. Let's get glammed up in Kildare first, though. I want to put together a capsule wardrobe.'

'A what?'

'You know, the kind of wardrobe where you only have a few key pieces that all match. Don't you follow the fashion blogs?'

'Not really,' Maddy had to admit. 'Where are you going to put it? The boot's full.'

Leanne shrugged. 'I'll just have to wear it, won't I?'

Kildare Village was packed with shoppers and there was a long line of cars crawling in through the entrance, where personnel in yellow vests were directing the vehicles into empty spaces. Leanne finally found a spot near the bus stop.

'Come on,' she urged after she had switched off the engine. 'Let's hit the shops.'

Maddy opened the door and uncurled her legs, wondering how she would manage the long drive ahead in such a low-slung car. 'This car was made for midgets,' she complained. 'I'll be crippled by the time we get to Paris.'

Leanne slammed her door shut. 'You'll get used to it. Being rich takes a little adjusting.'

'And a lot of pain,' Maddy muttered.

They headed to the shopping area, which was built like a village with Tudor-style houses and pedestrian streets lined with tubs of flowers. Piped music wafted through the walkways and outdoor cafés, and the whole place exuded glamour and money. Touted as the home of luxury fashion, Kildare Village was the go-to shopping centre for the well-dressed woman with an eye for a bargain. The clothes, shoes and handbags weren't cheap but a little less of a rip-off than in the shops in town.

'I've never shopped here, have you?' Maddy asked as they made their way along the pavement. 'Not really my thing.'

Leanne glanced at Maddy's navy trousers, H&M white shirt and Nike trainers. 'You have to get out of that nun's gear and upgrade a bit. Except for the runners. They're great.'

'Nun's gear?' Maddy protested. 'It's what I'd call a classic look. Very Katherine Hepburn, you know.'

'Well, she's been dead for quite some time,' Leanne quipped. 'But you do your own thing. I'm going to turn into a woman at last.' She gestured at her torn jeans and black Doc Martens. 'These'll have to go.'

'Where?'

'I'll chuck 'em in a bin. I want to get a whole new look. A bit edgy but more sophisticated or something.'

Maddy checked her watch. 'You have about an hour and a half to do that. Then we have to get back on the road.'

Leanne stopped on the pavement in front of the big ornate gates that led to the shopping village. 'Okay. But I think we should split up. I don't want you breathing down my neck if you don't approve of my fashion choices.'

'Great idea,' Maddy agreed. 'I've actually never shopped on my own. I either have Tom who'll say, "I'll meet you back at the car in twenty minutes" or my daughter moaning that she wants to buy something with a huge price tag. It's never been about me... always about them.'

Leanne laughed and patted Maddy's shoulder. 'Now it's totally about you. Spend, spend, spend, darlin'.' She walked off, leaving Maddy in the middle of the pavement, wondering where to start.

Suddenly dizzy at the thought of the large sum of money in the bank, Maddy didn't quite know where to go at first. In a daze, she looked up the paved avenue between the elegant shop fronts and saw a sign that said Gerard Darel. This was a label she knew from window shopping in Dublin. French, chic and expensive. But here it would be a little less so. She saw a floral dress in the window she immediately liked the look of and stepped into the shop with great determination. Time to ditch the boring, old, classic look. Katherine Hepburn was dead, but Madonna was still alive and kicking.

It proved to be the right choice of shop. Half an hour later, Maddy walked out of Gerard Darel with a bag into which the shop assistant had placed the dress in the window, a pair of white trousers, two silk T-shirts and a wide suede belt with a gold buckle. She was wearing the rest of her purchases: a grey pencil skirt and a navy linen jacket over a pink shirt. The boring navy trousers and white shirt were put in a separate bag in case she needed them 'for housework or gardening', the elegant shop assistant suggested, as if such activities were something to be avoided at all costs. The woman nodded approval of the Nike trainers. 'We're all wearing them these days,' she said and lifted her foot to show a pair of pink Adidas. 'They go with everything. But maybe you could get something a little funkier?'

Maddy immediately went to the shoe shop around the corner and ditched the white Nikes for a pair of Gucci sneakers with silver stars. It had a price tag of 400 euros, which she paid without blinking. Three times her weekly household shopping bill. What fun it was to be rich!

After a brief visit to the elegant ladies' room, Maddy bumped into Leanne on her way into the Victoria's Secret store. They both did a double-take and burst out laughing.

'Look at you,' Leanne exclaimed. 'The epitome of the wealthy-but-classy woman. It takes years off you, too.'

Maddy wiggled her hips. 'Thank you, love. And you…' She paused while she took in Leanne's new look: the purple Armani jeans, grey silk bomber jacket and embroidered sneakers. 'Incredible. Hot rock-chick or something.'

'That was kinda what I was aiming for. And now I want to get a few undies and then I'm finished. How about you?'

'Yeah. I want to get something special in here. Nothing like pretty underwear. Makes you look more confident even if no one can see it.'

Leanne frowned. 'No one? Well, that would be a hell of a waste. I'm going to make bloody sure *someone* sees it… when I meet the right guy, I mean.'

'Let's hope you do. I might show it off to Tom when I get home. If he's good,' Maddy added.'

Leanne winked. 'Or bad.'

'I hope that'll happen, too,' Maddy said wistfully, thinking of their sex life that had gone from hot to lukewarm in just a few years. *Ever since fecking golf,* she thought bitterly, wondering if it could also have been her fault. Looking at her reflection in the mirror of the changing room, she felt a jolt of pride at her still-firm breasts and shapely hips. Her tummy could do with a bit of work, and there were stretch marks on her hips. But her thighs were toned and her arms rippled with muscles, not from hours in the gym, but housework and gardening.

'Not bad,' she said to herself, pulling in her stomach. The ivory silk of the knickers felt sensual but she could only try on the bra, which pushed her breasts into round orbs. The teddy she tried on next made her look and feel sexy in way she had never experienced before. The black set edged with lace was even better, and she decided to buy everything she had picked out… even the French knickers and the suspender belt. There would be no golf in Tom's head when next she stripped in front of him. In fact, she thought, it would be the first time she'd ever stripped for him. They had never done anything even slightly kinky, she suddenly realised. Why not? Was it because of the way Tom had been brought up, by very strict, conservative Catholics? Or because his mother was an overbearing control freak?

Her own upbringing had been fairly liberal, even though the nuns in her boarding school had preached purity and keeping your virginity until you got married, which her mother had labelled as prissy and old-fashioned. Maddy mentally blessed her fun, eccentric mother who had died of cancer far too young. *You'd love this, Mum,* she thought with a fleeting pang of sadness. She gathered up the piles of silk and wire and paid for her purchases, adding, on a whim, a red bikini as Leanne emerged from the changing rooms.

'I see you're stocking up.'

'It was all so delicious I decided to get it all.'

'Good idea. Me too.'

'Never had so much fun,' Maddy said as they walked out of the shop. 'I usually get my underwear in Marks and Sparks. Not too exciting, I suppose.' On an impulse, she kissed Leanne on the cheek. 'Thank you for doing this with me.'

'Buying underwear?'

'No, the whole trip. It's such fun. I'm so looking forward to—' She suddenly froze and stared ahead in shock.

'Forward to what?' Leanne asked. 'What's the matter? You've turned pale green.'

'Oh my God,' Maddy mumbled, staring at two women coming out of the Jaeger shop. 'It's them.'

'Them who?' Leanne followed Maddy's gaze. 'Oh, you mean the grey-haired woman with the tight perm and sensible shoes?'

'Yes,' Maddy hissed. 'And the younger one with the stringy black hair, tight nylon dress and six-inch heels. That's my mother-in-law and her daughter from hell.' She tried to slide behind Leanne but it was too late.

The younger woman waved at Maddy. 'Hello, Maddy. Long time no see, eh?'

'Yes,' Maddy mumbled as they came closer. 'Quite a long time. Hi there.' She gestured at Leanne. 'This is my friend, Leanne. And this, Leanne, is my sister-in-law, Jacinta, and my mother-in-law—'

'Fidelma Quinn,' the older woman said and held out her hand.

'Howerya?' Leanne shook the older woman's hand.

'Nice to meet you, Leanne. I suppose you're here on a little shopping spree?'

'Yes.' Leanne waved her Victoria's Secret bag in the air. 'We got a few little goodies to liven up our sex lives. You should go in and take a look. Great bargains. Especially the crotchless panties and cut-out bras.' She winked. 'Kinky but fun, dontcha think?'

Fidelma stiffened, her face red. 'I don't know what you mean. I don't wear that sort of thing. Not for ladies, is it?'

'Ah sure, who's gonna know?' Leanne smirked. 'Only you know you're wearing them things, but it gives you a glow and sass in your step.'

'Uh, okay,' Jacinta said, pulling her mother away. 'I don't think that's for us. We got some nice things in the Jaeger shop. It's for a wedding.' Her eyes focused on Maddy. 'My cousin, Greta, is getting married. Did you know?'

'At last,' Maddy said without thinking. 'I mean she is over fifty after all. But better late than never, eh?' She paused. 'Well, nice to see you,' she breezed on. 'But we have to get going.'

'Yeah, we have a long drive ahead,' Leanne said. 'We're on our way to the continent, you know. A girls' getting-away-from-it-all kinda thing. Especially men.'

Fidelma looked confused. 'The continent of – Europe?'

'What other continent is there?' Leanne asked. 'But we have to go now. Nice to meet ya, ladies.' She pulled at Maddy. 'Come on. The ferry will leave without us.'

'Oh, but—' Jacinta said. 'I thought we might have coffee? I haven't seen you for such a long time, and I wanted to hear all about Tom and what he's up to these days.'

Fidelma nodded. 'Me too. He hasn't called me for at least a week.'

'Not much to tell,' Maddy said. 'He's been elected captain of the golf club, and now he's off on this golf break in Lahinch. Some kind of tournament, I believe.'

'Captain?' Fidelma said, beaming. 'Of the golf club? Well, that *is* very big news, isn't it? Why didn't he tell me?'

'Why don't you call him?' Maddy suggested. 'I'm sure he'll be delighted to hear from you.'

'Lahinch?' Jacinta said with a suspicious look in her eyes. 'Tom went on his own? And you're off to the continent with—' She paused. 'Are you and Tom having… problems?'

Maddy laughed. 'Of course not. We're just giving each other a bit of space, that's all.'

'Really?' Jacinta lifted an eyebrow. 'But if you're off on your own, why do you need—' She gestured at the Victoria's Secret bag.

Maddy grinned, enjoying Jacinta's confusion. 'You never know when it might come in handy.' She smiled and waggled her fingers at the two women. 'Say hi to Tom. Tell him I'll be in touch when I get to Paris.' Without waiting for a reply, she took Leanne by the arm and they ran across the parking lot to the car, where they collapsed against the bonnet, laughing.

'Oh God, the look on that old biddy's face when she spotted the underwear bag,' Leanne giggled. 'Priceless.' She stopped laughing. 'Shit, I'm sorry. That's your mum-in-law, isn't it?'

Maddy smiled. 'Yeah. Old biddy is a good description. A bigoted, judgemental old biddy. Poor Tom finds it hard to cope with her. He left home at eighteen just to get away from her. His dad had already left by that stage. But Tom is at least polite and pretends to like her just to keep the peace. She hates me with a passion, of course. So does that bitch, Jacinta.'

'But where did your hubby get those hunky looks? Not from either of them as far as I could tell.'

'He's the spit of his dad. A very good-looking man. And so nice. God knows why he married Fidelma. Maybe because she seemed motherly? But I can tell you as a mother-in-law, she's interfering and nosey at the best of times. We had a huge falling-out years ago when I had to tell her to stop getting involved. And for once Tom took my side against her. She had to back off but it's been very chilly between us since then.'

'I didn't think such women existed in real life. I mean, you read about old battle-axes but I thought it was some kind of joke.' Leanne went to the boot and opened it. 'Here, let's stuff our loot in here and get going. No more stops until we get to Rosslare, even for a pee, okay?'

'What about lunch?' Maddy asked, suddenly hungry.

Leanne tossed her a paper bag. 'I bought two sandwiches and some water in that posh French bread shop. We'll eat on the way.'

'Okay.' Maddy nodded and got into the passenger seat, wondering if this trip was a good idea. Leanne was showing a bossy side she had never noticed before. Ah, well, it would be easy to bail out once she'd had enough. So far, it was fun. No need to jump ship just yet. *Onwards and upwards*, she said to herself, quoting her granny.

They reached the ferry port at Rosslare late that afternoon after a drive through some stunning countryside with rolling green hills, winding rivers and lush pastures where cattle grazed in bucolic bliss. Maddy was nearly sorry they weren't going to stay in Ireland and drive across the south and do the Wild Atlantic Way, until she spotted the big white ship docked at the quayside. The line of cars crawling forward into the ship's hold, the passengers already on the upper deck, the flags snapping in the breeze and the blue sky meeting the sea in the distance gave Maddy a dart of excitement. This was it. It was real. She was going on a long trip that might, if not change, at least widen her life and her horizons. The thought gave her a pleasant buzz.

Chapter Four

Settled in the comfortable club seat in the upper salon, with the Irish Sea stretching before her and seagulls circling the ship, Maddy sipped wine and turned on her Kindle. She had loaded it with a number of books she had always wanted to read but never got around to. This was a good opportunity to start. They had four hours ahead of them before the ship docked at Pembroke on the Welsh coast, where they had booked two rooms in a four-star country-house hotel.

'Just to have a rest before we set off across England,' Leanne said.

Maddy agreed. There was no reason to rush their trip. 'A drive in the dark on winding Welsh roads is not my cup of tea,' she stated.

'It's a spa hotel, too, so we can get a bit of pampering while we're at it,' Leanne said from the adjoining chair as if reading Maddy's thoughts. She brought the foaming glass of Carlsberg to her lips. 'Mm, this is the life, eh?'

Maddy put her head against the headrest and sighed. 'Oh yes, it is.'

'Do you want to drive tomorrow?'

'I thought you'd never ask.'

'It's an amazing machine. Wait till you get the feel of it.'

Maddy sipped some more wine. 'Looking forward to that.' She turned to Leanne. 'But you said you'd tell me. About your dad, I mean.'

Leanne put her beer on the little table in front of her, running her finger around the rim of the glass. 'Yeah. My dad.'

'If it's too painful…'

'No. It's not that. It's just…' Leanne looked thoughtfully at Maddy. 'He disappeared, you see. After the divorce.'

Maddy nodded. 'So I gathered from the little you've told me. You haven't seen him since then? How old were you?'

'Twelve. But my mam couldn't face telling her family. She told them he'd died.'

'What?!' Maddy exclaimed. 'She said he was dead?'

'That's right. She's from a small village in County Clare. Very old-fashioned and Catholic. She couldn't admit the marriage had failed and her husband had done a bunk. So she pretended he died while on a visit to his hometown in Norway and was buried there. She acted the grieving widow as if she was going for an Oscar. Had it been a movie, she'd have won it, hands down.'

Maddy couldn't help letting out a little giggle. 'Sorry, but the way you tell it is both funny and sad.'

'I know.' Leanne sighed. 'The tragicomedy that is my life.'

'Have you always known the real story?'

'Yes. But I promised Mam not to tell the family back in Clare. Not easy for a twelve-year-old to keep pretending her dad was dead. But I kind of believed it because I never saw him again. He might as well have been dead.'

'That's appalling. How hard it must have been for you. Do you know where he went when he left?'

'Not until quite recently. I stumbled on something a few months ago. As you know, I've always loved fragrances and soaps and stuff like that. That's why I did that cosmetics project with my science class. While we did the research into how to make our own skin care products, I looked up a few companies in the South of France. Thought I'd see if I could learn how to make perfume. I found this guy, looking just like my dad in the photographs we had at home. And I just knew it was him, even though he's changed his name.'

'So you want to go and look him up?' Maddy turned her Kindle off. This was far more exciting than any book.

'Yes. I want to make him tell me why he abandoned me like that. Why he never called or sent me as much as a postcard. How can anyone do that?'

'I don't know. It would be impossible for me. I mean, your own child…' Maddy touched Leanne's shoulder. 'I'm sorry. What do you plan to do when you see him again?'

Leanne's eyes gleamed. 'I want to give him the fright of his life and just turn up and say, "Ta-da! Here I am, your long-lost daughter." That should make him choke on his morning croissant.'

'He deserves worse than that.'

'Yeah,' Leanne said flatly.

'If you can find him.'

'Oh, I will. I have a knack for these things. In more ways than one.' Leanne's nose twitched.

Maddy laughed. 'What do you mean?'

'I've always had this amazing nose. I can smell things miles away.' Leanne closed her eyes. 'Someone just walked past with a bag of cheese and onion crisps.'

Maddy craned her neck and looked around the salon. She spotted a man at the far side with something in his hand. 'I can see a guy over there with something that looks like a bag of crisps. But he hasn't opened it yet.'

Leanne smiled and nodded. 'See? I can smell it through the packaging from miles away.' She touched her nose. 'See this? Could be my destiny. Never really thought of it before. It was just something I could do, like a party trick. But now that I have this money, I want to go down there and see if I can get into that line of work. Perfume, I mean. I love smelling things, especially flowers and plants and stuff like that.'

'Have you been in touch with this man? The one you think is your dad?'

'No. I want to surprise him. Or give him a fright. That'd serve him right after all he's put me through.'

Maddy didn't know what to say. How hard it must have been for Leanne to have lost her father and then have had to make up lies and pretend he was dead just to please her mother. It made her own story seem pale and ordinary in comparison.

Leanne sighed and stretched. 'That's my tale of woe. Now yours. Come on… dish.'

Maddy sighed and drained her glass. 'I'm not sure I want to go there yet.'

'Well, I do,' Leanne said sternly. 'This whole trip is about sorting out our baggage. We both have reasons to want to go to France. I just told you mine. It's your turn to delve into the dirty linen.'

'Dirty linen?' Maddy said indignantly. 'That's not what I'd call it.'

'Okay, the painful event that changed your life, then. Or something. You want to find someone and say something like, "What the hell happened? Where have you been for the past hundred years?" right?'

'I don't know what I'd say, to be honest. It happened twenty-three years ago. Can't believe it's that long since—' She stopped, amazed the memory still hurt so much.

'Time flies when you're having fun.' Leanne sat back and closed her eyes. 'I can see it now... the beautiful young au pair girl falls for the older brother in the family or—' She gasped and her eyes flew open. 'It wasn't the dad, was it?'

Maddy rolled her eyes. 'Please. No, it wasn't. And I wasn't even an au pair girl. My parents wouldn't let me. They said I'd be treated as a maid and asked to do a lot more than just babysitting.'

'Too right. Those poor creatures are worked to the bone by horrible rich families and given hovels to sleep in.' Leanne sat back again. 'Okay, you weren't an au pair girl. What were you then?'

'I was a student at the Sorbonne. Studying French as a foreign student. I was nearly at the end of my course when I met him.'

'Who?'

'Ludovic Maximilian de Montrouge.'

Leanne snorted. 'Jesus, what a mouthful. Sounds kind of posh.'

Maddy didn't reply. Saying the name out loud had suddenly catapulted her back in time to those days at the end of spring over twenty years earlier. 'He wasn't really,' she said. 'Just his name. We met by accident the day before I was to take my finals...'

*

She bumped into him in the sun-dappled courtyard as she dashed to classes from her little maid's room under the eaves of a sixteenth-century house on the Left Bank.

'Oh!' she exclaimed trying desperately to hang on to the pile of books she was clutching as she ran, an apple in her mouth and a pencil stuck in her hair. The books slid from her grip and tumbled onto the flagstones. She took the apple out of her mouth and fell to her knees at the same time.

He crouched down to help her. '*Excusez-moi,*' he said. 'How clumsy of me.'

'*Non, pas du tout,*' she replied as she stacked the books, one on top of the other. 'It was my fault. I wasn't looking where I was going.'

'Neither was I.' He took her elbow and helped her up. Then he studied her for a moment. 'You're the girl across the courtyard. The Irish girl.'

'Yes,' she said, suddenly awkward as she finally came face to face with him. 'How did you know I was Irish?' she asked, blushing under the gaze of dark eyes fringed with thick black lashes.

'Someone told me when I arrived. You speak very good French.'

'Thank you.' She rearranged the books in her arms. 'I've been studying at the Sorbonne for a year. Almost finished. Are you staying here too?' She looked at him more closely. With his nearly shoulder-length curly hair and denim shirt, he looked more like an artist than a student.

'Yes.' He gestured at the windows opposite hers. 'I've been studying up there, across the way from you. My family owns the apartment below and the maid's room above it. And your room, too, of course.'

'Of course,' she mumbled, wondering where his apartment was.

'I'm right across from you,' he said. 'In the other maid's room.'

Her eyes widened in shock. 'What? But there's nobody across the courtyard. Madame told me when I moved in.'

'I've only been there a week. I moved up there to get some peace. Away from the family.' His smile widened. 'I'm afraid I spotted you dancing the other night. Must have been a good song you were listening to.'

'Shit,' she said in English, looking at him in shock. 'You didn't.'

He grinned. 'Um, yes.'

She backed away, realising he had seen her dancing around in her underwear while Prince sang her favourite track on the radio.

'What was the song?' he asked.

'None of your business.' She started to walk away. 'I have to go now. I have an exam.'

'Yes. Me too.'

She stopped and looked at him over her shoulder. 'At the Sorbonne?'

'No, the school of Alain Ducasse. I'm training to be a chef.'

'Oh.' She started walking again until she reached the heavy oak door to the street. 'Good luck,' she called over her shoulder.

'You too,' he called back.

The door banged shut behind her before she had a chance to reply. She hugged the books to her chest while she walked the short distance to the Sorbonne, her mind whirling. Bloody hell, that guy had seen her nearly naked. Dancing and making faces, singing into her hairbrush. Well, she had only a week to go before she went back to Dublin. Hopefully she wouldn't meet him again. And from now on she would keep her curtains drawn.

Chapter Five

'What was the song?' Leanne asked.

'"Cream" by Prince. With sexy dancing.' Maddy brought her hands to her face as Leanne laughed. 'It's not funny. I cringe when I think about it even now, so many years later.'

'I know, but I think it's quite a hoot. Great song, too. I used to sing it when I was twelve and didn't know what it meant. So what happened next? Did he ever see you in your underwear up close and personal?' She leant closer. 'Did you eventually, you know, *do it?*' she whispered.

Maddy looked out across the water and noticed they were about to dock at Pembroke harbour. 'Look, we're here,' she said, relieved she didn't have to reply. Digging up the past was proving to be more painful than she realised.

'Saved by the bell, huh?' Leanne said, looking disappointed. 'We'll take this up later. Can't wait for the next instalment.'

The country-house hotel just outside the small harbour town of Pembroke looked like something from a Jane Austen novel on the outside; a three-storey Georgian building set in a lush garden with roses climbing up the old walls on one side and crumbling pillars flanking the massive entrance door. The sash windows glinted in the setting sun and a thrush could be heard singing at the top of a tall oak.

'Wow,' Leanne exclaimed as they pulled up at the front steps. 'You'd practically expect Mr Darcy to come out and scowl at us for arriving so late.'

'It's only nine o'clock.'

'Yes, but too late for dinner. They used to eat early in them old days.'

The door opened and a young man in hotel livery appeared, running down the steps and opening the driver's door. 'I'll park this car for you.'

Leanne tried to close the door again, an expression of horror on her face. 'What are you doing? This is my car, so get your dirty paws off it.'

The young man smirked. 'I'm sorry, ma'am. As you wish.'

'What kind of hotel is this, anyway?' Leanne demanded. 'Trying to drive the guests' cars, now?'

'It's called valet parking,' the young man said. 'Usually appreciated. But it's up to you.'

Leanne's face turned crimson. 'Oh, okay. Yeah, I knew that.' She handed the keys to the young man. 'Do it, then, but be careful.'

'Of course. But we'll get your bags first,' he said and gestured to a hotel porter who had just appeared by his side. 'Take these bags to the garden suite.'

'Suite?' Maddy asked. 'I thought we'd booked single rooms.'

'They only had the suite,' Leanne replied. 'Come on, let's go and inspect it. We could do room service too, if the dining room is closed already.'

'Dinner is served until eleven every evening,' the porter remarked as he took both bags and their shopping from the boot.

'Okay, great.' Maddy led the way up the stairs. 'Let's check in first, Leanne. Then we'll freshen up and go and have some dinner.'

'Yes, sir,' Leanne muttered and padded after Maddy up the steps. 'This had better be good or we're leaving.'

It was better than good: the suite was gorgeous. Two bedrooms with double beds stacked with pillows covered in linen and lace, a huge bathroom each with a bath 'the size of a small swimming pool', Leanne declared, looking in awe at the fluffy towels and luxury toiletries on the shelves. 'Molton Brown and Crabtree & Evelyn,' she sighed. 'And the bathrobes are amazing. Maybe we should just stay here for the month?'

Maddy sniffed a bottle of shower gel. 'I think I'd get bored.'

'Yeah. Me too.' Leanne picked up a bottle of body lotion. 'In any case, we can nick a few of these.'

'Will we have to?' Maddy asked. 'I mean, aren't we staying in a few places like this on the way? They'll all have similar stuff in their bathrooms.'

Leanne shook her head. 'Ah, sure they will. Jesus, I'm so thick. But maybe it's from never having lived the good life before. You seem to know all about it, though. How come?'

Maddy shrugged. 'Don't know. I've only stayed in a luxury hotel once when Tom was on an official trip to New York. He took me as the department paid for his trip and the hotel room. Never forgot it.'

'All on tax payers' money, no doubt.'

'Of course. Happens a lot. You've no idea how those top civil servants milk the system.'

'I'm sure they do. And those left-wingers are the worst, I bet.'

'I have no idea,' Maddy said with an innocent air.

'Yeah, right. Let's go and have dinner. I need to practice this high-living thing.'

Maddy laughed. 'That's not too hard. Just remember to think rich.'

'And bitch,' Leanne added. 'If you act like a bitch, they'll think you're loaded.'

'Hm.' Maddy frowned. 'Not sure I can do that. I was brought up to be nice.'

Leanne grinned. 'I wasn't. This'll be a waltz in the park for me.'

'You mean walk.'

'No, I don't. I like misquoting clichés. Gives them a new twist.'

'You're a nutcase.'

'I know.' Leanne pulled at Maddy's sleeve. 'Come on. Let's hit the dining room and act like rich bitches.'

The elegant dining room was already emptying by the time they got there. The maître d' showed them to a table near the window with a view of the floodlit garden and what must have been the stable block in the old days.

'Looks like some kind of annex,' Maddy said. 'But in the eighteenth century, it would have been the stables and coach house.'

'It's the spa, ma'am,' the waiter said behind her. 'And the swimming pool.'

'Cool,' Leanne chortled.

'No, it's quite warm,' he replied.

Leanne giggled. 'Not that kind of cool. I meant—' She thought for a moment. 'How splendid.'

He nodded and took out his notepad. 'I'll take your order now.'

'But we haven't even looked at it yet,' Leanne complained. 'Give us a moment. But get us some wine, willya? I'll have white. I think my friend likes a glass of red. Right, Mads?'

'I'll get the sommelier to come over and advise you,' the waiter said and glided away.

'Oh, shit,' Leanne muttered. 'I don't have a clue about wines or fancy restaurants. I'm getting a headache looking at this menu. It's all in French, fer God's sake! Oh, here he comes. The wine guy with the wine list. See if you can find something drinkable on it.'

Maddy tried not to roll her eyes. She let out a little sigh. Leanne had no idea how to behave in a posh restaurant. Even at thirty-two she must have done most of her socialising in pubs and hamburger joints. Her uncouth ways were jarring at times. How would they be able to spend several weeks together travelling in a tiny sports car?

The sommelier, a good-looking young man with red hair and a ring in his left ear, walked up to their table. 'The wine list, ladies,' he said and handed it to Maddy.

She scanned the list, trying not to gasp at the prices. 'Do you have a house wine?'

'I'm afraid not. But if you turn the page, you'll see that we have some light reds and a good number of dry whites that aren't too... pricey.'

'I was thinking more of the alcohol content,' Maddy remarked. 'Some of these are very strong. Fourteen per cent? That's more like sherry.' She looked at the list again. 'As I'm not quite sure what we'll be having yet, I think a rosé would be good. It goes with both fish and meat. What about this St Croix?'

He nodded. 'Yup, that one would be perfect for the two of yez.'

Leanne laughed and grabbed his arm. 'You're from Dublin, aren't you? The north side?'

He beamed at her. 'Guilty. Inchicore. And you? Howth?'

'Sutton.'

He nodded. 'Thought so.' He took the wine list back from Maddy. 'Thank you, madam. I'll get the waiter to come and take your order. Enjoy your meal.'

He was about to walk away, but Leanne pulled at his jacket. 'Just a minute. When do you finish tonight?'

He looked only slightly taken aback. 'Eleven.'

'Great. How about we meet in the bar then?'

He pulled away from Leanne's grip. 'Uh, no. I'm expected at home. My wife...'

Leanne put her hand to her mouth. 'Oh, feck, you have a wife?'

'And two kids,' he added. 'But hey, no hard feelings. Very flattered and all that. See ya around, girls.'

Maddy shook her head at Leanne. 'Really. Hitting on the wine waiter. What next? A fling with the parking valet?'

'But he was cuuute,' Leanne hissed as the head waiter came back with the menu. 'I want to make the best of this holiday, and that includes cute men.'

'Behave yourself,' Maddy said sternly. 'You can't hit on every man you see. What do you want to eat?'

Leanne glanced at the menu. 'It's all in French. You order.'

Maddy quickly ordered shrimp cocktail followed by pork medallions for them both.

They sat in silence for a while, looking out at the garden. The first course arrived, a tiny pile of shrimps artistically arranged on a bed of baby spinach and sliced avocado.

'Have you noticed how small the helpings are in posh restaurants?' Leanne said as she wiped the plate with a slice of bread. 'I could murder a plate of chips right now.'

'Rich people have smaller stomachs,' Maddy said, glancing at Leanne's plate.

Leanne stuffed the bread into her mouth. 'Yeah, I know. And I shouldn't be mopping the plate, should I? But the dressing is so good and the bread is yummy. Sorry.' She sat up straighter and crossed her hands in her lap. 'I thought we'd have fun. I thought this would be a laugh. But here we are, miserable, and you sitting there, looking like a prune. If this is being rich, I don't want it.'

The pork medallions arrived, saving Maddy from having to reply. Leanne sighed and picked up her fork, attacking the slices of meat and the tiny roast potatoes with gusto. They ate in silence for a while, sipping wine and nibbling at the bread while the waiters hovered around them, filling their glasses and bringing fresh bread rolls. Maddy ordered blackcurrant sorbet for dessert, and Leanne asked for a double helping of chocolate mousse.

'How about a swim in the spa place?' Maddy asked. 'If the pool is open this late. It'd stretch our muscles and help us sleep.'

'Yeah, sure, if your ladyship can stand the company of a scrubber like me,' Leanne muttered.

'You? A scrubber? Don't be melodramatic.' Maddy laughed. 'Ah, come on, Leanne. Snap out of it. Let's enjoy this place and all it has to offer.'

'I didn't bring a swimsuit.' Leanne winked. 'But maybe I can swim in the Victoria's Secret stuff?'

'They'll have suits for guests at the spa.'

Leanne rolled her eyes. 'Gee, of course they do.'

Maddy got up. 'Come on, then.'

Leanne knocked back the last of her wine and got to her feet. 'Lead on. Show me the good time, boss.'

Chapter Six

The next morning, Maddy woke with a start as a roll of thunder shook the room. The curtains billowed at the open window, and she ran to close them as torrential rain struck the panes. She peered out at the grey wet garden, where the trees were being bent over by strong winds. What time was it? She checked her phone. Six-thirty.

She yawned and got back into bed, resting her head against the soft pillows and pulling the silk duvet over her. Leanne wouldn't be awake yet unless the thunder had woken her up. She had laid into rather a large brandy in the spa bar after their swim, unlike Maddy who had opted for a cup of camomile tea. They exchanged sleepy chatter, planning the following day's drive before going back to the suite and their respective bedrooms. And they were supposed to drive to Oxford for lunch and sightseeing. Weather permitting. But the weather didn't seem to want to cooperate, as the rain turned from violent bursts to a steady downpour, and the thunder rolled away in the distance.

Maddy stretched her back and luxuriated in the comfortable bed, the soft pillows stacked under her head and the feel of the silky sheets. It reminded her of a similar bed a long time ago, but then she hadn't been alone in a hotel. She had been in a bedroom in a château south of Paris. With a man who wasn't her husband. She smiled at the memory. How young she had been: only twenty-one and passionately in love, the way one can only be at that age. Later, love was deeper, steadier, more lasting. At that time, she hadn't thought much about the future or if they would stay together. It was all about here and now and him. Ludovic. *Ludo*, she thought, *where are you now? What happened to us? Why did we...* She screwed her eyes shut and tried to think of something else, but the images were too vivid, like a technicolour movie playing on the wall opposite her bed.

It had all started so innocently that day in Paris.

*

Of course, they met again. How could they not have? Drawn to each other like moths to a flame, they managed to cross the courtyard at exactly the same time the following morning.

'*Bonjour,* Madeleine,' he called as he walked towards her.

'*Bonjour,* Ludovic,' she replied, her face hot.

'How did you know my name?' he asked.

'Madame, your mother, told me. How did you know mine?'

'Ditto.' He smiled, showing slightly uneven white teeth in an unshaven face. 'But she's not my mother. She's my aunt. I'm the poor relation, you see. That's why I have to sleep in the servants' quarters.'

Maddy laughed. 'I don't believe you.'

He came closer. 'It's true. I'm known as "poor Ludo" in the family. They' – he flicked his head at the windows above – 'think I should have followed in my father's footsteps. But I don't have the talent or the desire to grow wine. I want to be a chef and set up my own restaurant one day.'

'They grow wine?' Maddy asked, impressed.

He sighed. 'Not any more. It was all going well for many years, but then there were a few cold winters. A few more bad years, and poof, all the money was gone. We had to sell up or go broke. The vineyard was bought up by some Englishman, but we still have the château and a few acres. My dad is now running a business selling sports equipment. Helps to keep the wolves away. Sad story, *hein?*'

Maddy nodded, bubbling with laughter inside. 'Very sad. But not true. Your aunt told me the real one. Your father is a lawyer in a small town in Provence. Digne, I think she said.'

He laughed. '*Merde*, and I thought I'd seem more romantic this way.'

She smiled. 'Good story, though.'

'Thank you.' He looked at her more closely. 'No books today?'

'No. The exams are over. I'll be going home soon.'

He frowned. 'Soon?'

'In ten days.'

'Oh.' His brown eyes were suddenly thoughtful. He picked up a strand of her hair from her shoulder. 'Only ten days to get to know each other.'

Suddenly flustered by the close contact with his body, the intense look in his eyes and the scent of soap and herbs from his clothes, she backed away. 'Who says I want to get to know you?'

His eye widened. 'You don't? But I can feel it. The… the vibes, the electricity between us. Don't you?'

Of course she did. But she didn't want him to know it. 'Don't know what you mean,' she said airily and started to walk away. 'I'm going to get some bread for breakfast. See you around, er, Ludo.'

She could hear him laugh and then his footsteps behind her. She looked at him over her shoulder.

'I need breakfast too,' he said with an innocent air. 'That's not a crime, is it?'

She had to laugh. He was so beguiling, with his tousled dark hair, big eyes and unshaven chin. 'No, of course not.'

When they were on the street, he touched her shoulder. 'Why not have breakfast together? The café across the street over there have the best croissants, all hot and buttery. And their coffee...' He kissed his fingers. 'Divine.'

She could smell the coffee and the fresh bread as they approached and her stomach rumbled. 'You make it sound irresistible.'

He took her hand. 'Just like you, Mademoiselle Meehan. Irresistible.'

She blushed yet again. He made her feel both awkward and special. She didn't quite know how to handle his obvious attraction to her. She had never been the subject of such ardour before. It felt strange and exciting. 'Thank you,' she whispered.

He stopped and looked at her with tender eyes. 'You're like a bird, all nervous and fluttery, as if you'd fly away if I get too close. Don't worry, little bird, I won't hurt you.'

'I know.'

He pulled out a chair beside a table outside the café. 'Let's enjoy the lovely morning and the sunshine.'

She sat down on the chair, and he joined her on the other one after ordering two café crèmes and croissants. 'That's what we call it, not café au lait like the tourists.'

'I know.' She laughed. 'I even knew that before I came. My French teacher taught us all sorts of things like that during my final year in school. She was from Marseille. Excellent teacher.'

'Except you have a touch of a Midi accent.'

She laughed. 'I know. Didn't realise that until I came to Paris. I'm trying to lose it.'

He shook his head. 'Don't. It's charming. And that way you sound French instead of foreign.'

Their order arrived and before Maddy had a chance to scrabble for her purse and wallet, Ludo threw a fifty-franc note on the table. 'This is on me.' He dipped his knife into the small pot of apricot jam on the tray and spread it on a croissant before handing it to Maddy.

'Apricot jam goes beautifully with a croissant and a café crème.'

'Thank you.' Maddy bit into the flaky, buttery croissant, its texture and flavour almost sensual in her mouth. She sipped some of the steaming café crème and declared both 'heavenly'.

'True,' he muttered through a big mouthful. He picked a flake from her chin. 'But a little messy. What are your plans for today?'

She licked her fingers. 'I have to go and empty my locker at the Sorbonne. And then I'll be sorting out a few things. I have a letter to write and then not much, I suppose. Why?'

'I'd like you to come with me to the Marais. My uncle runs a restaurant there. He wants me to work with him as sous-chef when I've finished my course, and then he'll retire when he's satisfied I can take over.'

'Oh. That sounds great. Yes, I'd love to see it. And meet your uncle.' Maddy's heart beat faster. He already wanted her to meet someone from his family and share his plan for his future. 'I'm looking forward to it.'

Ludo nodded, stuffed the last of his croissant into his mouth, drained his cup and got up. 'Good.' He picked up the receipt from the table and scribbled something on it. 'It's called Les Deux Toques. Here's the address. Very easy to find. It's near the Musée Carnavalet. The metro stop is Hotel de Ville. The restaurant is two streets away from there.'

'I have a map, so I won't get lost.'

'*Magnifique.* I'll meet you there at one o'clock. *A bientôt.*' He bent his tall frame to kiss her, not on both cheeks as she expected but on the mouth. Then he was gone, leaving Maddy slightly dizzy. Was this really happening? Was this gorgeous Frenchman truly interested in her?

She sat there in a daze, looking at his receding figure, still feeling his kiss that tasted of apricot and sunshine, wrapped in the sexiest voice she had ever heard.

Chapter Seven

Maddy was pulled out of her reverie by Leanne wandering into the room. She plonked herself down on the bed. 'Morning.'

Maddy sat up. 'Good morning. Sleep well?'

'So-so. Got a bit of a headache, but the super-deluxe bathroom had some paracetamol in a cute little box. Helped a lot.' Leanne stared out the window. 'Gee, that's a change from yesterday. I just watched the weather forecast on Sky News. Wall-to-wall rain all the way to London.'

'Oh noooo,' Maddy moaned. 'And I so wanted to walk around Oxford and have lunch there.'

'Me too.' Leanne made a face. 'Not really, though. I'm not into old buildings and history. But I wouldn't have minded a little shopping spree. I didn't even bring an umbrella. Did you?'

'No.' Maddy sighed and got out of bed. 'Sightseeing won't be much fun in this rain even with one.'

Leanne lay down on her stomach and propped her face in her hands. 'I have an idea. Let's skip the scenic route and the culture. Why don't we drive to the Cotswolds and stay in some country hotel? Have dinner, do a little walking around and see that amazing area? Loads of film stars and rock singers live there. I'm desperate to see how the other half live.'

'But they'll probably be behind high walls and security fences.'

'I know, but the villages are so cute. Loads of history, too.' Leanne produced her phone and held it out for Maddy to see. 'Look at this gorgeous hotel. It's in a real Tudor house. Fifteenth-century.'

Maddy looked. 'Gorgeous. But the Cotswolds is not exactly on the road to Harwich, is it? It'll mean a huge detour.'

'So what?' Leanne argued. 'We have the time. We don't have to be in Harwich until tomorrow evening. I want to see the real England.'

Maddy sighed. 'Okay. Why not? Looks like the kind of place that would have a cosy library with a fireplace and books. Perfect for a rainy day.'

'Great. It's a four-star too. The rooms look fabulous. I'll book us two rooms, then.'

'But if it stops raining, we could still go to Oxford.'

'It's not going to stop. According to the met office, anyway, but what do they know?'

Maddy thought for a moment. 'Yes. Okay. Book the rooms. Let's order breakfast. Then we'll check out and get going.'

Leanne jumped off the bed. 'I'll book the hotel and order brekkie, you go and have a shower.'

After a long hot shower and extensive slathering of body lotions and hand cream, Maddy put on one of the fluffy bathrobes. Her phone rang as she walked into the lounge, where a waiter was laying out a sumptuous breakfast on the table by the window. She glanced at the number on the screen. Nobody she knew. Maybe one of those scam calls. Or Sophie calling from Australia?

She replied on the fifth ring. 'Maddy Quinn.'

'Hi there,' said a breezy woman's voice. 'This is Brenda McIntosh. I'm the editor of *Women Now*.'

'*Women Now*? The—' Maddy was about to say 'rag' but stopped herself in time. 'The free magazine?' she asked.

'Yes. And the website. I'm calling about your blog.'

Maddy frowned and sank down on a chair by the table. 'My blog? What blog? This must be a mistake.'

'You're travelling with Leanne Sandvik through Europe? In a sports car? I believe it's a red Merc cabriolet?'

Maddy blinked. 'Uh… yes?'

'Leanne and I met at a party just before you left. She told me about your trip. We thought it would be a hoot if the two of you ran an online blog about your adventures.'

'You did?'

'We both did. I thought Leanne might have mentioned it by now? It's called "The Great Euroscape". A day-by-day account of your Thelma and Louise-type adventure. We've already run a teaser for it. We got some sponsors from some top cosmetic brands, too. It'll be a great boost to our little paper and the website especially.'

'Oh.' *Jesus, I'll kill her*, Maddy thought. She didn't read *Women Now* but had seen it at the hairdresser's and thought it a trashy publication. It contained mostly sleazy gossip about film stars, their love lives and their plastic surgeries. She had never even looked at their website. 'I'm sorry, but Leanne hasn't spoken to me about this. How on earth did you get my number?'

'Your number is listed in the school directory. I have a niece there.'

'I see. Just a small detail, but has Leanne signed some kind of contract with you?'

'Contract?' Brenda sounded confused. 'No, but we agreed on a fee per blog post.'

'How long would these blog posts be?'

'Just a short little snippet really. With selfies. She's already sent one from Kildare Village of herself in a cute underwear set. Got a huge amount of likes on Instagram. We use #OnTheRoadWithMaddyandLeanne as a hashtag. It's beginning to trend.'

'Holy mother,' Maddy said and hung up. She marched across the floor of Leanne's room and tore open the door to the bathroom, from where she could hear water gushing and Leanne singing 'Dancing Queen' at the top of her voice.

Maddy reached in through the glass door of the shower cubicle and turned off the water.

Leanne, covered in soap suds, her hair plastered to her head, turned around. 'What the—?' she screamed and snatched the towel from the rail to cover herself.

Maddy folded her arms and glared at Leanne. 'Yeah, "what the—" is what I thought, too. *Women Now*? Blog posts? Selfies on Instagram? Hashtags with our names?'

'Oh, that. Well, er…' Leanne let out a nervous giggle. 'Forgot to tell you. Fun idea, though, no?'

'No,' Maddy snapped. 'Finish your shower. Then you have a lot of explaining to do.'

Leanne turned the water back on, and Maddy marched out again, banging the door shut. She was sipping her tea when Leanne appeared in a bathrobe, all pink cheeks and her hair in little spikes. Maddy would have thought it was cute had she not been so angry.

Leanne sat down opposite Maddy, eyeing the array of fresh bread, cheese, cured ham, pots of jam and honey and hardboiled eggs. 'Wow. This is what I call breakfast.' She reached for her phone and took a few shots of the table. 'Gorgeous.'

'Yes. Very,' Maddy said between her teeth. 'But never mind that. You were going to tell me about that phone call and what it was all about.'

Leanne squirmed. 'Okay. I should have told you. But I didn't know how you'd feel about it, so I thought I'd wait until you were in a good mood. Didn't know they were going to call you. How did they get your number?'

'Through the school directory. Brenda has a niece there.'

'Yeah, I know. She told me.'

Maddy tightened the belt on her bathrobe. 'Whatever. Please explain to me why you agreed to this. And then go to why you didn't run it past me. After that we might continue to why the hell you want to have us plastered all over the Internet.'

Leanne picked at a roll. 'Yeah, well, it seemed like a brilliant idea at the time.'

Maddy lifted an eyebrow. 'After how many drinks?'

'Not that many. Is there any coffee?'

'In the coffee pot over there.'

Leanne poured coffee into a cup, added sugar, broke a roll in two and slathered it with butter and honey. She took a big bite, looking thoughtfully at Maddy while she ate. She swallowed, took a swig of coffee and wiped her mouth with the linen napkin by her plate. 'Right, let's discuss this. I'm sorry I didn't tell you. That was really stupid of me. But here's the deal...okay, so it was something

I agreed to over a few drinks, and I shouldn't have said yes straight away. But, when I thought it over, I told myself it would be a great way to earn some extra cash as we go along and that maybe we could turn the whole thing into a book or something when all this is over.'

'We don't need extra cash. We have two hundred thousand each. Should last a little while, even with your shopaholic tendencies.'

'Yeah, but a little extra wouldn't hurt, would it? If we decided to stay on somewhere? Or maybe even…' Leanne paused.

'Even what?'

'Well, maybe we'll decide not to come back at all?' Leanne looked wistfully at Maddy. 'You never know.'

Maddy stared at Leanne. 'Never come back? What do you mean? That might apply to you, but I have a house and children and a job and – as far as I know – a husband.'

'Your kids have grown up and left home. And you mentioned your husband last.' Leanne took another swig of coffee, looking at Maddy over the rim of her cup. 'Maybe, if he sees how much fun you're having, he might realise golf isn't all it's cracked up to be.'

'He won't see it. He doesn't read *Women Now*. Or visit websites for women.'

'But others might and tell him. How about his sister? She looked like she'd read stuff like that.'

'Probably. That doesn't make me want her to see a blow-by-blow account of our comings and goings on the Internet.'

'Well, you can't stop me doing it, can you? Legally, I mean,' Leanne added defiantly.

'Suppose not.' Maddy stared into her teacup. Their lovely escape didn't seem so lovely any more. 'How did you explain about the money? You know I don't want anyone to know about it. Least of all Tom or any of his family.'

'I said I had a bit of luck at the races.'

'Good story. I'm glad you didn't spill the beans about the lottery. At least that was a good thing. But count me out of any of this. I'd appreciate it if you could get my name out of that hashtag too.'

'Ah, come on, Mads,' Leanne pleaded. 'Don't be such a holy Mary. It'd be fun. A finger to all those boring people out there. A "Hey, look at us, we're doing it and you're not". They' – Leanne swept her teaspoon at the window – 'have to go to boring jobs and look at boring people across their desks. They can't drive through Paris in a sports car. But we can.'

'Like in the song? "The Ballad of Lucy Jordan"?'

'Yes. I heard Marianne Faithfull sing it just before we won that money. It made me cry. It made me realise that life was passing me by. That I was stuck with my mother in a crappy house in a crappy suburb and that if I didn't get out now I never would. I get what you're saying about the blog and the exposure, but I think it could cheer a lot of women up. Let them experience the adventure vicariously through us. Could be women who're sick or poor or desperate. It'd be like reading a great novel, only it doesn't end. It goes on and on through the summer. We could inspire them. Give them something to look forward to each day.'

Taken aback by the passion in Leanne's voice and the glimmer of tears in her eyes, Maddy softened. Then she thought about the women who were like she had been only a few years earlier: stuck at home, struggling with children, day care, a job and a house to run without much fun in between. 'When you put it like that, it looks a little different. And that was me, minus the kids, just a few days ago. So, okay. God help me, we'll do it. For them out there. All the sad and lonely and desperate women. All the hard-working mums, the women stuck in boring jobs, those who can't afford a proper holiday, all the—'

'Jaysus, will you stop.' Leanne started to laugh. 'You'll have me in tears. We're not solving a humanitarian crisis or anything.'

'Humanitarian.' Maddy sat up. 'Oh my God! That's *it*! Brilliant!' Leanne looked confused. 'What is?'

'The idea I just had.' Maddy beamed. 'We'll give the money we earn from the blog to charity. We'll pick something like Doctors Without Borders, or Oxfam or any of those organisations and maybe do a different one every so often. Plus, we'll mention it on the blog to get others to donate something, too.'

Leanne looked dazzled. 'Oh my God, yes! That's fabulous!' She jumped up and hugged Maddy. 'Now we can have fun without the guilt. You're a fecking genius, my friend.'

'I know,' Maddy said with fake modesty. 'But there's one thing we absolutely must do before we start, and that is, secure our rights. Copyright, I mean,' she explained when Leanne looked confused. 'I gather you haven't signed a contract with them, so right now they could grab the copyright to anything we write on their blog. They could nick and use it, and anyone could write a book based on what we post. We need a solicitor to draw up some kind of agreement before we get started.'

'Shit, that'll cost a lot of money,' Leanne grumbled.

'Nah, it won't. My dad's a solicitor. He's retired now, but he used to do litigations and stuff like that. He'll draw up a brief agreement and email it to me.'

Leanne nodded. 'Okay. I'll call Brenda and explain what's going on.'

'Tell her we won't write a word on that blog until we have the signed contract. Please explain why I hung up on her, too. I was in a state of shock.'

'Sorry,' Leanne mumbled through her second bread roll. 'My fault.'

Maddy fixed her with a stern look. 'No more surprises, please. And you'll keep your mouth shut about anything private, okay?'

'I will, yeah.'

Which, Maddy realised with a sinking feeling, was Dublin-speak for the exact opposite.

Chapter Eight

When the car had been delivered by a dripping-wet valet, generously tipped by Maddy despite Leanne's dirty looks, they drove off into the sheeting rain, Maddy at the wheel.

Leanne picked up her phone. 'No need to give him that much,' she muttered, scrolling through her newsfeed on Facebook.

'He was sopping wet and still delivered the car. I think he deserved that fiver and more.'

'Yeah, but those were pounds not euros, remember.'

'The pound has gone down since the Brexit vote,' Maddy remarked, slowing down at the exit. 'And we must be generous to those a lot less fortunate than us. Especially young guys with jobs like that. Now, pay attention and tell me how to get to the M4.'

'Turn on the GPS,' Leanne muttered, her eyes on the screen of her phone.

'Okay.' Maddy found the switch and turned on the GPS. A tinny voice told her to turn right and keep going. 'What did the woman say? Brenda whatshername?'

'McIntosh. She was a little pissed off but had to agree when I said the deal was off if there was no contract. She cheered up when she heard that the contract would be with her by courier this afternoon and that we'd have ours signed by the time we left the UK. If we find a place with a printer, that is.'

'We'll be stopping for lunch at Windsor, rain or no rain. I'm sure we can find a hotel or a post office with a printer there.'

'Windsor?' Leanne squealed. 'Can we go and see the castle?'

'We might manage a quick look,' Maddy grunted as she turned into a narrow street. 'Why does that thing tell me to go here? I'm sure it isn't the right way to the main road.'

'They get it wrong sometimes.'

Maddy turned off the GPS and pulled up. She turned to Leanne. 'Get the map out. We don't have the time to get lost. You'll have to navigate.'

Leanne kept her eyes on the screen of her phone. 'Yeah, but I was just about to get the score to this thing. Ninety-seven percent of people don't know half the answers to this test, but I think I just cracked it.'

Maddy rolled her eyes. 'Those stupid tests are just a ploy to get into your Facebook profile data. They'll get to your friends list, your contact details, your address and your bra size, and then they'll use it to manipulate you with ads and worse.'

'You made that up. About the bra size.' Leanne sighed, put the phone in her bag and got the map out from the glove compartment. 'Okay, I'm on the job. Where are we?'

'That's what you should be telling me. We're still in Pembroke in a one-way street. We need to get to the main road that will take us to the M4.'

The rain drummed on the roof of the car while Leanne scanned the map. 'Ah, okay,' she said finally. 'I know where we are. You need to reverse out of here and then go left. The main road is very close. I don't think the GPS knows anything about one-way traffic.'

'Obviously.' Maddy started the engine and reversed, doing a U-turn as soon as the street widened. Only minutes later, they were on the main road and Maddy began to enjoy driving the amazing car. Despite the bad weather, its smooth gears and fast acceleration were a true joy. 'Gosh, this is fabulous,' she said to Leanne. There was no reply. Leanne had fallen asleep, and the map was slipping off her knees. No matter. They would soon be on the motorway, and then there would be a few hours' drive to their next fabulous hotel: that Tudor manor in the Cotswolds. Maddy smiled and told herself to loosen up a little. What harm could the blog do? They would be living the dream of so many women and perhaps light up their dreary lives for just a moment each day. An act of charity while having fun. Maddy laughed out loud and revved the engine, overtaking a truck. A champagne lifestyle for charity. What a hoot.

The rain was still teeming down when they reached the small village of Maidenhurst, right in the middle of the Cotswolds.

'Lovely place,' Maddy said as they drove up the village street lined with old houses in mellow Cotswold stone.

'Very cute.' Leanne stretched and yawned. 'What time is it?'

'Five o'clock. Just in time for tea. Should have been here earlier, but the rain and the traffic jam at the exit of the motorway held us up.'

'Let's just find the hotel and settle in. I could do with some scones and tea.'

'The big gates, there at the end of the street, must be the entrance,' Maddy said.

'There are no hotel signs,' Leanne remarked.

'Probably very discreet. This is a seriously posh area.'

They drove through the gates and up an avenue lined with beeches, their branches swaying in the strong wind. Leanne leant forward and peered through the rain. 'You'd think it was January instead of June. It's only five and it's nearly pitch black out there.'

'Spooky.' Maddy pulled up at the front steps of a big house.

Leanne looked at the Cotswold-stone façade. 'This doesn't look very Tudor to me.'

'That's because it isn't. It's early Victorian. It's not a hotel at all, either, by the looks of it.'

'But there are lights in some of the windows. Why don't we go in and ask if they can tell us where the hotel is? Maybe they'll give us a cup of tea?'

'Okay. I'll just park the car away from the steps.' Maddy turned the wheel and drove slowly to the side of the house and parked between a battered Land Rover and a vintage Jaguar. She grabbed her bag and opened her door. 'Let's make a run for it.'

In the teeming rain, they sprinted across the gravel, up the wide steps and came to a stop at a massive oak door under an imposing pillared portico. Leanne grabbed the enormous knocker and hammered the door a few times, the blows echoing inside.

There was a long pause while they waited, shivering in the chilly wind. Then the door swung open. A tall elderly blonde in a Liberty-print dress and three rows of pearls stared at them.

'You're late,' she exclaimed. 'Come in. Don't stand there letting in the cold.'

Chapter Nine

Speechless, Maddy and Leanne walked into a vast entrance hall with chandeliers hanging from the ceiling. Huge logs blazed in a big fireplace, beside which two Great Danes snoozed without bothering to open their eyes.

The blonde woman heaved the door shut with a loud bang. 'You have to get started straight away. Fortnum's delivered the canapés an hour ago, and everyone will be here in about twenty minutes. It's a drinks party, and then we'll go on to dinner at another house. You can change into your uniforms in the staff room beside the kitchen. It's this way.' She clattered across the marble floor on her kitten heels, shooting an impatient look over her shoulder. 'Come along, gals, there's no time to lose.'

'Feck, she thinks we're some kind of catering staff,' Maddy whispered as they followed the woman. 'We have to tell her.'

'No,' Leanne hissed. 'Let's pretend we are. She's throwing some kind of posh party. This'll be great for the blog.'

'Are you nuts?' Maddy pushed Leanne aside and touched the woman's arm. 'Listen, there must be some kind of mistake. We don't—'

'What?' The woman pulled open a door that led to stairs going down into a basement.

'We don't have uniforms,' Leanne said, shooting a warning glance at Maddy.

'Oh,' the blonde said as she picked her way down the stairs. 'Okay. No problem. I have some big white aprons. You can put those on, and we'll pretend this is the new look for serving staff. It might catch on in a big way.'

They entered a big bright kitchen with state-of-the-art appliances and two huge fridges humming discreetly at the far wall. The vast table was covered in an array of large cardboard boxes with the Fortnum & Mason logo and stacks of silver platters and dishes. An open door led to what looked like a butler's pantry lined with cupboards, with a small table and two easy chairs by an empty fireplace.

Their hostess was about to say something when the mobile she was carrying trilled. 'Just a minute,' she said and answered. 'Lady Huntington-Smith. Yes, that's right, it's me. Edwina. The party is tonight, darling. You can't come? Why not? I know the weather is filthy, but—' She listened while the caller chatted at the other end. 'You're stuck in London with the Beckhams? That's such bad luck. For me, I mean,' she added with a laugh. 'Right, darling, see you soon. Hugs and kisses.' She hung up. 'Kate,' she said. 'Can't come. Bloody rude to call at the last minute, I have to say.'

'Appalling,' Maddy agreed.

'But we must carry on.' Edwina made a sweeping gesture at the butler's pantry. 'You'll find the aprons and napkins in the cupboards in there. All you have to do is arrange the canapés on the silver platters and then start serving as soon as Alistair, my butler, gives you the signal. He and his team will serve the champagne. Horace, my husband, will open the door and welcome the guests. Is that all clear?'

Leanne nodded. 'Okay. Shouldn't be too much of a challenge. We'll manage.'

Edwina peered at her. 'Strange accent. Are you Polish?'

Leanne grinned. 'No, we're Irish.'

'Oh.' Edwina stepped back. 'We haven't had Irish staff for simply yahs.'

'Well, we're coming back,' Maddy said, enjoying the confusion on the woman's face. 'Because of Brexit, you see.'

'Ah. Of course. That's it. Brexit. Things will be like they were before—'

'—before the war,' Leanne filled in, her face bland but her eyes dancing.

'Splendid,' Edwina said, looking a little confused. 'But, where were we? Oh yes, the champagne, Horace at the door, the food. Champagne. So, all is taken care of.'

She was interrupted by a whining at the door. It was pushed open, and a small black bundle, which proved on closer inspection to be a miniature poodle, trotted in.

Maddy was immediately entranced. 'What a cute little doggie,' she cooed and crouched down, putting her hand out. 'Come here, sweetie.'

The little dog sniffed at Maddy's hand and wagged its short woolly tail.

'This is Gidget.' Edwina swept the dog up in her arms. 'She's not mine. I'm minding her for a friend for the summer. Sweet, isn't she?'

'She's divine.' Maddy stroked the soft curly fur. Gidget licked her hand. 'Isn't she beautiful, Leanne?'

'Adorable,' Leanne agreed.

'Yes, but naughty,' Edwina said. 'Horace is very cross with her. She keeps getting into his study and chews on the rugs there. Must be some kind of smell she likes. I have to keep her out of his way while she's here. And now, darlings, I have to lock her up so she doesn't get trampled on by any of the guests. She's inclined to nip if pushed. See you upstairs in a little while. Toodle-oo.'

'Toodle-oo,' Leanne mimicked, waggling her fingers as the door closed behind Edwina.

When they were alone, Maddy faced Leanne across the canapés. 'I don't know how you talked me into this mess, but let's do our best, serve the food and get out of here fast.'

'It's a deal.' Leanne proceeded to open the boxes. 'Wow, this is what I call finger food.' She stuffed two tiny sandwiches into her mouth. 'Mm, lobster.'

'Stop eating the party food.' Maddy delved into another box and started to arrange the tiny open sandwiches on the platters.

Leanne took a bite of a smoked salmon sandwich. 'Just one more. I'm starving. And in any case, I doubt if the women guests will eat much of it. Those celebs are always on a diet.'

'I suppose.' Maddy slipped a cracker topped with foie gras into her mouth and had to agree it was divine. Another with shrimp went the same way, followed by a caviar canapé. She nearly choked as the door opened to admit a tall man with a tuft of white hair on top of an otherwise bald head. His kindly eyes twinkled behind gold-framed glasses.

'Hello,' he said. 'You're the Irish girls Edwina told me about?'

'That's us,' Leanne said. 'Are you Alistair, the butler?'

'No, I'm Horace the husband. For my sins,' he added. 'Not too fond of these parties, I'm afraid.'

'Well, this one will be short and sweet,' Leanne said. 'Then on to dinner in some other mansion, I heard.'

'Good show. And I won't be going on to dinner.' He pointed at his head. 'Frightful headache, you see.' He winked. 'But nobody will miss me. Not really the fashionable type.'

Maddy laughed. 'I see what you mean.' She lifted one of the platters. 'Does this look okay?'

Horace glanced at the food. 'Jolly good. Do a few more, and then take them up to the conservatory. That's where her ladyship is receiving guests. It's through the drawing room. Glass dome full of the most horrid plants. You can't miss it.' He looked around the kitchen. 'I hope the mutt's been locked up? Have you seen her? Small black bundle of trouble.'

'You mean the cute little poodle?' Leanne asked. 'Gidget?'

'Cute, my eye,' Horace said, his voice laced with venom. 'A nasty little horror. Can't stand the beast, but Edwina's promised to keep it for the summer.'

'She's been locked into the boot room, I think,' Maddy said.

'Jolly good.' He rubbed his hands. 'Right-o. Into the fray, then. I'm supposed to greet people at the door. But I'm just going to leave it open and let them all drift in as they arrive. I saw a spiffing red sports car outside. Someone must have just arrived.'

'No, that's ours,' Leanne said.

Horace looked surprised. 'Really? Catering must be very lucrative these days.'

'Oh, it is,' Leanne said. 'Very lucrative.'

'Splendid,' Horace said. 'Must go. See you later.' He clicked his heels, saluted and left.

Leanne giggled. 'Jesus, these people are like something from *Downton Abbey*. Did ya hear the accent? Nice old fella, though.'

'A real dote,' Maddy agreed. She put on one of the big white aprons she had found in the butler's pantry and handed the other one to Leanne. 'Put this on, and when you're ready, let's hit the conservatory.'

Leanne tied her apron. 'Let's go. But remember, the first celebrity is mine.'

'Be my guest,' Maddy muttered, rolling her eyes. Celebrities, how are you. This old fogey party was more likely to be full of other old fogies. But as she entered the conservatory, she stopped and gasped. The cavernous conservatory, its domed ceiling soaring above her, was like a tropical forest full of exotic birds. And bursting with famous people.

Chapter Ten

Leanne gasped behind Maddy and would have nearly dropped her tray had a tall man not gripped it and steadied her. 'Easy,' he boomed. 'Don't let the dogs get all that scrummy food.'

Maddy knew that deep voice. Could it be…? She turned around and gazed up into the twinkling eyes of… 'Jeremy Clarkson,' she whispered. 'Oh my God.'

'Oh, come on,' he said with a laugh. 'I haven't been promoted to God just yet.'

Maddy felt her face go red. 'That's not what I meant.' She shoved her platter at him. 'Here, have a bite.'

He winked and laughed. 'So very tempting, darling. But I'll just have a sandwich or two instead.' He picked up five sandwiches in his big hands and put them in his mouth.

Leanne shoved her own tray at him. 'Have one of mine, they're even better.'

Jeremy's laugh boomed louder. 'How lovely! Two pretty Irish girls offering me delicious food.'

'Hold my tray for a moment, willya,' Leanne ordered Maddy.

'What?' Maddy took Leanne's tray, balancing both awkwardly.

'Let me help you,' Jeremy said, taking one of the trays.

'Thank you,' Leanne simpered and hauled her phone out of her back pocket. 'We just want to take a selfie with you, if that's all right?'

'Of course,' he said and chortled. 'But we could make it more interesting if we can get Hugh to pose with us. That should make all your Instagram friends green, won't it?'

'Hugh – Grant?' Leanne croaked.

'Is there any other?' Jeremy waved at a man half-hidden behind a rubber plant. 'Hey, Hugh,' he called. 'Come here and make two Irish cuties happy.'

'A pleasure,' Hugh Grant said and walked towards them. 'I love Ireland, just as much as you do, Jeremy, old fruit.'

'Don't we all? They want a photo for their friends,' Jeremy replied. 'But instead of a selfie, maybe we could get someone else to take it? More like a group hug?'

'Brilliant,' Leanne squeaked.

Jeremy put the tray on a rusty wrought-iron table. 'There. You can pick it up later.'

'Here, let's get rid of this one,' Hugh Grant said and put Maddy's tray beside Leanne's. Then he waved at someone in the crowd. 'Joanna! We need a hand here.'

An attractive older woman with short blonde hair approached. 'Anything for you, Hugh. Within reason, of course.'

'We just want our picture taken with Jeremy and Hugh,' Leanne said and handed the woman her phone. 'A couple of them please.'

Joanna took the phone. 'Okay. Put your arms around each other and say cheese.'

'No, say sex,' Jeremy corrected. 'That gives you a better smile and a light in your eyes. I always say sex in my head when I have my photo taken.'

Maddy laughed. 'Never thought of that.'

'But now you'll never forget it, I bet.' Hugh put his arm around her and they all lined up in front of Joanna.

'Okay, everyone say sex,' Joanna called, and clicked the phone three times. She handed the phone back to Leanne. 'There. Hope it came out okay.'

Leanne checked her phone. 'Perfect. Thank you so much.'

'No problem.' Joanna waved her hand in the air and disappeared into a thicket of bamboo.

'Where did she go?' Hugh asked. 'I want to have a chat with her about a part in that Aga saga that's being made into a movie. Just what I need right now.'

'No idea where she went,' Jeremy said. 'Just dive in through the jungle, old boy. I must toddle off, too,' he added after Hugh had left. 'Got to have a chat with my producer. Nice to meet you, girls.' He kissed them both on the cheek and disappeared into the throng around a slowly trickling fountain surrounded by banana plants.

'Aga saga?' Maddy said when they had retrieved their trays. 'Was that Joanna Trollope? I thought she looked familiar.'

Leanne frowned. 'Shit, we missed her. She should have been in the picture, too.'

'Don't be greedy.' Maddy lifted her tray. 'Come on, let's get to work. Edwina will have our guts for garters if we don't do as we're told. That butler seems a little grim, too,' she said, looking at a portly man in black and white taking charge of the champagne trays as if he was directing traffic.

Leanne nodded. 'Yes,' she hissed in Maddy's ear. 'He said he wanted to speak to us afterwards. Something about a mix-up at the catering firm.'

'Maybe he's on to us?' Maddy mumbled. 'Let's just get this done and get out of here before he has a chance to ask questions.'

They pushed through the array of tropical plants and proceeded to offer the delectable canapés around the chatting, laughing, drinking crowd. Edwina seemed to be in her element, knocking back the champagne, not even glancing at either Maddy or Leanne. They went back to the kitchen three times to reload the trays, and when the guests started to take their leave, there was hardly anything left except a few crumbs and some of the decorations.

When they had rinsed the trays and stacked the boxes in the recycling bin, Leanne threw her apron on the table. 'Get your bag, and we'll get out of here before the butler or anyone else gets here.'

'Too late,' Maddy said, as the door was pushed open. 'Here he is now.'

But it wasn't the butler. It was Horace, his cheeks flushed and his bow tie crooked. 'So you're off then?'

'Yes… we…' Maddy started.

He laughed and winked. 'Did this for a lark, did you?'

Leanne smiled. 'Yeah. Just for the craic, as we say in Ireland.'

His eyes widened and he looked suddenly nervous. 'Oh.'

'No, no,' Leanne exclaimed. 'We're not into illegal substances. I meant craic. C-R-A-I-C. Irish for fun.'

'Doing something for the hell of it,' Maddy filled in.

Horace exhaled. 'Thank goodness for that. For a moment, I thought – well, I know that sort of thing goes on here, there and everywhere, especially here. But we don't mention it.'

'Of course not,' Leanne said reassuringly. 'Just like you won't tell Edwina, I mean Lady Whatsit about—'

He put his finger to his lips. 'Won't tell, promise. You did ever such a good job, in any case. Nobody would have guessed you weren't professionals.'

'But how did *you* know?' Maddy asked.

'The catering firm called just after you arrived to say they had a staff problem. Double booked or something, so they couldn't provide the serving staff we'd ordered. They were frightfully sorry and it won't happen again. Damn right it won't. We won't use them again.'

Maddy put her apron on the table. 'Does Edwina – I mean Lady, eh…'

'Huntington-Smith,' Horace filled in. 'No. She doesn't know. I took the call.'

Maddy nodded. 'Oh good. Thank you for not telling on us. It was all a mistake, really. We got lost in the rain and called in to ask for the way to Tudor Manor Hotel, where we booked a room. And then—'

'Then Edwina mistook you for serving staff and didn't give you a chance to explain,' Horace filled in. 'But you didn't mind because it all seemed a bit of fun, and you could get those dreadful selfies to show your Internet friends.' He grinned. 'Am I right?'

'Spot on,' Leanne laughed. She took her phone from the pocket of her jeans. 'Why don't we do a selfie with you?'

Horace laughed. 'Well, why not? I've never been in one. Are you going to post it on the Internet?'

'Only with your permission,' Maddy said.

Horace beamed, showing all his crooked teeth. 'You have it. I could do with fifteen minutes of fame. It's always all about bloody Edwina and her good works and her hostess-with-the-mostest rubbish.' He positioned himself between Maddy and Leanne, putting his arms around them both. 'So what do we do now?'

'I take the picture.' Leanne stretched out her hand with the phone. 'Everyone, say sex.'

'Sex!' they all shouted.

Horace's laugh boomed around the kitchen. He laughed even louder when Leanne showed him the photo. 'Excellent. That should make Edwina rather ill, I should think, if she sees it on Facebook.'

'I hope it won't cause you any trouble,' Maddy said.

Horace shrugged. 'I don't care. This was such fun, dear girls.'

Leanne stuffed her phone into her bag. 'We'll be off now. Could you just give us directions to Tudor Manor?'

Horace nodded. 'Of course. It's not far. At the other end of the village, a little lane around the corner from The Highwayman pub. Can't miss it.' He sighed. 'Well, good luck, dear girls. It was a pleasure to make your acquaintance. Do call in if ever you're in the neighbourhood.'

'We will.' Maddy grabbed her bag and her jacket. 'Bye, Horace, so nice to meet you.'

'And you.' Horace groped in his breast pocket, pulled out a crumpled card and handed it to Leanne. 'Here's the number to the house.'

'Thanks.' Leanne put the card in her bag.

Horace slapped his forehead. 'Nearly forgot. What about your fee? For the work you did tonight, I mean.'

Leanne shrugged. 'No need for that. Give it to charity.' She blew him a kiss. 'See you around, Horace, baby.'

'I'll see you out.'

'No need,' Maddy called over her shoulder as they left. 'We know the way.'

As the big entrance door slammed shut behind them, Maddy and Leanne ran through the still teeming rain to the car and drove down the avenue on the tail of the last departing guests.

'Look at all those SUVs. I wonder where they're going on to,' Leanne mused.

Maddy sighed. 'Who cares? All I want is a long hot bath and dinner.'

'Me too. I'm glad that particular adventure is over.'

'I hope none of those celebs will be annoyed at appearing on the blog,' Maddy muttered as she drove up the village street on the lookout for The Highwayman pub.

'Sure, they'll love it,' Leanne said. 'Just think of what it'll do for the blog. And those celebrities adore any kind of exposure. There is no such thing as bad publicity, ya know.'

'Or good,' Maddy said darkly, still unsure about the whole blog idea. What had she let herself into?

Chapter Eleven

The weather improved the following day, and after a full English breakfast at the Tudor Manor Hotel they paid the inflated bill and drove into the Cotswold hills in the morning sunshine.

'Wonderful day,' Maddy said as green pastures and lovely stone-faced cottages flashed past.

Leanne fished her sunglasses from her head and put them on her nose. 'Yeah. A change from yesterday, thank God. Must say that breakfast was pretty filling. Not like a full Irish, though.'

Maddy sighed and undid the button on her trousers. 'No, you're right. There was no black pudding or fried potatoes and only one egg. But it was pretty good all the same. Don't think I'll want to eat for at least a week.'

'I'm sure you'll change your mind around dinnertime.'

Maddy checked her watch. 'It's only ten o'clock. We'll have time to visit Oxford.'

Leanne's shoulders sank. 'Oookayyy. Let's do that, then, since you're so hooked on culture and learning.'

'Thanks. Sounds like you're making some kind of sacrifice. Must say I'm confused. I mean you have a science degree from Trinity. Must have taken a little learning.'

'Learning, yes. But science needs a different kind of mind. It's technical and very specific. Far from the arty-farty realm of literature and art.'

Maddy considered this for a moment. 'Oh. Yes. I suppose you're right. Never thought of it like that.'

'I love science, especially chemistry. But literature and art leave me cold. Give me mountains to climb, oceans to swim in, snow to ski on and things to smell and feel, and I'm happy.'

'I had no idea we were so different,' Maddy exclaimed.

'You live in your mind, I live in my senses. But we're still on the same wavelength about everything else, I feel. Don't you?'

'Oh, yes. I do,' Maddy agreed with a surge of warmth towards Leanne. She had never had a friend with this depth of understanding. Maybe this was how it felt to have a sister?

They travelled in silence for a while, the only sound the soft purring of the engine and the distant swish of the traffic outside until Leanne let out a laugh. 'So, what about your man, then? Sir Horace? Isn't he a dote?'

'Oh yes. I loved him. I could adopt him as my uncle and take him home.'

'Me too.' Leanne looked thoughtful as she drove. 'I kind of recognise that name. Huntington-Smith. It reminds me of something… Edwina Huntington-Smith, especially. It has a *Hello* magazine ring to it somehow.'

'Not to me,' Maddy argued. 'I never read those magazines.'

'Not even at the hairdresser's?'

'No. I usually do my emails on my phone and glance through *Vogue*.'

Leanne sighed. 'You're so not clued in. Are you even on Facebook?'

'Of course. Isn't everybody? But okay, I only have fifteen friends,' Maddy admitted, feeling stupid. 'And I hardly log in at all.'

'But don't you think it's a great way to keep in touch with friends?'

'Not really. In any case, I don't have many,' Maddy confessed. 'I went to a boarding school in Kilkenny. Most of the girls were from all over the country, some of them lived abroad. We all seemed to scatter after graduation, and then I went to France, came back and got married. I didn't really have much time to hang out with friends. And when my mother died, I found that I couldn't connect with people my own age. I became a bit of a hermit in a way.'

'Oh. I had no idea. Must have been lonely sometimes.'

Maddy shrugged. 'I'm an only child, so I wasn't used to a lot of people my age around me. My mum was my best friend, in a way. She was my rock, you know?'

'Really?' Leanne glanced at Maddy. 'I'm so sorry. I never had that kind of thing with my mam. You must miss her a lot.'

Maddy sighed. 'I never stop missing her. It's not that I don't have friends these days, but those I have prefer to meet up for coffee, not chat on Facebook.'

'I see. Good for you. But what about Twitter?'

'God forbid.'

'How about Instagram?'

Maddy laughed. 'Yes, a bit. I put up holiday snaps and such things just so the kids can see what we're up to. And I can keep an eye on them too. But not that often.'

'Typical. You need to catch up, my friend. This will be a learning curve for you. A chance to join the twenty-first century.'

Maddy laughed. 'Yeah, that's a thought.'

'Anyway,' Leanne continued, 'do us a favour, willya? Google your woman. I want to find out who she is.'

Maddy picked up her phone. 'Okay. Try to slow down a bit.' Maddy quickly typed Edwina's name into the search box on Google.

'What's coming up?' Leanne asked, her eyes on the road. 'Tell me quickly, before we get to the motorway.'

'Lots of things. Photos in *Hello*, *Tatler* and the *Sunday Times*, where there's an article about their house. Did you know it's called Toadhead Manor? It's an old name. The original house was built in Tudor times by Sir Horace's ancestors but was burnt down at the end of the eighteenth century. The present house was built on the foundations of the old house by John Nash in the early nineteenth century. That's interesting. Edwin Nash, who was a distant relation, built a lot of the protestant churches in Ireland. Did you know that?'

Leanne waved her hand impatiently. 'Yes, yes, whatever. What else does it say?'

'It says…' Maddy scanned the article. 'Oh my God, this is amazing!'

Leanne stood on the brakes, and the car came to a screeching halt on the hard shoulder, accompanied by much tooting and blinking of headlights from other cars.

'What? What?' she shouted. 'Tell me. I can't drive and listen to you at the same time.'

'Calm down. I'll read it to you.'

Leanne snatched the phone from Maddy. 'I'll read it myself.' She looked at the screen, scrolling down, her eyes widening. 'Edwina

Huntington-Smith, née Abbingley, is a distant cousin and close friend of the duchess of – wow. So, she's very well connected. She was flower girl at the duchess's first wedding, it appears. And,' Leanne continued, 'her husband, Sir Horace, is a former chairman of the boards of several well-known car manufacturers such as Jaguar and Ford UK, among others. He is also high profile in local farming in the area, his farm having switched from beef to tillage and organic fruit and vegetables. And he breeds Leghorns and Bantam hens. Edwina,' Leanne read on, 'is a well-known hostess in the area and often throws parties attended by her many famous neighbours.'

'Like the one last night,' Maddy said. 'Gosh.'

'Golly gosh, indeed. This'll be brilliant for our blog.' Leanne handed the phone back and started the car. 'I hope we can get the contract sorted so we can start.'

'I got the email with it attached from my dad this morning. He says he'll go through it so we don't have to. We'll just sign it once the *Women Now* people get back with their signature. It'll all be done electronically too and then we're off in a hack.'

'Great.'

Maddy put her phone back into her bag. 'I hope they'll accept the terms. We agreed to their fee, but we wanted a certain percentage of the profit from advertising too, so they might balk at that. Plus, we have full rights to photos and whatever we write.'

'Pretty stiff terms,' Leanne muttered. 'But I get the point. This could be something we – or I, in any case – might develop, so it's a good thing to have everything settled. Your dad's great to do this for us.'

'He's a true brick.'

'Here's the exit to the motorway now,' Leanne announced. 'We'll be in Oxford before you know it.'

'Well, in about an hour anyway. But this car is such a smooth ride. I might have a little snooze while you drive.'

'Snooze away,' Leanne said. 'And dream pretty dreams of Prince Charming and his beautiful castle in the hills. That's what my dad used to say when I was little girl.'

'How sweet.' Maddy smiled and closed her eyes. The purring of the engine and the gentle motion of the car was almost hypnotic, and her mind drifted to the past and that real castle she had been to once in her distant youth.

*

The afternoon at Ludo's uncle's restaurant was fun and filled with laughter. Les Deux Toques proved harder to find than Ludo had said. Maddy walked around the Marais turning into narrow lanes, finding herself down dead ends and in tiny squares, where washing hung from the windows of old houses and music could be heard here and there. The air was thick with the smell of garlic, herbs and newly baked bread. After a lot of asking around, she finally found it in the middle of a sunny street lined with cafés and quaint shops selling arts and crafts and second-hand books. She pulled the red door open and entered the little restaurant, where guests, engaged in lively conversations, were finishing their lunch. Infused with the smell of excellent food, the restaurant felt instantly welcoming.

A waiter sprang to attention as she approached the counter. 'Mademoiselle? A table for one?'

Maddy smiled. 'No, I'm not eating. I'm here to meet Ludo and his uncle.'

'Ah.' He nodded and pushed the door behind him open. 'In the kitchen.'

'*Merci.*' Maddy entered the kitchen, where two chefs were busy preparing the last orders and the head chef – Ludo's uncle, Maddy supposed – was arguing with a young boy in a stained white apron.

'I will not tolerate this kind of sloppiness,' the head chef shouted, gesturing with a ladle. 'You'd better sharpen up or you're fired. Go and work in McDonald's for all I care.'

The boy hung his head. '*Oui*, chef,' he whispered. 'I'm sorry. I was careless.'

Maddy backed towards the door. She would wait for Ludo outside. But someone caught her by the arms from behind. She twirled around. 'Ludo!'

He kissed her on both cheeks. '*Ma petite* Madeleine. You found us. Don't worry. My uncle runs a very tight ship. Anyone not doing his job gets strips torn off him. He's really quite sweet.'

The head chef, a stocky man with thick black eyebrows and a bulbous nose, stopped shouting. 'Ludo!' he exclaimed, his angry expression swiftly changing like the sun coming out of a dark cloud. He clapped the young boy's shoulder. 'Go on. That's enough. You'll do better tomorrow, okay?'

The young boy melted into the shadows, and the head chef went to kiss Ludo and shake hands with Maddy. '*Bonjour,*' he said. 'I'm Jean Montrouge. Please call me Uncle Jean. I see Ludo did not exaggerate your Irish beauty. That porcelain skin, those blue eyes… The little freckles on the nose… *Très belle!*'

Maddy blushed. Nobody had said she was beautiful before. 'Thank you.' Up close, with his smile lighting up his rough features, this man was charming.

He put his hand on Ludo's back. 'But you want to eat, no?'

Maddy shook her head. 'Thank you. I've already had lunch.'

'A little dessert, then? With coffee?'

'We'll have some crème brûlée,' Ludo said. 'And if there's a table free out there, we could all sit down. I'm a little tired after the lunch rush hour. I had to wait tables today. My uncle is a real slave driver.'

'You have to learn how to run a restaurant,' Uncle Jean remarked.

'I know.' Ludo took Maddy's hand. 'Let's go and sit in the restaurant. I have a proposition for you.'

'A what?' Maddy followed Ludo back into the now nearly empty restaurant.

'A proposition,' he said, after they had sat down at a table by the window.

Maddy looked into his melting brown eyes and thought whatever it was, she would say yes. She wanted to be with him, in his space. 'Tell me.'

'I have been asked to do a job tonight. A catered event in a castle just south of Paris. Beautiful place by a lake. It's a wedding. Could be very busy. But I have been offered free accommodation once the dinner is over in the old part of the castle, far away from everyone else. The wedding party will be staying in a nearby hotel, as the château is not taking overnight guests. So…' He paused. 'I was wondering if you'd like to come with me?'

'To the château?' Maddy asked. She laughed. How stupid that sounded. 'I mean will we…?'

'Separate rooms,' Ludo said. 'Adjoining. With a shared balcony.' He touched her cheek. 'We won't do anything you're not comfortable with. Will you come with me tonight, Maddy?'

Unable to reply, she looked down at the pink linen tablecloth.

'I know we've only just met,' Ludo said, his voice a near whisper, 'but I have a feeling I've known you all my life.'

'I bet you say that to all the girls,' she teased, trying to lighten the mood.

He took her hand. 'No. I've never said that to anyone, because it wouldn't have been true. But you haven't replied to my question.'

His eyes were burning into hers; Maddy was suddenly speechless. She knew what would happen if she went with him. She shouldn't go. But a night with him, in an old French château... how utterly irresistible. She leant back, away from his dizzying closeness and his scent and his warm breath on her face. 'I...' She swallowed. 'Yes,' she heard herself say. 'I'd love to go with you to the château.'

Chapter Twelve

A sudden squeal cut into Maddy's daydream. She sat up. 'What? Are you in pain?'

'N-n-noo,' Leanne stammered. 'But there's something moving.'

'Moving? Where?'

'Under your grey pashmina in the back seat.'

'What do you mean? I don't have a grey pashmina.' Maddy craned her neck to look behind her. 'That thing? It's not mine. I thought it was yours.'

'No,' Leanne snapped, trying to keep the car from swerving into the next lane, narrowly missing a van. 'Not mine. But whoever it belongs to, it's hiding something. Can't you see? It's moving. I just noticed it in the rear-view mirror.'

Maddy glanced at the heap of soft grey cashmere. Nothing. 'I can't see what you're going on about.' She twisted around and put her hand on the crumpled pashmina. There was something underneath. She could feel it. Then it moved and Maddy screamed, snatching her hand away. 'Oh my God! You're right! It's... I don't know... a rat?!'

'I'm taking that exit,' Leanne shouted and turned the wheel. 'We have to get off the motorway and – don't touch it! If it's a rat, it'll bite you. They're dangerous.'

'I know.' Rigid with terror, Maddy stared at the bundle. It moved and then was still, then moved again. 'We have to get rid of it. When you stop the car, I'll grab the bundle and throw it out.'

Leanne drove up the exit from the motorway. 'Good plan. Don't take your eyes off it. I can stop after the roundabout over there.'

'Okay.' Shaking, Maddy kept her eyes on the wriggling grey bundle while Leanne took the roundabout on two wheels and turned into a narrow road, finally coming to a stop on the grassy verge.

Leanne turned off the engine and opened her door. 'Get out! We have to get rid of that thing.'

Maddy got out of the car, her legs trembling, and opened the rear door. She was about to grab the bundle to throw it in the ditch when it made a sound. 'It's whining,' she said. 'Rats don't whine, do they?'

Whatever it was writhed under the pashmina and then let out a different sound.

'It's barking. Can't be a rat, then.' Leanne took the bundle out of the car and put it on the grass. 'It's a dog.'

'Not just any dog,' Maddy said as a curly black head peeped out from under the heap of cashmere. She knelt on the grass and peeled off the cover to reveal a small black poodle that immediately started to lick her face. 'It's Gidget. That dog Edwina was minding.'

Leanne stared at the dog. 'Holy Mother, how on earth did she get into our car?'

Maddy cuddled the little dog. 'More importantly, how on earth are we going to give her back? We only have a few hours before we get on the ferry. We can't drive all the way back to Edwina's today.'

'Maybe we can pop her into a police station in Oxford? Tell them we found this dog and ask them to contact the owner. I'm sure she's microchipped.'

'Yes, but the owner, Edwina's friend, is away. Edwina is only minding it. So the microchip won't be much help there.'

'Maybe we can give Edwina a call and tell her Gidget ended up in our car? Agree on somewhere we can leave her and then…'

Maddy kissed Gidget on the nose. 'It's okay, sweetheart. We'll soon have you home again.'

Gidget struggled out of Maddy's arms, crouched on the grass and made a big puddle.

'Look, she's housetrained,' Maddy squealed. 'What a good girl!'

'Thank God for that,' Leanne muttered, taking her bag from the back seat. 'We have to call them and tell them we found her. Horace gave me a card with their number. Should be here somewhere.' After a little digging around, Leanne found the card in the bottom of her bag and handed it to Maddy. 'Here, you call him.'

'Why me?' Maddy protested.

'Because,' Leanne said and took Gidget in her arms. 'We're going to get you back to Edwina, darling. Aunty Maddy is going to call the nice Horace and he'll sort it.' Gidget licked Leanne's face and nestled into her arms with a contented sigh. 'Oh, isn't she sweet,' Leanne cooed. 'Like a real live cuddly toy.'

'Don't get too attached,' Maddy warned. 'We can't keep her.' She found her phone and dialled the number on the card. It rang several times before there was a reply.

'Toadhead Manor,' a haughty voice said.

'Is that Horace?' Maddy asked.

'No. This is the butler. I will get Sir Horace for you. Who will I say is calling?'

'I'm Maddy, one of the Irish waitresses who helped out last night.'

The voice suddenly changed. 'Oh, it's you, dear girl. Horace here. Sorry about that. I have to make sure it's not any of the tabloids. There's a bit of a kerfuffle here today.'

'Oh. Hope it's not serious.'

'Nothing much, really. Just Edwina having kittens about something as usual. What can I do for you?'

'It's about the dog. The little poodle. Gidget. She, well, she seems to have sneaked into our car last night, and we have only just noticed her.'

'Oh. You found the dog.'

'Yes,' Maddy said, puzzled by the sudden chill in his voice. 'Unfortunately, we can't come back with her, so I was wondering what we should do? Maybe leave her at a police station in Oxford? Then you or Edwina might come and get her?'

'No,' Horace said.

'What?' Maddy stared at Leanne and made a what-the-hell face. 'What do you want us to do with her, then?'

'Keep the bitch,' Horace said and hung up.

'What did he say?' Leanne asked.

'Keep the bitch.'

'What?'

'That's what he said.' Maddy stroked Gidget's silky fur. 'Maybe we should. I'd love to keep her. She's adorable.'

Leanne hugged the dog to her bosom. 'I know. So cute. But you have to call him back. We can't take a dog on the ferry.'

'Why not?' Maddy asked, an idea forming in her mind. 'I was just thinking what a terrific mascot she'd be. And how great she'd look in all the photos. Nothing like a dog to attract attention on the Internet. I'm sure we'll go viral if we have her as our star.'

'You're nuts,' Leanne said. 'We can't take a dog on a ferry to Holland. It's against the law. She needs a passport and microchips and stuff like that. We could end up in jail. Go on, call your man now and tell him it's not possible.'

Maddy sighed. 'Oh, okay, then.' She dialled the number. When Horace answered, she started to talk very fast. 'Listen, Horace, we can't keep this dog. She belongs to Edwina's friend who, I'm sure, will want her back soon.'

'No,' Horace said morosely. 'We have to keep her for the summer. I tried to make Edwina see reason, but she wouldn't listen. I'd be eternally grateful if you could keep the little monster for the next few weeks, at least.'

'But why?' Maddy asked, confused. There was a note of panic in Horace's voice that seemed odd considering the size of the dog. 'What have you got against her? I mean you have two ginormous Great Danes, so what harm can an itsy bitsy little poodle do?'

'Plenty,' Horace snarled. 'All over the house. And she's been at my prizewinning hens too. Not to mention that she sleeps in our bed and farts all night. Possibly the result of being fed foie gras and smoked salmon. Edwina dotes on her and baby talks to her. I can't stand it any more. When she disappeared last night, I was hoping she'd never come back. Please, please keep her. At least a couple of weeks. I'd be willing to pay.'

'But we're on our way to Holland,' Maddy cut in. 'We're on a long journey around Europe. We can't take a dog without a passport with us to the continent.'

'Ah, but she does have a passport,' Horace said, a note of triumph in his voice. 'Just look in the glove compartment. And she's been microchipped too. She was supposed to travel with the owner, but it turned out the husband didn't want her, so Edwina volunteered.'

'What?' Maddy exclaimed. 'So you put the dog in our car?'

'I'm afraid I have to plead guilty to that one. You must have been tired. You forgot to lock that wonderful machine.'

'Oh, feck.'

'A lucky break, I'd say,' Horace remarked.

'I could contact Edwina and tell her what you did,' Maddy said.

'Please don't.'

'But she must have told the owner the dog is missing by now.'

'No, she hasn't. Too chicken to face the wrath of that particular woman. Edwina won't say a word until she has to. When the dog is found or her friend returns – whichever comes first. Edwina might even tell her the dog caught some kind of flu and died.'

'She wouldn't.'

'You don't know Edwina. But there's something else…' Horace's breathing became laboured. 'I didn't want to alarm you, but I haven't been very well. Heart trouble. I'm having surgery in a couple of weeks. I need peace and quiet until then.'

'Oh,' Maddy said. 'I'm so sorry. Okay… I'll consult with Leanne, and if she says yes, we have a deal.'

Horace heaved a huge sigh. 'Splendid.'

'Just one thing before I hang up. What if Edwina sees pictures of the doggie on the Internet? We might include her in some pictures for a website we're taking part in, you see.'

Horace let out a laugh. 'Edwina hasn't a clue about the Internet. Or computers. She wouldn't know a laptop if it bit her in the arse.'

Maddy couldn't help giggling. 'Okay, then. I think we can help you out. But only for the month, okay?'

'You have saved my life, darling girl,' Horace said and hung up.

'What was that all about?' Leanne asked after Maddy had put her phone away.

Maddy smirked. 'Turns out we just got ourselves a new passenger.'

Their visit to Oxford cancelled due to a lack of time, they drove on, making a quick detour to Windsor to buy food suitable for a spoilt poodle. In the Posh Pooch shop, they purchased dog food of the dry variety, a soft dog bed, a collar and lead decorated with little red hearts and two bowls for food and water. Maddy steered Leanne away from the dog rain capes, squeaky toys and other unnecessary items.

'But it's all so cute,' Leanne cooed, stroking a dog cardigan in soft blue. 'This must be what it's like to buy clothes for a new baby.'

'No, it's not,' Maddy said with feeling, her thoughts going back to those days when she had first discovered she was pregnant with Sophie. The joy mixed with fear. The miracle of the first little kick, the knowledge that life would never be the same again and that a new little person was growing inside her. 'Having a baby is a true miracle. A dog is just a dog.'

Leanne looked contrite. 'I know. Sorry. I didn't mean – it was a stupid thing to say.'

Maddy put her hand on Leanne's arm. 'It's okay. No harm done. It was just that what you said made me realise how much I miss them. The babies, I mean.'

'I know.'

'Dogs can make wonderful companions, especially for people living alone,' Maddy continued, not wanting to upset Leanne. 'But you can't turn them into your baby. Or a fashion accessory,' she added, eyeing a woman in the opposite aisle trying to fit a pink sweater on a tiny Chihuahua with sad eyes. 'Dogs don't need clothes. They have fur.'

'I know that too,' Leanne said, hugging Gidget to her chest. 'But can I love her anyway?'

Maddy laughed. 'You can. And you may buy her that chicken toy too. Come on, let's get out of this hot shop before you end up spending a fortune. I want to go and see the castle.'

'Just one more thing,' Leanne said as they walked back to the car with Gidget on her new lead. 'I want to change her name. I hate Gidget, don't you?'

'With a passion. But that's her name, and she knows it and comes when you call her.'

'Yeah, but if we call her Bridget, she won't know the difference.'

Maddy nodded. 'Of course! Brilliant idea. Love the name. Suits her, too, doesn't it, Bridget?'

The little dog wagged her tiny tail.

'She loves it,' Leanne said.

Having fed the renamed Bridget and settled her in her new bed in the back seat, they drove the short distance to Windsor Castle

car park and set off for a quick view of the famous castle, leaving
the dog asleep in the back seat with the windows half-open.

The castle proved to be even more incredible than the pictures
in the guide book. As they walked through the state apartments
admiring the grandeur and fine art, including paintings by Rembrandt, Rubens and Canaletto, Maddy felt an eerie sense of being
in a parallel universe. This couldn't be real, being here, walking
through such beauty and history without a care in the world. She
wondered if she really was dreaming and would wake up in her own
bed on a dreary Monday morning with a full day of teaching surly
teenage girls ahead of her. She glanced up at the ceiling soaring
above them, at the gilt wood carvings and the faces in the portraits
looking haughtily down at them, the sound of their footsteps on
the marble floors echoing through the long galleries. It was difficult
to take in all that had happened in the short space of two days. But
here they were, looking at all the magnificence of the British Empire,
which now seemed a lot more real than if she had seen it on TV.

Leanne shivered beside her as they entered the Waterloo Chamber
with its magnificent décor and rich furnishings. 'Can you smell it?'
she whispered. 'That kind of musty history smell of dried flowers
and old books?'

Maddy sniffed the air. 'No. Well, maybe. Like all old places, I
suppose. A whiff of the past.'

'In this one, it's especially strong. But I suppose my nose is extra
sensitive.'

'It is. I can't smell half the things you do,' Maddy said, realising
Leanne's sense of smell was highly unusual, scarily so. She could
smell people a mile away and know exactly what soap they used or

what they had had for lunch. She would know without looking that someone was eating an orange from a distance and smell cigarettes before anyone had even taken their first puff. It was a strange talent, if you could call it that, and had to be very difficult to live with. Imagine being assaulted by your senses all day long.

'My nose will lead me to my dad,' Leanne said.

Maddy put her arm through Leanne's. 'Maybe it will also help me find who I'm looking for.'

'If he smells good.'

Maddy sighed. 'As far as I remember, he smelt divine.'

A pinging sound echoed through the vast room. Maddy checked her phone. A text from her father. *Contract signed by other party through Docusign. They will send it to you to do the same. Love, Dad.* Maddy showed the text to Leanne. 'I presume you know what Docusign is.'

'Yes. It's electronic signing online. Very modern!' Leanne smiled as she read the text. 'Cool. Now all we have to do is sign it!'

Maddy raised her right hand and they high-fived. They were on their way.

Chapter Thirteen

The trip on the ferry started off in calm waters, despite the promise of high winds later.

'I have a tendency to get a little queasy in high seas,' Maddy warned as they settled at a table in the dining room, Bridget at their feet.

Leanne gazed out across the sea. 'Looks pretty calm now. Maybe the weather report is wrong?'

'I certainly hope so.'

'Fingers crossed.' Leanne picked up the menu. 'What do you want? Maybe something light? I'm not that hungry. How about Caesar salad and toast?'

'Sounds good. And a bottle of Dutch beer.'

Their order arrived within minutes and they ate in companionable silence for a moment.

Leanne finished her beer with a smile on her face. 'Great stuff. But strong. You want another one?'

Maddy shook her head. 'No. I'm grand.'

'Okay.' Leanne leaned back and stared out the window across the blue-grey water. 'This view reminds me of Norway. And my dad.'

'Do you remember him clearly?'

'Yes. He left when I was twelve. He was this tall, handsome hero-type to me. And he was fun and adventurous. Loved the great outdoors. We used to go on these lovely holidays in the west, just him and me. We went sailing and fishing.' Leanne looked wistfully at Maddy. 'If –I mean when – I meet him again, I'm not sure how I'll feel. He left and never came back. Mam made it sound as if he deserted us. But maybe there's more to it than that? Maybe there was some reason why he walked out and didn't keep in touch? That's what I want to find out.'

'You're willing to give him the benefit of doubt, then?'

Leanne nodded. 'Yes, of course. Wouldn't you?'

'If it were my dad, yes,' Maddy replied after a moment's hesitation. 'But not—'

'But not in the case of that guy who didn't keep his promise?' Leanne filled in. 'I'm guessing now, but isn't that what happened?'

'Yes. Something like that. We parted on the promise of him contacting me when he came to Dublin. But I never heard from him again. I want to know why.'

'Could make you sad though,' Leanne remarked. 'The truth often hurts. And then what good would it do? I mean if you could live your life again, would you change anything? Would you not have married Mr Golf Pants, stayed single and waited for the French lover to appear again, even if it took years?'

'But then I wouldn't have my children,' Maddy argued. 'No. I don't think I'd change much. Except perhaps…' She thought for a moment. Was the failure of her marriage her fault? Or Tom's? Or just a series of circumstances and misunderstandings? 'It's difficult to pinpoint the exact cause of why Tom and I seem to be drifting apart, as the saying goes,' she remarked. 'But maybe some of it is because I always had this regret – this kind of wishful thinking about Ludo and what could have been. There's a part of me I never shared with Tom. A part that only Ludo has seen.' She sighed and stared out the window, trying to focus on the present. 'There are more waves now.'

Leanne nodded. 'Yes. It's getting a little rocky too. But I like it.'

'I don't.' Maddy rose unsteadily. 'I'm going to go to bed before it gets worse. Will you mind Bridget?'

Leanne looked at her with concern. 'Of course. Do you have seasick tablets?'

'In my bag. Might be too late though,' Maddy said and stumbled to her cabin, where she collapsed on her bunk and fell asleep.

Amsterdam on a June morning was enchanting. The water in the canals reflected the sunlight in glittering waves, and the façades of the narrow old houses glowed with vivid colours. Flowerpots crammed with petunias, geraniums and roses hung from the railings of the humpback bridges, under which floated a procession of quaint barges. Maddy had imagined a seedy town full of sex shops and dodgy cafés selling drugs, but she was pleasantly surprised by the intricate canals and beautiful architecture. Everywhere she looked, people were cycling across the cobblestones, having coffee outside picturesque restaurants or queuing to visit museums and art galleries. Leanne had booked rooms for them at a boutique hotel overlooking the beautiful Herengracht Canal, where they had thought of every comfort, even a water bowl and a cushion on the floor for Bridget in Leanne's room.

'That's what I call service.' Leanne bounced on the large bed. 'Very comfy. I bet yours is as well.'

It was. Once settled in, Maddy lay back on top of the bed in her room, looking up at the ceiling with its cornices painted lime green and the brass chandelier. Her gaze drifted to the large window, through which she could glimpse a bridge across the canal crammed with barges and smaller rowing boats. A cool breeze laden with coffee and cinnamon buns drifted in, making Maddy feel surprisingly hungry. It was lovely to relax after the rough seas that had made her more than a little seasick. She hadn't been able to appreciate the plush cabin on the ferry, the nice dining room and the gourmet food on offer like Leanne, who had stuck her head in later that night and, when she saw Maddy's green face, just said, 'Ugh, don't move. Scream if you need me.' There was no screaming, however, just a lot of heaving, ending with her dinner in the toilet followed by fitful sleep and a splitting headache.

Leanne, having what she called 'Scandinavian sea legs', had enjoyed all the perks of first class and emerged glowing from her cabin with Bridget under her arm the next morning. 'You have no idea what a great fashion accessory a little doggy can be,' she declared. 'And what a magnet it is, especially when it comes to hunky men. Last night, I was chatted up by this gorgeous Dutchman, and we had a nice little flirt until his wife arrived. That put an end to the fun. Talk about a battle-axe in blonde clothing.'

Maddy had to laugh despite her lingering nausea. 'I can imagine. Pity he was married.'

Leanne shrugged. 'Yeah. But that's life. All the great men are usually taken.' She produced her phone from her bag. 'Hey, I have a bunch of photos I want to send off and a little bit of a blog post I wrote as our first effort. I'll show it to you when we get to the hotel, and then we can tweak it a bit and get it off to the *Women Now* people.'

'Oh, God, I'm not sure I feel strong enough to see it.'

'What?' Leanne squealed. 'Are you chickening out already?'

'No,' Maddy said. 'I'm just a little apprehensive. I'm sure it'll be great.'

'You bet your butt,' Leanne said. 'You'll love it. I swear.'

In her hotel room, Maddy closed her eyes and drifted off, happy to be on dry land and on a bed that wasn't moving. But she only managed a few minutes' snooze before Leanne knocked on the door. Maddy got up, wobbled across the soft carpet and let her in, scooping Bridget into her arms. 'My turn for cuddles.'

'Yes, sure. Be my guest.' Leanne sat down on the sofa by the window and took out a small travel laptop from her tote. 'Here, take a look. Our first post. The champagne reception with the celebs.'

Maddy sat down beside her, Bridget on her lap. *Bubbly with the Best,* she read. 'Great title.' *How about this for a fun evening in the Cotswolds?* it continued. *Accidentally landing at a stately home in pouring rain and ending up as serving staff to the rich and famous. We parked the car and rang the bell to ask where we were. But before we knew what was happening, the hostess with the mostest, a real lady of the manor, pulled us in and dolled us up in waitress gear serving trays of caviar and champagne to none other than Hugh Grant and Jeremy Clarkson, as you can see by the photos taken by*

Joanna Trollope, queen of the Aga sagas. We kept pinching each other, but nothing happened, so it was real and true. Afterwards, we met Sir Horace. Yes, a real live sir, who thanked us for being more fun than any real waitresses they had ever had. He was happy to be included in our selfie, as you can see. What a guy! A good time was had by all, especially us.

A great way to kick-start our Great Euroscape. Next stop Amsterdam. Who knows what will happen there. Stay tuned! Love and kisses from Leanne, Maddy and our new mascot, a poodle called Bridget.

P.S. All proceeds of the blog will go to the Simon Community in Dublin, and Oxfam.

The photos under the post were of the two of them setting off from Dublin, taken by Tom with Leanne's phone, followed by Leanne in her Victoria's Secret underwear. Then the photos taken at the party in the Cotswolds, one of the two of them at Windsor and finally a cute shot of Bridget in the front seat of the car.

Maddy laughed and handed the laptop back. 'Love it. The photos are great.'

'Glad you liked it. I thought we'd skip the ferry crossing. Not much fun to show you puking or me trying to deal with a pissed-off Dutch blonde.'

'Could add a touch of realism, though.'

'Who wants realism? We're living the dream,' Leanne declared.

'Lucky we got Bridget through all the controls at the ferry port.' Maddy sighed.

'They were more interested in her than us.' Leanne got up. 'Let's hit the town. I've already booked us a trip on the canals.'

Maddy glared at her. 'Are you mad? I don't want to go on another boat trip for at least twenty years.'

Leanne plopped down on the sofa again, scaring Bridget, who jumped up and started to bark. 'So, what the feck do you want to do, then? We can't stay all day in this hole.'

'A four-star hotel like this is a hole now?' Maddy said hotly. 'Jesus, you're getting awfully spoilt.'

Leanne grinned. 'I only said that to get a rise out of you. You were looking so pale and wan. And it worked. Look at you... all red-faced and excited.'

'Ha, ha.' Maddy twiddled Bridget's ear, racking her brain for ideas. 'Okay. Don't scream, but I want to see the Rembrandthuis, otherwise known as Rembrandt's—'

'—house,' Leanne cut in. 'Okay. Fine. Not a bad idea. Then I get to pick the next thing. I want to go and see NEMO. Fantastic museum, or exhibition, or – gosh – I don't know what to call it.'

Excited, Maddy nodded. 'Yeah, yeah I know. It's a kind of living museum on top of the entrance to the IJ Tunnel. Slanted-roof green-copper building, almost surrounded by water, right? I think I've seen pictures of it.'

'That's right. Its rooftop square has great views and water- and wind-operated hands-on exhibits. Inside, everything is interactive, with three floors of investigative mayhem. You can lift yourself up via a pulley, make bubbles, build structures, divide light into colours, race your shadow and all of that. Something you'll love if you're into physics.'

'Or a teenager. Sounds fun,' Maddy agreed. 'That'll be your treat. But then I want to go to a restaurant called Greetje for lunch. Typical Dutch food, I've heard.'

Leanne rolled her eyes. 'And you were puking your guts out only a few hours ago. But if that's what you want, let's do it. After that I want to go to Micropia.'

'What's that?' Maddy waved her hand. 'No, don't tell me. Something to do with bacteria?'

Leanne grinned. 'Yes. Absolutely fascinating. But you'll never want to go into a bathroom again.'

Maddy made a face. 'I think I'll give that one a miss. I'll take Bridget for a walk, instead. All around the canals. How's that, sweetheart?' She kissed the little dog on top of her head.

'That's all sorted, then,' Leanne said. 'All we have to do is find a fun place for drinks and dinner. Not too much booze, though. Makes one look like a floozy in photos,' she added, with a cheeky grin.

'That's very true. Especially at my age.' Maddy looked for her phone and found it on the bed. 'I'll look up the Lonely Planet. They have the best tips.'

'Okay. Then let's get going.'

After a bit of scrolling, Maddy found the perfect dinner venue. 'Here it is! Right in the middle of the red-light district. D'Vijff Vlieghen. Means the five flies, apparently. Lots of character with Delft blue tiles and work by Rembrandt. More Dutch food but we can just take a nibble. Looks amazing.'

Leanne looked doubtful. 'In the red-light district?'

'Yeah, but I'm sure that has become very touristy. In any case we don't look like Dutch hookers, do we?'

'What exactly do they look like?'

Maddy shrugged. 'Who knows? But we'll be fine if we stick together.'

'This is one of those very rare moments in life when I wish I had a man to escort me,' Leanne muttered.

'We don't need men. We're strong, independent women,' Maddy said. 'Aren't we?'

Leanne nodded and made a thumbs-up sign. 'You betcha.'

Chapter Fourteen

Life had suddenly become very difficult for Sir Horace. The day after the champagne party, there was a hue and cry over the disappearance of the tiny poodle called Gidget. The house was turned upside down, as they were all ordered to 'find her at once'. But as the day wore on and there was no sign of the wretched dog, the house fell into an uneasy silence. After the initial panic, Edwina swore everyone to silence. Nobody was to breathe a word about the fact that this precious little poodle was missing. The owner, who was away at a secret location abroad, would be none the wiser until Edwina confessed or the owner returned asking for her pet, whichever came first. Edwina discussed several alternative options with Horace in the library the following morning.

'We could say she got colic and died. Or maybe someone stole her?' She shook her head. 'No, either way I'd be blamed, and she'd never speak to me again or invite me to dinner. You know how unforgiving those people are. And she'd tell everyone and we'd be social outcasts. Pariahs.' Edwina shuddered. 'That would be the end.'

'Not as I see it,' Horace muttered. 'I'd finally have time to take up bridge and maybe spend more time with my flock.'

'You sound like the vicar.' Edwina rose from the leather chester-field sofa. She pressed her fingers to her temples. 'I feel a migraine coming on. I'll go and lie down for a bit.'

'All right, my angel,' Horace said absentmindedly from behind his laptop. 'I hope you feel better soon.' He knew it was likely to be days before Edwina emerged from her bedroom. Her migraines were epic but provided him with a break from her constant nagging and the social whirl she was so addicted to. 'I'll just look up the papers online, and then I'll go out to check on the girls.'

'I really think you should stop calling the hens "girls".' Edwina shrugged her thin shoulders. 'But they're your pets, of course. Ridiculous.'

After Edwina had glided out of the room, Horace switched from the cricket scores to the *Women Today* website and the new blog called 'The Great Euroscape', chuckling at the text and the photos. Those girls were a hoot. And very pretty, both of them. He couldn't decide which one he liked best: the sassy platinum blonde with her dark eyes or the tall older girl with the glossy dark-honey hair and dazzling blue eyes. Both fun with that Irish repartee he could listen to for hours. What a combination. He found he suddenly missed them. They had lit up the old place with their laughter and jokes. Some of the guests even called the next day asking to book them for their parties. But Edwina herself hadn't been impressed. 'Not very professional, were they?' she snorted. 'And they got too familiar with the guests. I have a good mind to complain.'

Little did she know that they had written about the party and included Horace in some of the photos. He laughed to himself as he scanned the pictures, wishing he could show them to Edwina.

He looked good there, between the two girls. Younger than his sixty-two years. And happier than he had been for a long time.

But then Edwina discovered Gidget was missing and forgot all else except finding that dratted thing. Horace thought it a blessing the dog was gone. Now he didn't have to lock his wardrobe so the dog wouldn't pee in his shoes or fret about what mayhem a poodle could create in his hen house. Peace at last. He sighed happily and read the last item in the blog post with a beautiful view of the canals of Amsterdam and the flower-decked bridges. So quaint. He remembered the city from his student days when he would go there with friends to live it up a little, smoke some excellent pot and find a cuddly Dutch woman to make him happy for the night. In those days, Amsterdam had been the go-to place for sex and drugs. Probably still was.

He read the last line, nostalgia mixed with envy rising in his chest. *After a cultural afternoon, we're off to see the sights and have peek at the red-light district tonight. If we're not back by tomorrow morning, send in the troops!*

He smiled fondly at the photo of the two women waving from their sleek red sports car. Darling girls. He hoped they were being careful. Amsterdam was a dangerous city behind all the charm and quaintness. And now they were going to the red-light district for dinner. How he wished he could be there to guide them. He sighed. You couldn't put an old head on young shoulders. But… maybe one could give them a helping hand somehow…

*

After a fun day visiting all the sights and museums on their lists, Maddy walked Bridget and stopped for coffee outside one of the coffee houses overlooking the canals, enjoying the boat traffic on the waterways, and Bridget asleep at her feet. The feel of the sun on her skin, the smell of coffee and the taste of apricot jam on her mini croissant had taken her instantly back to her days with Ludo. Such a short time when the intensity of their feelings for each other and the sadness of an imminent separation made their brief love affair bittersweet. They were both sure they would meet very soon again and perhaps make a life together. They had made promises to one another but it was not to be.

Maddy took the old photo from her handbag and looked at it. It had been taken in a photo booth and they had laughed and kissed while the camera flashed. Then Ludo tore the strip in two and gave her half, which she had kept and gazed at from time to time. Their faces were a little fuzzy but still recognisable. Maddy sighed and put the photo back in her bag, her thoughts still stuck on those few weeks in Paris. Such a long time ago, but sometimes it seemed like only yesterday. Their paths crossed only to separate again at the next turn, Maddy going back to her studies and then meeting Tom, getting married and bringing up two children. Ludo doing whatever he did with his life, while she worked as a teacher in a girls' school in Dublin. How strange that life had turned out like this, so differently from the way she had expected. Maddy always thought that meeting special people was meant to be and that their romance would end in them being together for life. The perfect Parisian love story. But she was wrong. The night in the château and then the few weeks afterwards were all they had in the end. But what a night it had been, that first time...

*

A small room, he said, in the less comfortable part of a little château that was more like a manor house. Although the building was smaller than the châteaus she had visited in the Loire Valley, it was nevertheless a castle of Cinderella standards, built of sandstone with two tall towers ending in pointy roofs at each end, from which gargoyles grimaced at visitors from a height. The front windows glowed with candlelight, and they could see staff running to and fro inside, laying tables and arranging chairs. Ludo drove his small Citroën around the back and parked near the kitchen door. As they went inside, a smiling man in a chef's uniform showed them a narrow winding staircase, at the end of which they would find their rooms. After they had climbed the stairs, Ludo quickly inspected the two interconnecting rooms before he kissed Maddy, told her he would be up as soon as he finished work and put his bag on the bed in one of the rooms.

'Not that late, I think,' he said. 'The cutting of the cake will be around nine, and then I'll be free after we've cleaned up. You won't be bored?'

'No. I brought some books and magazines, and I saw there's a TV set in one of the rooms. I'll be fine.'

'And don't forget to go for a walk in the gardens before it gets dark.' He smiled, kissed her again and left. Maddy was free to inspect her room, which was bigger than she expected, with a balcony overlooking a lake and woods beyond. Leaning over the balustrade, she could see into the cobbled courtyard with a herb garden and pots overflowing with geraniums. The hustle and bustle of the wedding party was but a faint murmur at this part of the building. She stood there for a while, unable to tear herself away from the lovely view, thinking, wishing, as the thin crescent of a new moon rose above the oaks, *Please let this moment last forever.* Then she turned away, crept down the winding stairs and walked to the garden, where she wandered around breathing in the scent of flowers and newly mown grass until dusk fell. Next she went upstairs, settled on the bed and picked up her book: *La Chartreuse de Parme* by Stendhal, one of the French classics from her college course, which had enchanted her from the very first page.

She had drifted off into a light sleep when Ludo entered the room. Suddenly aware of being studied, her eyes flew open. 'Oh, I must have nodded off. Is it late?'

He kept looking at her. 'No. We've just finished. They're dancing downstairs. Can't you hear the music?'

She sat up and listened. 'Yes. They're playing "La Vie en Rose".'

He took her hands and pulled her up from the bed. 'Let's dance. It's my favourite song.' He put his arms around her waist, and as if by instinct, she put hers around his neck and her cheek to his. Their bodies seemed to fuse together as they danced slowly to the faint music, while Ludo softly sang the words into her ear, his hot breath tickling her neck. The scent of him and his body against hers made her feel like she was drunk on champagne, as he sang the first lines of the song.

'What's the next bit?' he mumbled in her ear. 'You sing it.'

She sang it in English, remembering the Louis Armstrong version. 'That's what it sounds like in my language. Not as divine as the French.'

'It's lovely.' He kissed her mouth then her neck and pulled her down on the bed. '*Je t'adore*,' he whispered into the neckline of her open shirt.

'*Moi aussi*,' she whispered back, French coming out of her mouth as if she was born to it. Oh, God how strange it was to feel so deeply for a man she had only met a short time ago. But maybe this was what they meant by love at first sight? When they sank down on the bed, her body ached for him. She didn't know if it was true love or if it would last forever, she just wanted him as much as he seemed to want her.

Not exactly a virgin, nevertheless, she was not very experienced. But he soon brushed away her awkwardness with his kisses, sweet touch and smooth movements that invited her to a rhythm as sensual and loving as if they had been lovers for a long time. There was no pulling back now. She wanted only to melt into his embrace and consummate this new love, whatever happened in the future. How sweet it was to be here in this enchanted place with the soft darkness outside enveloping them, the fragrance of flowers mingling with the cooing of doves and the distant music from the wedding below.

Later, as they lay in each other's arms, naked under the soft linen sheet, he asked her how she felt.

'Happy,' she whispered. 'And hungry.'

He sat up and swore. '*Merde!* The food. I forgot. You were so beautiful lying there, and then...'

'And then I forgot, too.' She laughed softly into the dark.

'But the food—' He switched on the lamp beside the bed. 'I put it outside. Leftovers from the wedding.'

He went outside and fetched a basket full of covered bowls, plates, glasses, forks and a bottle of champagne, which he opened with a loud bang. 'Our wedding meal.'

They sat up in bed, still naked, and he fed her delicious morsels of foie gras, roast veal, tiny tomatoes, ripe camembert and, finally, a slice of wedding cake all washed down with vintage champagne.

When she declared she couldn't eat any more, they lay back, their arms around each other and slept until the early morning sun poked rays of gold through the window they had forgotten to cover.

'You go home tomorrow,' Ludo said as they lay there, their arms around each other. 'But I was thinking... maybe you could stay a bit longer? Ask my aunt if you can keep the room until the end of the month?'

Maddy thought for a moment, her heart leaping with joy. He wanted her to stay. 'That would be fabulous. Yes, I think I could organise that. The rent isn't that much. I could get a job minding children or something – or teaching English.'

His eyes lit up. 'Fantastic! That gives us more time to be together.'

'I can't wait.'

The arrangements were made; Maddy stayed on in the little room for another two weeks. Ludo spent most nights with her, while he did his finals at the cookery school. Despite being busy with his finals, Ludo managed to squeeze in moments with Maddy during those weeks. He showed her parts of Paris not known to tourists. They walked through the Marais, along the Canal St Martin, an area popular with Parisians on Sundays. There, they picnicked on the banks of the canal, listening to guitar music and joining in with sing-songs, visiting quirky cafés and browsing in cute little boutiques. They walked hand-in-hand across the iron footbridges, stopping to look at the view, their arms around each other. They made love and then talked late into the night, sharing their hopes and dreams. It was a magical, dreamlike time that stayed in Maddy's heart and mind for the rest of her life.

They made the most of the time they had left before Maddy had to go back, but the last morning dawned far too soon.

'You're leaving tonight,' Ludo said regretfully as he got dressed.

'I know.' Maddy sat up in bed, watching him, wanting to remember every little detail. 'But you'll come to Ireland, you said.'

'Yes. Later this summer. Then we'll be together again.'

'That'll be wonderful.' Maddy groped in her bag. 'Here, I'll write down my address and phone number so you have it.' She found a piece of paper and the stub of a pencil, scribbled down the street address and the phone number and handed it to him.

He put it into the breast pocket of his shirt. 'I'll put it in a safe place.' He handed her a card. 'The number of my uncle's restaurant. Just in case. I'll be staying there, in the flat upstairs in a few weeks. My aunt and uncle are selling their apartment. They're moving to Nice.'

'I know.' Maddy put the card in her bag. 'My room is being let as soon as I move out.'

'The end of an era for them. And us.' He held out his hand. 'Let's go and have breakfast in the little café across the street one last time.'

'Then it's goodbye,' she said, tears welling up in her eyes.

'No.' He put his finger under her chin and lifted her face. 'Just *au revoir*. We'll soon meet again.'

She nodded. 'Yes,' she whispered. 'Soon.'

*

The lobby of the hotel was very crowded when, after a brief rest and settling Bridget for the night, Maddy and Leanne went downstairs. They were both dressed rather demurely in order 'not to attract the wrong kind of impression', as Leanne put it.

'After all, the red-light district—'

'—is full of hookers and pimps?' Maddy filled in.

'Yeah.'

'Oh, come on, it's very touristy these days. A bit like Soho in London or Temple Bar in Dublin. I can't imagine we'll have any trouble.'

Leanne looked a little sheepish. 'I suppose. God, I'm such a chicken.'

Surprised, Maddy stared at her. 'You? Chicken? Are you feeling okay?'

'I'm grand. Just a little apprehensive about walking around a strange city in the dark. Don't mind me.' Leanne took Maddy by the arm. 'Come on, let's hit the tiles. We promised our fans we'd go, so we have to.' She stopped. 'Did you see all the comments on the first post?'

'God, I forgot to check. Were there a lot?'

'Hundreds.' Leanne laughed and pulled her phone from her handbag. 'Here, you take a look.'

Maddy took Leanne's phone, logged into the blog and scrolled down to the comments section. Her eyes popped as she saw the number of comments. 'Jesus, there are loads!'

'Read some of them,' Leanne ordered.

Some of the comments were hilarious, some were deeply touching. 'You saved my dreary life, you fab hussies,' someone had written. 'Swoon city, darlings,' said another under the picture of Jeremy Clarkson and Hugh Grant. 'You're in my dream, move over,' said yet another. And on and on in the same vein. This first post had obviously hit home and lit up the lives of so many women out there.

'Incredible,' Maddy breathed and handed the phone back.

'And we have like twenty thousand new followers. We're going viral.'

'Scary.'

'But fun.' Leanne's eyes sparkled as she walked on. 'Let's go. I'm looking forward to seeing this weird restaurant you told me about.'

'That's the spirit.' Maddy pushed the main door open and together they marched into the street and across the cobblestones to the narrow lane off the canal.

They had only walked a few minutes in the dark lane, when Leanne nudged Maddy. 'Don't look now, but I think we're being followed,' she whispered.

Maddy shot a furtive glance behind her and noticed the shadow of a tall man a little further down the street. 'Maybe just a tourist?' she suggested, trying to sound brave despite the knot in her stomach.

'No,' Leanne hissed. 'He came around the corner right behind us, and then when I looked, he dashed into a doorway. Now he's there again.'

Shaking, Maddy took her phone from the pocket of her jacket. 'Should we call the police?'

'Don't know the emergency number here.' Leanne started to walk faster. 'Let's get to the main street ahead. There'll be more people there, and he might lose his nerve.'

'Okay.' Stiff with fear, Maddy linked arms with Leanne, and together they half ran up the street, wobbling on the uneven paving. They could hear the rasping breath of the man behind them. Just before they arrived at the brightly lit main street, Maddy looked over her shoulder again. The man had stopped, his shape illuminated by the dim streetlight. Then he started walking again, shouting something they couldn't hear. Leanne broke into a run, Maddy behind her, but the man caught up with them. 'Hello, wait a minute I want to talk to you,' he wheezed, his hoarse voice echoing through the still night.

Suddenly, Leanne stopped dead and stared at Maddy. 'Is it—?' she panted. 'It couldn't be!'

'Who?' Maddy asked, so out of breath she could hardly get the words out.

Leanne started to laugh as the man came closer. 'It's him! What the hell is *he* doing here?'

Chapter Fifteen

'Sir Horace!' Leanne exclaimed, laughing so hard she had to hold on to Maddy to stay upright. 'It's you!'

'Indeed it is, dear thing,' Horace said, panting hard, his face purple. 'You nearly killed me.'

Maddy gasped and stared at their stalker. 'Jesus Christ, you scared us shitless.'

Horace put his hand on his chest and coughed. 'Well, if you'd stopped and looked, you'd have known I wasn't a stalker or anything.'

Leanne couldn't stop laughing. 'We thought you thought we were hookers.'

'And I thought you thought I was some kind of weirdo following you. I ran as fast as I could so you would see me, but you were too fast for me.' He took out a large hanky and wiped his brow. 'Must try to get in a little sport now and then. I'm too out of shape for this kind of thing.'

'Did you follow us all the way from the hotel?' Maddy asked.

Horace pocketed his hanky. 'Yes. I was just asking about you at the reception desk when you came out of the lift.'

'Oh God, your bad heart!' Maddy exclaimed. 'You said you might need surgery. This could have killed you. Are you feeling all right?'

Horace blushed. 'I'm fine, darling. I might have stretched the truth a little bit. I do apologise.'

'Hmm, I thought so,' Maddy muttered.

'But what are you doing here?' Leanne enquired.

'I came to see you,' Horace replied. 'I read your blog post this morning about going to the red-light district and thought...' He coughed. 'As I know Amsterdam rather well, I told myself it wasn't very safe for two pretty young girls to walk around in this part of town at night. Or any part of this town. It might look charming and picturesque in the sunlight, but after the dark, the rats come out of the sewers, believe me.'

Maddy looked at him thoughtfully. 'I'm sure that's a slight exaggeration, but you have a point.'

Leanne smiled fondly at him. 'So you came all the way over here to protect us?'

Horace nodded. 'Yes. I saw there was a flight at two o'clock, so I hopped into the car and drove to the airport. Finding you was no problem, as you'd posted a photo of the view from your rooms.'

Maddy clapped her hands. 'Bravo! Great detective work. But what about her ladyship? What did she think about you taking off like that?'

Horace adopted a sad expression. 'I'm afraid she came down with one of her migraines. She'll be out for several days. I'll be back before she comes out of her room. She'll be none the wiser as to my little, ahem, fling.'

Leanne giggled. 'You snuck out behind her back? Brilliant. But what about the farm? Your prize hens?'

'All taken care of. Alistair, our butler, will see to them. As usual.'

'As usual?' Maddy's eyebrows shot up. 'Is this a permanent arrangement?'

Horace squirmed. 'Weeell… whenever the old girl has one of her turns, I have little holiday. Nothing much I can do to help her, so I stay out of her way and do my own thing, so to speak. And Alistair is my confidant of sorts.'

'A partner in crime?' Leanne suggested.

Horace smiled. 'I suppose so. But enough about that. Where are we going?'

'We were planning to have dinner at something called the five flies,' Maddy replied.

Horace nodded. 'Ah, yes, d'Vijff Vlieghen.'

Leanne looked impressed. 'You sound as if you speak Dutch like a Dutchman.'

Horace laughed. 'Not quite. But I spent some of my misspent youth here, if you get my drift. Sowed a few wild oats and so on. Before I met Edwina, of course,' he added.

Leanne winked. 'Of course.'

'Nice place, that restaurant. Used to be quite an elegant joint in my day,' Horace remarked. 'I hope I'm up to standard.'

Maddy looked at him. With his polished brogues, corduroy trousers, tweed jacket, Viyella shirt and Eton tie, he was almost like a pastiche of the English country squire. But she knew it wasn't contrived; it was simply how he had always dressed. 'You're grand,' she said.

'Splendid.' Horace linked arms with Maddy and pulled Leanne to his other side. 'But let's get going before someone thinks we're standing here discussing the price for a threesome.'

Leanne giggled. 'Horace, you're a scream.'

He squeezed her arm. 'That's the nicest thing anyone has said to me for a long time. I was wondering,' he continued as they turned into the main street, 'if you'd consider—' He stopped. 'No, that would be an imposition.'

'What?' Leanne said. 'Come on, don't hold back. You're among friends, here. Except if it's something smutty. We don't do that.'

'No, of course it isn't.' He stopped abruptly in front of a shop selling sex toys. 'Nothing remotely sordid. I was just wondering if you'd take me with you to Paris?'

His wistful expression touched Maddy's heart. He looked so forlorn and slightly lost, like someone whose life was passing him by. Just like her, like so many other middle-aged people in the world, stuck in loveless marriages with no way out except a major upheaval that would break a lot of people's hearts. He needed a bit of fun.

'Of course we will,' she heard herself say. 'Won't we, Leanne?'

But Leanne wasn't listening. She was staring at the display in the window. 'Can't believe all this is out there for all to see. I mean…' She pointed at an item. 'What's that for? The chain and leather thingy?' She looked at Horace. 'Any ideas?'

He looked uncomfortable. 'Well, it's…' He leant forward and whispered something in Leanne's ear.

She pulled back and stared at him. 'Wow. No idea that was even possible. How come you're so knowledgeable?'

Horace reddened and cleared his throat. 'I picked it up here and there.'

'Mostly here, I bet,' Maddy suggested, nudging Leanne with her elbow.

'Yeah, he seems to know Amsterdam like a local,' Leanne agreed.

'So that's okay, then?' Maddy asked.

'What?' Leanne looked confused.

'Horace wants to come with us to Paris,' Maddy explained. 'I said we'd love to have him.'

There was a long silence, during which Horace appeared to hold his breath. Then Leanne shrugged. 'Yeah, sure.'

'Really?' Horace looked as if someone had handed him a ticket to paradise. 'You are both angels from heaven.'

Maddy laughed. 'Not quite, but we're working on it.' She glanced at Leanne, trying to get her to chime in. But all she got was a dirty look behind Horace's back.

'What were you thinking?' Leanne demanded an hour later in the ladies' toilet of the restaurant.

Maddy put away her comb. 'What do you mean?'

Leanne gestured at the door with her lipstick. 'Him. That British chinless wonder. Inviting him to join us.'

'Why not? He only wants to hitch a lift to Paris. Then he'll get on the Eurostar back to London and Gloucestershire. He won't make any trouble.'

'But he'll ruin the whole *experience*,' Leanne moaned. Her eyes bored into Maddy's as she continued. 'I've dreamt of doing this for ages. Driving through Paris with the wind in my hair, just like in the song. And now I have to do it with fecking Horace!'

Maddy tried not to laugh. 'It might be raining.'

Leanne applied lipstick and pressed her lips together. 'Then I'll wait until it stops.' She glared at Maddy. 'Listen, the blog is about *us,* not bloody Horace anyway! You read those comments from our fans. This will ruin the fun.'

'I know.' Maddy put her hand on Leanne's arm. 'Come on, cheer up. It won't be that bad. In any case, the Eurostar leaves from Gare du Nord. We can let him off there and then continue on through the city. We'll drive down the Champs Elysées and on through to Rue de Rivoli and cruise through the best areas. It'll be fun. And no Horace. I promise.'

Leanne glared at her. 'I'll hold you to that. If you wreck this, I'll dump you at the nearest metro station. And that's also a promise.'

'I won't wreck anything. In any case, I want to go and see someone when we get to Paris.' Maddy felt suddenly breathless as she remembered her own agenda. Finding Ludo. Getting some kind of closure on the sense of loss that had haunted her for the past twenty years.

Leanne's eyes softened. 'Of course. You want to settle some scores.'

'Not exactly. I just want to find out why it ended like that. Why he never got in touch.'

'I know. Sorry.' Leanne put her lipstick away and opened the door. 'We'd better get back to Horace. He'll have drunk all the wine.'

They made their way through the crowded restaurant to their table, where Horace was having a lively discussion with a pretty waitress. She smiled and walked off, saying something over her shoulder.

'*Ja, hoor,*' Horace shouted after her.

'Did you hear that?' Leanne muttered. 'He's insulting her. The eejit! Calling her a—'

'That's horrible!' Maddy exclaimed.

'What the hell do you mean?' Leanne glared at Horace when they reached the table. 'Calling women names like that. I think you should leave right now, you disgusting pig.'

Horace shot up, his face red. 'What? I simply said—'

'We heard,' Maddy interrupted. 'You said "ya whore".'

Horace sighed and shook his head. 'No, dear. I said "*ja, hoor*". That's Dutch. It means "yes, indeed". We were talking about the town and how *moy* it is. I mean nice. In Dutch. I was being perfectly polite, as a matter of fact.'

Maddy laughed and sat down. 'You were speaking Dutch? And we thought you were being insulting. That's hilarious.'

Leanne sank down on the other side of Horace. 'Sorry about that, Horace.'

Horace smiled and sat down. 'It's a rather strange language. I don't speak it very well, but I picked up a bit years ago. Not that I'm good at languages, actually. Horticulture is more my thing.'

Leanne leant closer to Horace. 'You might be a bit of a klutz, but you smell nice. What's that aftershave? Sandalwood with notes of verbena and a whiff of something else.'

'New-mown hay but just a touch,' Horace filled in. 'You have an excellent nose, there, m'dear. It's a special blend. I get it from a small firm in Provence. They hand-mix their scents to order. Quite unknown but I stumbled upon it when I was in Paris a few years ago. They have a little boutique on the Left Bank.'

Leanne looked excited. 'Really? I must go there. I love smelling things and detecting the different ingredients. Maybe they'll make up a scent for me. What's the name of the shop?'

Horace looked thoughtful. 'Let me think. They're called something odd, after the hometown of the owner, who is from one of the Scandinavian countries.'

'Try to remember,' Leanne urged, an anxious edge to her voice.

'Hovden,' Horace after a long silence. 'I think that was it. A village somewhere.'

'Hovden?' Leanne whispered, her face suddenly deathly pale. 'It's a small fishing village in Northern Norway.' She turned and stared at Maddy. 'That's where my dad was born.'

Chapter Sixteen

They decided to start for Paris early the next morning.

'It's a five-hour drive,' Leanne announced at breakfast in the hotel dining room. 'And we'll stop for lunch in Brussels.'

Horace beamed at her. 'Sounds exciting. I've never been there. A town much vilified by my countrymen. All bad things start in Brussels, it seems.'

Maddy tore herself away from the view of the canal. 'I wouldn't say that. But I know people in Britain view Europe differently.' She smiled at Horace, who looked like an excited schoolboy embarking on a new adventure. His sparse grey hair was neatly brushed and his kind eyes behind the gold-rimmed glasses sparkled with excitement. There was an innocence about him that was endearing. You just couldn't be annoyed at him for longer than five seconds. He had proven to be a useful companion, taking photos on their walk through the red-light district on the way back to the hotel the night before. He had a good eye for intriguing backdrops that gave a naughty edge to the photos that Leanne proceeded to post before she went to bed.

'Our brush with Amsterdam's dark side,' she called it, hinting at sex clubs and erotic movies, neither of which they had attended, but the photos told a different story. 'No need to be two goody two-shoes,' she said with a cheeky grin as she posted the piece. 'We have to play to the fantasies of our followers.'

'Not sure I like it,' Maddy said, hoping no one she knew followed the blog. Leanne got a bit carried away sometimes. But as the blog had gained a massive amount of followers, the editors were happy, as more sponsors asked to buy space on the website. The latest caper in Amsterdam would add a little spice.

Leanne leant across the table and looked Horace in the eye. 'I hope you realise you'll be travelling in the back seat with Bridget? You might even have to have her in your lap. She loves her cuddles, you know.'

Horace blanched and gulped. 'Yes. Very well.'

'But she is such a sweetie,' Maddy exclaimed. 'Why does she misbehave with you and not with us?'

Leanne shot him a dark look. 'I bet you've given her a kick now and then.'

Horace squirmed. 'Well… I might have aimed my slipper in her direction but she deserved it, believe me.'

'Some female dogs just don't like men,' Maddy stated. 'I read that somewhere. Could be the reason.'

Leanne nodded. 'Maybe. But you have to be nice to her, Horace, or you'll end up dumped at the side of the road.'

Horace gave her a sheepish look. 'I'll do my best, I swear. I know this is the price I have to pay to see Paris.'

Leanne looked confused. 'But you've been there before, you said.'

He nodded. 'Yes, but the last time was over five years ago. I've had to tighten my belt since then. The house had to be restored, as some of it was in danger of falling down. So, I've been a little stretched financially, so to speak.'

Maddy finished her tea. 'But I thought – I mean that lavish party and Edwina's designer clothes…'

Horace sighed. 'That's her money, not mine. She has a considerable personal fortune, none of which she wants to spend on the house. So, it all comes out of my earnings and what the estate produces. We used to be better off, but we've lost on the farm income lately. I've had to dip into the egg money for this trip.'

'Oh.' Maddy patted Horace on the arm. 'Must be hard.'

He shrugged. 'I manage.'

'So that visit to the perfume shop was a long time ago?' Leanne cut in. 'I looked them up on the web, but all I got was an address. No website or anything.'

'I wouldn't know,' Horace said. 'I usually put in my order by phone. The last one was a year ago when Edwina ordered some for me as a Christmas present.'

Leanne looked deflated. 'So, I have to call in to the shop if I'm to find out anything about them?'

'I presume you do,' Horace replied.

Leanne nodded and got up. 'Okay. Right, gang, let's check out and get going. Next stop Brussels.'

'And the dratted European Union,' Horace filled in.

They reached Brussels after a tedious drive on the motorway through Holland where the flat landscape and industrial developments did nothing to lift their spirits.

'If this is Europe, give me England any day,' Horace muttered from the back seat, where Bridget had crawled onto his lap, decorating his beige twill trousers with black curly hairs, much to his annoyance. 'Could we skip lunch and go on to Paris? I'm not sure Brussels will make my heart sing.'

Leanne shot him a withering glance over her shoulder. 'We have to eat. And I've heard the Grand Place is wonderful.'

'And I've heard Brussels is a dump,' Horace retorted. 'But, look,' he said, pointing at a road sign. 'There's the exit to Bruges. Can we go there instead?'

'No,' Leanne snapped. 'We can't. Too much of a hassle. We'll have to park outside town, and then it's a long walk. I looked it up in my European guide book. In any case, Bruges is always crammed with tourists and it's impossible to get into any restaurant.'

'But Brussels will be crammed with those horrible EU people,' Horace said with a shudder, trying to shift Bridget off his lap, making her growl.

'What are you doing to her?' Maddy asked. 'Please be gentle. She doesn't like rough handling.'

'I was just trying to get her off me. But okay, she's the boss.' Horace looked morosely out of the window, admitting defeat. 'Bloody Brussels,' he muttered under his breath.

The town proved to be a lot better than they expected. The Grand Place, with its amazing seventeenth-century buildings, was impressive, especially the guildhalls with their carvings, beautiful windows, balconies and crenulations.

'A true architectural jewel,' Maddy mumbled, reading aloud from her pocket guide. 'That's no exaggeration.'

They craned their necks to look at it all and nearly broke their ankles on the uneven cobblestones. They were spoilt for choice when it came to places to eat but finally settled on one in the cellar of a mediaeval house.

'Moules frites,' Leanne announced. 'That's the best thing to have here. Mussels and fries to you and me.'

'Not for me. There isn't an "r" in this month,' Horace protested.

'Ah, sure that's an old saying,' Maddy argued. 'Mussels are safe to eat all the year around now.'

'I hope you're right,' Horace said, glancing under the table, where Bridget had settled on his feet.

'You could just eat the frites,' Maddy soothed. 'Belgian fries are the best in the world.'

'I think my mother's roast potatoes in goose fat would give them a run for their money,' Horace said with a defiant air.

Maddy was about to reply when her phone rang. She glanced at the caller ID and blinked. Tom. What could he want? They had agreed not to contact each other except in an emergency. She got up from the table looking for a quiet spot. There was no one in the small lobby inside the entrance door, so she walked towards it while she answered. 'Hi, Tom. What's up? I hope nothing bad has happened.'

'So do I,' Tom snapped. 'I just heard about you and how you're exposing yourself on the Internet.'

Maddy's heart sank. 'What? I don't—'

'Don't try to deny it. The secretary of the golf club showed the blog to me. The photos. You and that… that tart in the red-light district in Amsterdam. She asked me if we were related.'

'Oh, that.' Maddy laughed. 'Just a bit of fun.'

'Not the kind of fun I approve of.' Tom's voice was ice cold. 'What did you say to her? About your connection to me?'

'I said we weren't related. Which is technically true.'

'Yes, technically. Of course.' Maddy said, with a nasty feeling he was disowning her. What a wimp. Couldn't even stick up for his wife. She could imagine Tom standing there in his hotel, all dressed up in his golf clothes ready for another round. 'Nobody could be less related to you than me.'

'What do you mean?' he demanded. 'I'd appreciate it if you didn't sneer.'

Maddy sighed. 'I'm not sneering. I'm sorry if the blog post upset you.'

'It made me feel like a total eejit. I had no idea you were planning to do this. I thought you were just going on a holiday with a friend.'

'So did I. This blog idea just kind of happened. But we're being paid for it, don't worry. It's all going to charity. And we have signed a contract, so it's all above board.'

'Above board? That's not what it looked like to me.'

Maddy felt her patience run out. 'For God's sake, Tom, try not to be so fecking tight-arsed. It's just a bit of fun. Loads of women out there love it.'

'What if the children see it? Their mother cavorting around Europe like some kind of—' He stopped.

'Please,' Maddy cut in. 'Don't say something you'll regret.'

'I'm trying, believe me.'

'Keep trying,' Maddy said and hung up. Swallowing tears of rage and hurt, she marched back into the restaurant, where she found Leanne digging into a steaming pot of mussels and Horace downing a huge tankard of beer.

Leanne looked up. 'You look like some rat bit you in the backside.'

'Yeah. Something like that.' Maddy sat down. A waitress approached with an identical pot to Leanne's and a plate of chips. 'Beer, madame?' she asked.

'If you have something weak,' Maddy said. 'I'm driving.'

'Oh, well, in that case, a Heineken would be fine,' the waitress replied. 'Our own Belgian beer is very strong.'

Maddy nodded. 'That'll be grand.'

'Grand?' Horace asked and wiped the foam off his lip. 'Why do you gals always say everything's grand?'

'Irish expression,' Leanne informed him. 'We say a lot of stuff that might sound weird to you foreigners.'

Horace bristled. 'Foreigners? The British are not foreign. You are.'

Maddy laughed. 'Isn't that the whole Brexit Eurosceptic thing in a nutshell?'

'What is?' Horace snapped, his eyes taking on a steely look.

'That fear of Europe some of you seem to have. Pity you didn't feel like being a part of it. I think Europe will be sadly lacking without a touch of British humour and heart. We'll miss you, believe it or not.'

Horace's eyes bored into her with unusual fire. 'Fear? We don't fear anything. We just don't want the bloody European Union to tell us what to do.'

'Yeah, there is that.' Leanne sighed. 'We don't like it much either. But we like the cheese and wine. I bet you'll miss that.'

Horace laughed. 'Who needs French cheese, when we have Stilton and port?'

'Gee, I forgot about Stilton.' Maddy winked and started on her mussels, the best she had ever eaten. 'Mm, divine,' she mumbled through a mouthful. 'Never had mussels like this before.'

'I hope they won't make you ill,' Horace said, looking as if he was hoping quite the opposite. 'I'm sticking to fries and bacon. Very nice too.'

'To each their own,' Leanne said and took a swig of her glass of Riesling. She put it down. 'But hey, we have to do our photo shoot. Come and sit beside me, Maddy, and take Horace's tankard.' She handed her phone to Horace. 'Here. Do your job. Take a picture of the two of us for the blog.'

'Just a minute.' Maddy dived under the table and hauled Bridget into her lap. 'The star of the show.' She lifted Horace's beer tankard, while Leanne held up a mussel. 'Ready! Say cheese!'

Grumbling, Horace snapped a couple of shots and then grabbed his tankard. 'I hope you didn't ruin the head.'

'It still looks pretty foamy to me,' Leanne chortled. 'But let's not linger too long. We'll want to get back on the motorway to Paris soon. I want to get there before the shops close. And I want to check into that little boutique hotel before we put Horace on the Eurostar back to London.'

Horace looked up from his plate of fries. 'Oh. Forgot to tell you. Not going back yet. I'm staying in Paris and then—'

'Then?' Leanne said, her eyes on stalks.

'I'm going with you down south!' Horace beamed at her and downed his beer in one go.

Appalled, Maddy and Leanne stared at each other.

'How do you mean?' Maddy asked. 'I thought you said you were strapped for cash or something? I can't believe your egg money would stretch much further. Unless the hens are laying like machine guns.'

'And won't Edwina wake up soon and find you missing?' Leanne filled in.

Horace burped loudly, surprising even himself. 'Oh goodness me, this beer is strong. I do apologise.' He patted his mouth. 'Won't happen again. Anyway, I must explain. I checked my bank account just before we went into the restaurant. And I saw a payment I didn't expect. A refund from my insurance company, who accidentally charged double a few months ago. I was wondering why they suddenly increased the insurance for the Land Rover, but it appears it was a mistake. So, I'm ahead in my budget for the rest of the year and can splurge a little. I plan to travel with you dear ladies all the way to Nice and then fly home from there.'

'And Edwina?' Maddy enquired.

'She can take a flying jump,' Horace said hotly. 'I need a holiday from her and her bloody social circle.'

Maddy and Leanne looked at each other again. Maddy's mouth twitched. 'The worm has turned.'

Leanne frowned. 'It's not funny.'

'No, it's not,' Maddy agreed. She looked at Horace. 'I don't think we can do this, Horace. I'm sorry, but it won't work. We shouldn't even have let you come this far.'

'What about this dog?' Horace poked Bridget with his foot, making her bark. 'I might tell on you and say you stole it. Report it to the police in Britain. To Scotland Yard, Interpol. You could be in a lot of trouble, dear girls.' There was a mean glint in his eyes as he leant back.

Leanne laughed. 'Interpol, huh? I imagine they'd be too busy with other stuff to worry about one little missing poodle.'

Maddy leant forward and stared at Horace. 'Yeah, and how would they react if we told them who put her into our car?'

Horace laughed. 'How do you know I did it? You can't prove a thing. The police would never believe it anyway.'

'They'd probably just dismiss the whole story,' Leanne said. 'I can't imagine they'd do anything but laugh at it.'

'Not if she belongs to someone with a rather high profile,' Horace retorted, looking smug.

'Yeah, like who?' Leanne sneered.

'Like a very well-known person,' Horace said. He glanced around the room, leant forward and lowered his voice. 'Quite a celebrity. You might have heard of her. A titled lady, you know.'

Maddy's jaw dropped. 'Who?' she wheezed.

'A member of the royal family,' Horace said, looking important. 'That's all I'm going to say for now.'

Leanne kept staring at Horace, her face pale. 'You're lying.'

'Try me.'

Maddy suddenly felt as if Horace had been replaced by an evil clone. This was not the jovial epitome of the British gentleman who would save any lady in distress; this was a calculating, cold-hearted member of the aristocracy.

'What a transformation,' she said out loud. 'The true-blue Brit takes out the guns. How disappointing. But I suppose the British Empire wasn't created on a bed of kindness and compassion.'

'Damn right, old thing,' Horace said.

Chapter Seventeen

The drive to Paris took them through some beautifully scenic landscapes as the motorway wound its way through the south of Belgium, where Horace wanted to do a detour and visit the battlefields of Flanders. But Maddy pretended she didn't hear him and continued on the A1 across the border, past Lille, and its flat landscape, over the Somme and through the forest of Compiegne. The countryside changed here, the road lined with a dense wall of trees, casting shadows onto the road. Chantilly and its magnificent château could be seen in the distance, a stark contrast to the urban blight of the outskirts of Paris.

'I'm just going to close my eyes until we get to the Porte Maillot exit,' Leanne declared as they drove through the suburb of St Denis and put her hands over her eyes.

'Rather ghastly,' Horace agreed as he looked out the window. 'But London isn't much prettier.'

'Or any big city,' Maddy said. 'Hang on to your pants, guys, we're about to hit the Périférique. Don't talk until we're out of this hell.' With the wheel slipping through her sweaty hands, she eased the car into the mess of the packed four-lane ring road that swings around Paris, where countless accidents happen every day and so many people have even been killed. Always busy, always terrifying, it's the most efficient way to get into Paris, even if you nearly have a heart attack every time.

Maddy clamped her teeth together, tightened her grip on the wheel and drove straight into the next lane, knowing she had right of way, and praying the drivers knew it, too. They did, even if their angry faces showed they didn't like it much. But Maddy smiled and gestured, pleaded with her eyes, tossed her hair, and little by little, the French male drivers let her pass, some smiling back and even waving.

'Frenchmen can never resist a pretty woman,' Leanne said with a laugh. 'But French women are different story. Watch out, Mads, that hatchet-faced blonde in the beamer is going for you.'

Maddy swerved, narrowly missing a big van, and tucked herself into the next lane behind a lorry. 'Okay. I'm in the inside lane. How do I get out of here when I want to exit?'

'Just go through the whole performance again,' Leanne said. 'Hey, Horace, where are you staying?'

'I thought I might stay in that charming hotel with you,' Horace said, still squeezing his eyes shut, hugging Bridget for comfort. 'Are we there yet?'

Leanne rolled her eyes. 'No, you wimp. And you can't stay with us. They're booked up. Did you think we'd foot your hotel bill too?'

Horace opened his eyes. 'Yes, why not?'

'Because we can't afford it,' Leanne retorted. 'You're forcing us to take you to the South of France, but that's all. You're not getting anything else. Right, Maddy?'

'Dead right.' Maddy narrowly missed a limo with the Ritz logo and slammed on the brakes, causing a cacophony of tooting from the cars around them.

Horace squealed and hid his face in Bridget's fur.

'This road is a total nightmare,' Leanne exclaimed, her face white.

'I feel sick,' Horace groaned.

'Please shut up, you two,' Maddy ordered as she changed gears and revved the engine. 'Horace, you got the deal, so don't push it, or you'll be a statistic.' She drove off so fast they were thrown against the back of their seats.

'But I—' Horace shouted.

'Shut the fuck up, Horace,' Leanne snapped.

'Charming,' Horace muttered, when the traffic slowed down.

When they finally reached the exit and could drive up the ramp to the relative calm of Porte Maillot, Leanne announced she had found a little hotel in the Latin Quarter that would suit Horace's budget. 'It's a two-star but looks okay,' she reported, looking at the images on her phone. 'Got fairly good reviews on Trip Advisor. Will I book that for you?'

Horace nodded reluctantly, looking stroppy. 'Yes. Fine.'

'Gimme your credit card, then.'

Looking miffed, he dug in his pocket and handed it to her. 'There you are.'

Leanne made the arrangements while giving directions to Maddy, who complained about the poor quality of the GPS. 'You'd think a car like this would have a good one,' she grumbled.

'The better one was extra,' Leanne replied. 'I thought you'd know Paris like the back of your hand.'

'It's been a while, you know. Twenty-three years, two children and a marriage kind of makes things like the back streets of the Left Bank slip into the dark recesses of one's mind.'

Horace snorted a laugh. 'You two. So funny.'

Leanne turned to stare at him. 'Glad to provide such entertainment. Hey, while we're at it, give me the address of that boutique. You said it was around here somewhere?'

'Why should I?' Horace sniffed.

Leanne smiled sweetly. 'Because we'll dump you right here and drive off if you don't, that's why.'

'I'll be on to the police in a flash,' Horace retorted.

'And then the fun will be over,' Maddy remarked. 'For all of us. How sad.'

'It's just off the Boulevard St Germain,' Horace said. 'Rue de Buci. Short street full of restaurants. That's all I'm going to tell you.'

'We'll find it,' Leanne said.

As she followed Leanne's directions, Maddy realised that there was one thing not even twenty-three years, a marriage and two children had erased from her memory. The way to Ludo's restaurant.

After leaving Horace at the dingy little hotel, they continued to the more elegant part of the Left Bank, and their hotel, which offered such luxuries as valet parking and complimentary afternoon tea served in their rooms.

'Ah, this is better,' Leanne declared, sitting up against a myriad of lace-edged cushions on Maddy's bed. 'I feel nearly human. What plans for the evening, madame?'

'Anything that doesn't include Horace,' Maddy replied from the window seat, where she was enjoying the breath-taking view of the rooftops of Paris. *Ludo,* she thought. *He's out there somewhere. He alone knows what happened, why he never came back to me. Finally, I'll get the closure I need. All I have to do is find him.*

'Sounds good to me. I told him we'd get in touch tomorrow morning. He said he wanted to revive some memories tonight. No idea what he meant, but do we want to know?'

Maddy poured herself another cup of Earl Grey from the Wedgwood teapot. 'No, we don't. Do you realise he's blackmailing us?'

'Of course.' Leanne nibbled on a mini *pain au chocolat*. 'But I doubt he'll do anything about it even if we dump him.'

Maddy shivered. 'Not sure I want to put it to the test. He could be a bit of a loose cannon. I don't want to end up in a British jail for kidnapping a royal pet.'

'That'd be surreal. Great for our exposure though!' Leanne got up from the bed and stretched, smiling at Bridget asleep on a cushion by the window. 'Isn't it strange how French hotels and restaurants don't mind you bringing in dogs?'

Maddy laughed. 'Yes, but if you try it with a baby they get all prune-faced and disapproving.'

'Typical. Uh, Maddy?'

'Yes?' Maddy tore herself away from the view.

'I want to go to the shop. You know, the one Horace mentioned. It's just around the corner. It's not that late, so they'd still be open. Will you come with me?'

Maddy looked at Leanne's pale face and realised how frightening it must be to consider confronting a father who had deserted his daughter twenty years earlier. A greater pain than that of a long-lost love like hers. The search for Ludo could wait. Leanne needed her now. She held out her hand. 'I'll come with you. Of course.'

Leanne took Maddy's hand in her ice-cold one. 'Thank you. I know you want to go and look for that guy who left you, but...'

Maddy squeezed Leanne's hand. 'That can wait. It's just a little blip in my life compared to yours. Do you want to go now and see if we can find the shop?'

Leanne nodded. 'Yes. It's four-thirty. I figure they close at six or even seven.'

Maddy got up from the window seat. 'Let's go.'

'What about you and—?'

'That can wait until tomorrow.' Maddy paused. 'I'm scared, to tell you the truth. I don't think arriving at his restaurant shouting "surprise!" would be a good idea. He might not even remember me. He might be married with five kids, or—'

'In a relationship with some babe twenty years younger,' Leanne filled in. 'Or a bitter, lonely man who never forgot you.'

Maddy sighed. 'No, I don't think that would have happened. But why didn't he get in touch after I left, like he said? I have a feeling he just threw away the bit of paper with my contact details and went on to the next woman.'

'And the next and the next. That's what Frenchmen are supposed to be like.'

'Not Ludo,' Maddy said hotly. 'He's not one of those typical Frenchmen, I just know it.'

'Of course not,' Leanne soothed. 'There must be exceptions.' She stopped, looking confused. 'But what about you? Did you try to contact him?'

'I had a card with the phone number of the restaurant. But it didn't ring through. I tried several times, but then I realised they must have changed their number or something. I tried to look it up on that Minitel website they had in France then, but couldn't find the name of the restaurant. So I gave up.'

'Oh. Bad luck.' Leanne picked up Bridget's lead and clipped it to her collar. 'Come on, sweetheart. Time for walkies.'

Bridget jumped on to the floor and wagged her tail, trotting to the door.

Maddy laughed. 'She loves her walkies.'

Leanne opened the door. 'Have you got the box with the poop bags?'

Maddy tucked it in to her handbag. 'Right here. Never thought I'd go to Paris to scoop up dog poo from the pavement.'

'No, but it's the law here, so we have to do it. Just thank your lucky stars we don't have a Great Dane.'

'I don't even want to think about that.'

When they were in the street, Maddy looked around. 'It's so quiet here. The traffic is just a distant murmur. Which way is Boulevard St Germain?'

'Follow me.' Leanne led the way down the street with Bridget trotting beside her.

Maddy followed, a poop bag at the ready, breathing in the soft Parisian air laden with coffee, fresh bread, petrol fumes and something else, particular to this beautiful city. If she had been dropped there blindfolded, she would have known it was Paris. She felt as if time was standing still and she was the young student rushing to lectures, books in hand, her whole life ahead of her. As they crossed the busy Boulevard St Germain and walked down the street on the other side, she knew she had to face Ludo soon and ask him the questions that had been troubling her for so long.

Bridget stopped to produce a few little turds and Maddy picked them up, her thoughts still far away, and deposited the plastic bag in the special bin nearby. 'Quite neat, really,' she remarked.

Leanne didn't reply, her mind obviously on the confrontation ahead. She turned a corner and gazed at the street name on the plaque above her head. 'This is it. Rue de Buci. Nice little street.'

'Lovely.' Maddy looked at the little restaurants lining the street, interspersed with small boutiques and coffee shops. 'They play live jazz here in the evenings, I read in the guide book. We should have dinner here tonight.'

Leanne shivered despite the warm weather. 'Please. I can't think of dinner now.'

They walked down the street until Leanne stopped in front of a green door with a small shop window beside it. The sign over the shop said: 'Hovden, *Parfums du Nord en Provence*.'

'*Parfums du Nord*,' Leanne whispered, Bridget's lead slipping from her hand. 'Does that mean perfumes from the north?'

Maddy picked up Bridget's lead. 'Yes. "Perfumes from the north in Provence" is the whole sentence.'

'Oh.' Leanne stood stock-still, staring at the sign. 'Hovden,' she whispered. 'I've been there. When I was eight. My dad took me there to meet his family. Never forgot it. So beautiful and stark. It smelt of salt fish and seaweed and woodsmoke. The seagulls screeching above us. Little wooden houses. The fjords and mountains plunging into the sea. And my grandmother. Tall and strong like a pine tree. So proud but so gentle too.' Leanne drew in a ragged breath and turned her attention to the display in the window. 'Look at the little bottles and boxes. Such a beautiful design. Blue, like the fjords and then a deeper azure like the Mediterranean. And the font of the letters. Art deco with a modern twist. I wonder who made those?'

'Only one way to find out,' Maddy said.

'I know.' Leanne's hand shook as she put it on the door handle. 'This feels like a watershed moment in my life.' She took a deep breath and pushed the door open.

Chapter Eighteen

Tiny bells tinkled as they entered the shop, where a light scent of lavender floated in the air. The shop was lined with shelves full of bottles in all colours of the rainbow, packages of soap and stacks of towels and tableware with Provençal designs. Maddy looked around. 'How enchanting. Like coming in through a magic door to somewhere in the south.'

'There's no one here,' Leanne whispered, looking around the empty store. 'Let's go.'

'We have to stay,' Maddy said sternly. 'We've come all this way and now we have to find out—'

'I'll write to him. Or call the shop.' Leanne started towards the door. 'I can't do this.'

'You must.'

'No. Let's go. There's nobody here anyway.'

But someone stirred in the doorway at the far end, and a tall silver-haired man dressed in a black polo neck and jeans poked his head out. '*Je viens toute de suite,*' he said in heavily accented French and disappeared again.

Leanne gasped and grabbed a hold of Maddy. 'It's him.'

'Are you sure?'

Her face white, Leanne nodded. 'Yes. Oh God. I can't—' She backed away and tried to hide behind Maddy.

Maddy pulled her forward. 'You must stay. I'm here. I won't leave you.'

Leanne nodded. 'Okay,' she croaked, her eyes on the doorway.

They waited while they heard the man talk to someone. Then he said goodbye and emerged from behind the counter, smiling. 'Sorry about that. What can I do for you?'

Maddy blinked. What an amazing man. At least six foot five with a lean body, that white hair and the most extraordinary eyes she had ever seen; blue-green, fringed with black lashes under thick dark brows. His handsome features bore an uncanny resemblance to Leanne's, she noted during the seconds before he recognised his daughter. He stiffened and gasped.

They stared at each other for a loaded minute. Then the man spoke. 'Leanne?'

'Dad?' she whispered, squeezing Maddy's hand.

His face ashen, he took a step forward. 'I... my God. I can't—' Tears welled up in his eyes. He reached out and touched Leanne's cheek. 'It's really you?'

She pulled back. 'Yes, it's me, Dad.'

The man looked bewildered and pushed a shaking hand through his thick hair. 'I can't believe you're here. It's like a dream.'

'Or a nightmare?' Leanne said, a bitter tone in her voice.

'I don't know what you mean. I've tried to reach you so many times. But this is not the place to discuss this. Can we... can we go somewhere and talk?'

Leanne nodded. 'Yes. That's why I'm here. To talk.' She stepped forward and glared at him. 'And to ask why the *hell* you deserted your wife and daughter and wrecked my life.'

'I… yes, that certainly has to be explained.' He looked behind him. 'I'll get my assistant to mind the shop and close up.' The man looked at Maddy. 'Sorry. You must a friend of Leanne. I'm Erik Sandvik.' He held out his hand.

'Maddy Quinn,' she said and shook his hand. Under normal circumstances, she would have smiled and cracked a joke, but the shock still lingering in his eyes stopped her. 'Yes, I'm a friend,' she added.

His smile was stiff. 'Good. Excuse me for a moment.' He disappeared through the door at the back and called for someone. A slim young woman with black hair appeared behind him.

'This is Jeanne,' he said. 'She runs this shop for me. Jeanne, these ladies are… friends from Ireland.'

'*Bonjour,*' Jeanne said and smiled. 'Nice to meet you,' she continued in English.

'Hi,' Leanne and Maddy said in unison.

'I'll leave you to it, Jeanne. I'll talk to you tomorrow before I leave for Nice.'

Jeanne smiled. '*D'accord, Jan. A demain.*'

'Does everyone call you Jan Hovden?' Leanne asked.

'Jan Hovden is my business name. My friends call me Erik.' He went to the door and held it open. 'Let's go to the bistro on the corner. It'll be quiet so we can talk.'

They filed out into the street, where the evening sun warmed their backs as they walked to the bistro. Once settled in a corner of the quiet restaurant with a carafe of wine Erik had ordered, Leanne drank from her glass and put it down, facing her father.

'So… what's the story?'

He sighed and folded his hands on the table. 'My story?'

Leanne leant forward. 'And mine. And Mam's.'

Erik cleared his throat and drank some wine. Then he looked back at Leanne. 'I have a feeling you've been told some things that aren't true. I want to tell you my side of this.'

'Yeah, I bet,' Leanne muttered bitterly. 'This had better be good.'

Maddy squirmed. The tension between this man and his daughter almost made the air crackle. They didn't need her now. She pushed her glass away and scooped Bridget into her arms. 'Look, I'll take Bridget for a walk in the Jardin de Luxembourg, and then I'll get back to the hotel.'

Leanne nodded. 'Okay. I'll call you later. Thanks for coming with me.'

Erik pulled out Maddy's chair and patted Bridget. 'Nice to meet you, Maddy.'

'And you, Erik.' Their eyes met. Maddy felt an undercurrent of something between them – an odd attraction or connection. She couldn't quite detect what it was, but it was there, like a light breeze on her skin that made her shiver. Then it was gone as he turned away. She walked out into the street, the sunlight blinding her for a moment, making her momentarily light-headed. She put the dog down on the pavement. 'What happened there?' she said out loud.

Bridget wagged her tail and barked.

Maddy laughed and looked up at the blue sky. 'You're right. Who cares? It's a lovely evening and I'm free. For a while.'

*

After a pleasant walk in the Luxembourg Gardens, Maddy returned to the hotel and settled Bridget on her cushion with a bowl of water and her favourite toy. After a quick visit to the bathroom and a glance in the mirror, she ventured out again in search of dinner, leaving Bridget asleep in her room. A little apprehensive about dining alone in a Parisian restaurant, she studied the menus and peered into windows but found nothing that appealed to her. Not actually hungry yet, she decided to take a walk on Pont des Arts, a pedestrian bridge that links the Institut de France and the central square of the Louvre on the other side of the Seine. As her feet pounded the wooden planks she stopped to linger at the railings for a moment, looking at the panorama of beautiful buildings that lined the blue water of the river, with Notre Dame just visible in the distance. The sun was dipping in the blue sky, and pink clouds floated over the towers of the ancient cathedral.

She and Ludo had stood there the day before her departure, his arms around her, talking about the future and when they would meet again. The railings were no longer weighed down by the myriad of padlocks lovers from all over the world used to hang there. They had all been removed by the *mairie*, as they were a threat to both the old railings and the river. Now there was only the odd one defying the law. She and Ludo hadn't bothered with a padlock; they knew they'd never forget each other. And she never did. But what about him? Had he remembered? Maddy suddenly felt an urge to find out. As soon as possible.

She continued her way to the other side, crossed the square and emerged on Rue de Rivoli, headed to the metro station and bought a ticket. She knew which line would take her to the Hotel de Ville stop, where she would get off and walk up that long street toward the Marais and the little back street where she would find Ludo's restaurant. *Easy, peasy*, she said to herself as she walked, smiling at the memory of her younger self wobbling on the cobblestones on her way to be introduced to Ludo's uncle. But now, the cobblestones had been replaced by proper pavers, the streets had been cleaned up, buildings restored and luxury shops moved in. The Marais had lost its seedy charm and was now annoyingly trendy and chic. Maddy only noted this in passing, her mind on a reunion that could end in tears.

What am I doing? she asked herself as she drew nearer to her destination. *What will I find?* She stopped for a moment, staring into a shop window without seeing its contents. *Go back now, before it's too late*, she said to herself. Then she shook her head. *You've come all this way, why chicken out at the last moment?* She pulled herself together and walked on, finding the street within minutes. And there it was. The restaurant.

She stopped and stared at the sign. The name had changed. It was now called La Pomme de Pin, according to the red sign, with 'cuisine Provençal' in smaller letters. He must have changed the name of the restaurant – and the cuisine. She checked the time on her watch. Seven-thirty. It would be quiet before the evening rush. A good time to seek out Ludo. He wouldn't be that busy yet. She pushed the door open and entered the cosy restaurant, her hands clammy, her mouth dry and her heart hammering in her chest.

Chapter Nineteen

Inside, she stood for a while getting used to the dim light, studying the décor of rough white walls, rustic furniture and red-and-white-checked tablecloths. There was a seductive smell of herbs, garlic and other spices in the air, and she was suddenly ravenous, despite her jittery nerves. Only a few of the tables were occupied, and a smiling waiter showed her to a table by the window.

'I haven't reserved,' Maddy said.

'That's fine,' he replied. 'We don't take reservations here. Everyone's welcome until we're full. Are you English?'

'No. Irish.'

He grinned at her. 'Ah, Irish. You're very welcome, pretty Irish lady. You come from a beautiful country.'

'Thank you.'

He handed her a menu. 'The special tonight *is l'onglet aux échalottes avec le petit gratin dauphinoise* with a special sauce by our chef.'

'Sounds lovely.'

'I'll let you look at everything else and come back when you've decided. Anything to drink?'

'A small carafe of rosé, please.'

'*Toute de suite, madame.*'

He was about to leave, but Maddy stopped him. 'Just another little thing,' she said, butterflies whirling in her stomach. 'Would it be possible to see the owner of this restaurant? Ludovic Montrouge?'

His eyes widened. 'Ludovic Montrouge? But that is not the name of the owner.'

Maddy stared at him. 'What? But… I mean… Ludo was supposed to take over this restaurant. Are you sure he isn't here?'

'I'm certain.'

What about his uncle?'

He shrugged. 'I don't know him either. I have only worked here a few years. But I can ask the chef. He's also the owner. Bought the restaurant about fifteen years ago. Then it was called—'

'Les Deux Toques,' Maddy cut in. 'I know.'

'You were here then?'

'Yes. A long time ago. When I was a student.'

'I see.' He nodded and smiled. 'Must have been different then.'

'Yes,' Maddy said in barely a whisper. 'Very different.'

'I'll ask the owner if he can see you after your meal. He might be able to help you.'

'Oh yes,' Maddy said, her voice shaking. 'Thank you. That would be—'

But the waiter had disappeared to get her order, leaving her sitting there staring into space, her stomach in a knot. *Ludo*, she thought. *What happened to you?*

Maddy fiddled with the menu, trying to come to terms with what the waiter had told her. Feeling the need for some Dutch courage, she downed a glass of the wine when it arrived, and nibbled on bread while she waited for her order. The restaurant was filling up with customers, and suddenly all the waiters ran around trying to keep up. Her grilled steak with potato gratin arrived with the sauce in a sauceboat and she dug in, the aftershock of what she had learned making her ravenous. Nerves always made her hungry, and this was no exception. Nobody paid much attention to her other than a quick glance. A woman eating alone in a restaurant was a common sight, she realised, as she saw others in the same situation here and there in the restaurant. Women must have had a much better deal in France.

When she had finished, the waiter came back and took her plate, asking if she wanted anything else. 'A dessert or coffee?'

Maddy shook her head. 'No thanks. I'll just finish the wine.'

'Right, madame. I will tell Chef that you want to speak to him. He'll have time to talk to you as soon as the rush is over.'

'Thank you.'

Maddy didn't have to wait long. Little by little, things calmed down and guests started to leave. A man in a chef's hat appeared behind the reception area and walked to her table.

'Madame, er—'

Maddy stood up and held out her hand. 'Please, call me Maddy.'

They shook hands and sat. The chef, a middle-aged man with dark hair and kind eyes, smiled at her. 'So, you want to know about the previous owner of this restaurant?' he asked in accented but fluent English.

Maddy nodded, her hands suddenly clammy. 'Yes. Do you know where he is?'

'You're a friend of his?'

She nodded. 'I knew his nephew. A long time ago. We... lost touch. But now I'm in Paris, I thought I'd look him up.'

'I see.' He paused. 'I don't know that much about him. I bought this restaurant from his uncle. Ludovic, the nephew, never owned this place. He left a few years before it was sold.'

'A few years?' Maddy tried to calculate how many years had passed since then. 'But if you bought it fifteen years ago, Ludo must never have realised his plans,' she said, as if to herself.

'Plans?' the chef said.

'Yes. He was going into business with his uncle after he finished training as a chef.'

'Oh. I didn't know this. I met the nephew only once, just before the sale went through. He was in town to help his uncle with the sale and other things. The uncle was very ill then. Had been for a long time. He leased the restaurant to someone who ran it as a pizzeria for a few years.'

'Oh,' Maddy exclaimed. 'That must have been why I couldn't find it in the Minitel thing.'

The chef shrugged. 'Perhaps.'

Maddy frowned. 'Ludo was in town, you said? Had he moved from Paris?'

'I believe he had.'

'Where to?' Maddy asked, a note of panic in her voice.

'To Provence. Near Gordes. That's all I know.'

'Oh.' Deflated, Maddy sat back. Her head swam. Why had Ludo moved to Provence? How would she find him now? 'Gordes, you said. Have you any idea what he's doing there?'

The chef shrugged. 'No.'

'And the uncle?' she asked, sensing what the answer would be.

The chef looked sad. 'He died shortly afterwards.'

'How sad for Ludo. They were so close.'

'So I understood.'

'Did the uncle have any other relatives besides Ludo?' Maddy asked.

'I don't think so. No wife in any case. And no children. Ludovic was like a son to him. And Ludo's father died just a year before this.'

'I see.'

The chef rose. 'I'm sorry. I have to go. The late-night customers will arrive shortly.' He held out his hand. 'A pleasure to meet you, Maddy. I hope you find Ludo.'

Maddy shook his hand. 'Thank you for talking to me.'

'You're welcome.' He kissed her hand. 'I hope you find him. *Au revoir.*'

Maddy stared at his departing back, her mind on Ludo. Why had he left Paris all those years ago? Why hadn't he stayed and fulfilled his dream? What was he doing in Provence? The disappointment of her search finishing in a dead end hit Maddy like a sledgehammer. Was this getting too impossible? Should she give up now? With all these questions whirling around in her head, Maddy paid the bill and left the restaurant. As her footsteps echoed down the empty street, she shivered despite the warm breeze. Where to now? Then she knew. She would not give up. She had to follow the lead to Provence.

Maddy bumped into Leanne at the entrance to their hotel. Her head still full of what she had discovered, Maddy started to tell her story but stopped when she saw Leanne's white face and eyes full of tears. She took Leanne's hand. 'What's the matter? What happened? Was your dad mean to you?'

Leanne wiped her eyes with the back of her hand. 'No.' She sniffed, touching her nose. 'Do you have a hanky? Why do I never have a tissue when I want to have a good cry?'

Maddy fished a crumpled tissue from her bag. 'Here. I haven't used it.'

Leanne wiped her eyes and blew her nose. 'It smells of herbs. In fact, you smell of herbs and garlic. Where have you been?'

'Long story. Have you had anything to eat?'

'No. Don't want anything.'

Maddy pulled at Leanne's arm. 'Of course you do. You haven't eaten anything since the mussels in Brussels.'

Leanne giggled. 'Mussels in Brussels.'

Maddy had to laugh. 'Accidental rhyming. But come on, let's get you some dinner. There's a little restaurant on the corner.'

A little while later, Leanne tucked into steak and chips in the bistro while Maddy sipped a cup of camomile tea.

After devouring the entrecôte and the accompanying fries, Leanne put down her knife and fork. 'Thank you. I needed that.'

'Thought so.' Maddy put down her cup. 'You don't have to tell me anything if you don't want to. I just want to know where we go from here.' She could see that Leanne was affected by whatever had just happened and she didn't want to push her.

'Where do you want to go?'

'Provence. And you?'

Leanne sighed. 'Yeah, that sounds great. I want to go to Nice. That's where Dad's business is. He wants me to see it.'

'Do you?'

Leanne nodded. 'Yes. I want to find out about him and his life. It was tough going there with him tonight. He told me some harsh things about my mother. And something I never knew.'

'What?' Maddy asked, despite her resolve not to pump Leanne for information.

'They were never married.'

Maddy blinked and stared at Leanne. 'Never married?'

'Nope.' Leanne smirked. 'That makes me a bastard, doesn't it?'

'Of course not. How come they never married? Didn't he want to?'

'It was Mam who refused. They had lots of arguments about it. But she always said no. It was all about religion. She's a Catholic, he's a… nothing. Never wanted to go inside a church of any kind. Didn't even believe in marriage, but when I arrived, he said he'd be prepared to go through a civil ceremony, but it had to be in Norway. She refused point blank. But she faked it by wearing a wedding ring. Then, when they split up, she made up that story about being a widow, so she wouldn't be labelled as a single mother in her village or anywhere else. Instead, she was a widow trying to make ends meet raising her child, blah, blah.' Leanne sighed, her shoulders slumped. 'Of course, it meant she didn't have to share me with him, despite him trying desperately to see me. He wrote to me often, but I never saw those letters. She must have thrown them away. And she never told me when he called or gave me his number. Then he went on about how manipulative and needy she is and a real control freak. As if I didn't know. Jesus, those two. I wonder how they ever managed to produce a child. But of course, Mam was stunning when she was young. Must have been hard to resist if she came on to him. And he, what a looker. I've seen the photos.'

'He's still a very handsome man,' Maddy remarked, remembering those luminous blue-green eyes.

Leanne smirked. 'He got to you, did he? The silver-fox thing, right?'

Maddy blushed and looked away. 'Not really.'

'Yes, he did. I could tell. He hasn't lost it.'

'How old is he?' Maddy asked.

'Fifty-four. A bit younger than my mother. Maybe that was the problem, too? Or one of them?' Leanne shrugged. 'But whatever. Tell me what you've been up to. Did you find your man?'

'No. But I know where he is. Roughly.'

Leanne smiled. 'Oooh. I see. Provence, right? Is that why you want to go there?'

'Yes. Somewhere near Gordes.'

'Must look that up. But sure, it's on the way to Nice, even if we have to do a little detour.'

'I think it'll be a nice trip too. That part of Provence is beautiful, they say.'

'That's okay.' Leanne drank some wine and looked at Maddy. 'Now, there's something I want to tell you about the rest of the trip. Two things, actually.'

'Okay.'

'First, my dad is travelling down at the same time in his own car. So we'll be meeting up with him along the way. You okay with that?'

'Of course. But I thought you'd sorted everything with him?'

Leanne nodded. 'Yes, some of it. We've opened the box, but now we need to sort out the contents, if you see what I mean. I need to get to know him. I need to find out who he is. And let him know who I really am. Does that make sense?'

Maddy looked into Leanne's troubled eyes. 'Yes. Perfect sense.'

'Good. Okay. So then, number two. I think you'll agree with that one too.'

'Just tell me.'

'We need to dump Horace.'

Maddy nodded and sighed. 'Oh yeah. I can't stand him. I thought he was kind of cute for a while, but then he turned nasty. He hasn't stopped moaning. And he hates Bridget.'

'And we want to hang on to her. She's adorable. I got some messages from the website to say Bridget is a huge draw and they want more photos of her. She's beginning to outshine us. We might have to rename the blog "Bridget's great escape".'

Maddy shivered. 'Better not. Then someone might twig who she really is.' She leant forward. 'A royal dog. Do you realise that?' she whispered. 'We might end up in jail.'

Leanne giggled. 'What a hoot. Could be safer to let Horace take her back, then.'

'No, he can't stand her. Let him go back on his own.'

'How are we going to make him do that?' Leanne enquired. 'He'll refuse point blank and threaten us again. He might even blow the whistle.'

'Don't look so worried. I've just had an excellent idea. Why didn't we think of it before?' Maddy took her phone from her bag.

'What?' Leanne hissed. 'Tell me.'

Maddy went onto Google. 'Just a minute. When I've finished, you might just find that Horace has magically decided to go home all by himself.'

Chapter Twenty

Maddy was right. The next morning, as they were enjoying breakfast in the dining room of their hotel, a flustered Horace suddenly appeared at their table.

Leanne smiled at him. 'Good morning, Horace.'

'Morning, ladies.' He eyed the basket of fresh bread and croissants. 'Er, would it be all right if I shared some of that? I checked out of my hotel and didn't—'

'Pay for breakfast?' Maddy asked sweetly. She pushed the basket towards him. 'Here. Help yourself. We'll get you a pot of tea.'

'So kind.' Horace pulled a chair from an adjoining table and sat down. He grabbed a croissant and stuffed it into his mouth. 'Rather nice,' he mumbled through his mouthful.

'They're scrummy,' Leanne agreed. 'So, dear Horace, are you ready for the next leg of the journey? We thought we'd stop off in Chartres to see the cathedral and then lunch in Amboise. Interesting château there.'

Horace swallowed noisily. 'Er, I'm afraid I have some bad news. I won't be coming with you.'

Maddy adopted a sad expression. 'Oh, that's disappointing. We were beginning to enjoy your company. You're not feeling ill, are you?'

Horace poured himself a cup of tea from the pot a waitress had just brought. 'No. I'm fine. Just a little shaken from the shock, don't you know?'

'Shock?' Leanne asked. 'What's happened? Did you get mugged or something?'

'No, nothing like that.' Horace slurped his tea. 'I had a phone call from Alistair, our butler. One of the girls is sick.'

'Your daughter?' Maddy asked, fighting to keep a straight face.

'No, one of my prize hens. Henrietta, the brood hen. One of the best. Worth thousands. She fell ill last night and hasn't recovered. I must go back and see to her.'

'Of course,' Leanne soothed.

Horace brushed pastry flakes from his trousers. 'There's a train from Gare du Nord in an hour and a half. So, if you could drive me there, I'd be most grateful.'

Taken aback by his sad and worried face, Maddy smiled and patted his arm. 'Of course. No problem, Horace. We can get on to the lovely Périférique from there and then onto the motorway. Right, Leanne? It's your turn to drive.'

'I know,' Leanne muttered into her cup of café au lait. 'So looking forward to that.'

Horace squeezed her on the shoulder. 'You'll be fine.' He reached for another croissant. 'So if you're ready, maybe we should get going? I'll wait here and finish breakfast while you girls go and pack up and get the animal.'

'We're ready,' Maddy said. 'Bridget is waiting in the car out front. Thought you might have seen her.'

'No. I didn't notice. So,' Horace continued. 'We say goodbye. Or maybe it's *au revoir*. I wish you the best of luck. Sorry about that little contretemps yesterday. I was so anxious to keep going with you. But now that my girl needs me, I must depart.'

'We understand,' Leanne soothed. 'And no hard feelings. The blackmail was a bit of a dirty trick, but you were desperate. In any case, if it hadn't been for you, I wouldn't have found – someone I was looking for. A happy accident.'

Horace turned to Leanne. 'Really? You found someone because of me? Maybe I brought you luck? That's terrific. Maybe I'll come join you again once I've seen to my hens. How about it?'

'Uh, thanks,' Maddy said. 'But we couldn't put you to that trouble.'

'No trouble, old thing.' Horace winked. 'I might not be able to get away, but I'll be keeping an eye on you.'

Having deposited Horace at the Eurostar terminal, they continued up Rue de Rivoli, driving slowly, the top down, with Leanne humming the tune of 'The Ballad of Lucy Jordan' while she drove. 'Oh, this is what I dreamed of,' she said with a blissful smile. 'I can die happy now.'

'Thank God for that.' Maddy managed to take a few shots of Leanne at the wheel with a backdrop of the shopfronts of Rue de Rivoli, and the Luxor Obelisk as they drove across Place de la Concorde. They continued up the Champs-Élysées, around Place Charles de Gaulle glancing up at the magnificent Arc de Triomphe while all around them traffic roared and car horns tooted.

'Have you had enough warm wind in your hair yet?' Maddy shouted, snapping away.

Leanne grabbed the steering wheel tighter, her face white. 'Jesus, yes. We got to get outta here, fast!'

'Hang on, take a left here so we can go down to Place Trocadero. We need a shot of the Eiffel Tower,' Maddy ordered.

'How? We're six lanes away.'

'Just drive across, you have right of way and they know it,' Maddy shouted.

They managed to get across the messy knot of traffic without bumping into anyone and Leanne expertly turned into the relative calm of Avenue Victor-Hugo. They drove around Place du Trocadéro and parked illegally in front of Palais de Chaillot, raced across the terrace and, breathless and laughing, got a confused Japanese tourist to take a shot of the two of them with the Eiffel Tower in the background. That done, they drove through the back streets to

Avenue de la Grande Armée and down to Porte Maillot.

'Okay,' Leanne said, taking a deep breath. 'It's calmer here. But we'll soon be hitting the dear old Périférique.'

'It doesn't look that bad,' Maddy said as they reached the slip road. 'Horace would be pleased.'

Leanne relaxed. 'Yes, we might have hit it at the right time. But talking about Horace,

what the feck did he mean – keeping an eye on us? Oh God, it's getting busy again.'

Maddy held Bridget in a tight grip. 'No idea what he meant. Let's get through this mess first and then we'll talk. I have to hold on to Bridget so she won't jump on top of you.'

'Okay.' Leanne swerved to avoid a truck trying to get ahead of her. 'Bastard French drivers.'

'That one was Italian.'

'Same kind of bastard,' Leanne said through clenched teeth.

They were quiet during the next tense half an hour and could finally breathe as they came out of the tunnel at Saint-Cloud and drove up the hill to the next junction. Leanne wiped the sweat off her forehead with the back of her hand. 'Phew. Glad we're out of that mess. The motorway will be easy after this.'

Maddy kissed the top of Bridget's head. 'You can lie down in the back seat now, Your Highness. Panic over.'

'We're meeting Dad in Chartres for lunch,' Leanne cut in. 'Is that okay with you?'

'Yes. Fine. Might be a tense meal, though.'

Leanne shot her a glance. 'I know. But there won't be any aggro. He just wants to do a little sightseeing. He said he's never visited the cathedral, and it's supposed to be spectacular.'

'But if he's such an atheist, why does he want to see this monument to Christianity?'

'No idea. Why don't you ask him?'

'I might just do that,' Maddy mumbled.

'But back to Horace,' Leanne ordered. 'What was that about keeping an eye on us? Was that another threat?'

'I think he was just trying to scare us. Or just that he'll be following the blog.'

'Probably. But how did you manage to get him to go back home? Is that chicken really sick?'

'Hen,' Maddy corrected, bubbling with laughter. 'Can't you guess? I phoned the house and got Alistair, the butler. I explained that, well, we needed to get rid of Horace, and he said it was a good idea. I think he was tired of poultry-sitting. So, we concocted this little lie between the two of us. And then, when Horace gets back, Henrietta will have had a miraculous recovery.'

'Brilliant.' Leanne's shoulders relaxed as she drove. 'Now we can enjoy the rest of the drive.'

'Until we meet your dad,' Maddy remarked.

Leanne shot her a glance. 'What's wrong? I thought you found him attractive.'

Maddy turned her head and looked out the window. 'Yes, he is. Very attractive. And I'm so glad you found each other. But do we need him to be involved in our trip?'

'We're just having lunch. Why is that a big deal?' Leanne wondered. 'Are you still recovering from last night?'

'Yes. It really shook me, to be honest. I'm still trying to get over what I found out about Ludo.' Maddy looked back at Leanne. 'I'm probably just being over sensitive. Ignore me, okay?'

'I'll do my best. You have your agenda, I have mine. Better not to mix them up.'

They spotted the cathedral about an hour later, its towers hovering above the golden wheat fields like a mirage in the distance.

'How amazing,' Leanne said.

'Majestic,' Maddy replied in awe. 'Imagine what it was like in the middle ages? Must have been even more impressive to the true believers.'

Leanne glanced at Maddy. 'You're not one of them?'

Maddy thought for a moment. Did she believe in God? Yes, she did. In her own way. But… 'I'm not sure about a lot of the stuff the

Catholic Church wants us to follow. But yeah, there is someone up there looking at us and maybe shaking his head in despair. And I do believe in an afterlife. What about you?'

Leanne changed gears and turned into the main street of the town. 'A bit like you. There is someone up there. Or something. But I'm more into the yoga-chakra kind of thinking. Spirituality is in nature and all things beautiful. And karma and stuff like that. It's all a mystery, isn't it? Trying to understand it just gives you a headache.'

Maddy laughed. 'True.'

They had arrived outside the cathedral, and they both craned their necks to look at the towers soaring above them. A car horn tore into their quiet contemplation.

'Shit, we have to park,' Leanne exclaimed, glancing in the rear-view mirror. 'We're causing a huge traffic jam. And there's a cute French policeman trying to wave us through.' She stuck her head out the window. 'We'll be outta here in a sec, sweetheart,' she shouted at the angry policeman and surged forward, taking the corner on two wheels.

Bridget started to bark, scratching on the window with her paws. Leanne pulled up at the kerb. 'Let her out, willya? She needs to pee. Could you take care of that while I text my dad?'

'Okay.' Maddy scrambled out, clipped the lead to Bridget's collar and walked out into the warm sunshine. They were on the edge of a small park, and she walked Bridget a bit down the way, which was perfect for little dog. Maddy let her off the lead, and she scampered away between the bushes. Minutes later, she scampered back, tongue lolling in a huge doggy smile. Maddy pulled her phone from her pocket and took a shot. A voice behind her made her jump.

'Very cute.'

Maddy twirled around and saw Erik approaching on the path. 'Oh. Hello.'

'Hi there.' He was even more handsome than before, the tension of yesterday replaced by a huge grin and a glint in the blue-green eyes that made her cheeks flush. 'Leanne told me you were here, so I came to fetch you. Lunch, then the cathedral. How does that sound?'

'Perfect,' Maddy squeaked. What was happening to her voice? It was him. He had this incredible charisma she couldn't resist. *Could anyone?* she wondered, confused by her reaction. Even though this was only the second time they had met, she could feel vibes between them that spelled trouble and complications. She didn't need this right now.

He scooped Bridget into his arms, and she immediately started to lick his face. Another victim of that northern charm. Maddy shook her head and laughed. 'She's such a tart.'

'She's adorable,' Erik declared, ruffling Bridget's fur. 'But come on, Leanne's waiting. She found a great spot to park just outside the restaurant. Nice and cool, so we can leave Bridget there after lunch while we look round the cathedral.'

'Grand,' Maddy said, not trusting her voice while her heart did a strange somersault in her chest.

They walked along the path, crossed the little square and continued down a leafy street, where Maddy spotted the car parked under a large plane tree in front of a restaurant with tables both outside and in. Leanne was already sitting at a table outside, taking shots of the car and the street with her phone. She aimed the phone at them and shouted, 'Smile!'

Erik stopped and pulled Maddy closer, the dog still in his arms. 'This okay?'

'Fabulous,' Leanne shouted back. '"Close encounter with handsome man in mediaeval town" will be the caption. You're a huge improvement on Sir Horace, Dad. Hope you don't mind adding a little sex appeal to our blog.'

'Only if you mention my firm,' Erik shot back. 'I'll take every chance to get some exposure for my products.'

Leanne made a face. 'That's my dad. Ever the opportunist.'

Ever the flirt, Maddy thought, as she detached herself from his grip. But she smiled at him, suddenly realising how alive she felt. And young and beautiful. With a newfound pep in her step, she bounced forward, her head up and her back straight, smiling for no particular reason.

Leanne smirked and put her phone on the table. 'Do you two actually need lunch? It seems like you've got some kind of energy already.'

'We need lunch,' Erik declared and kissed Leanne's cheek. He put Bridget down and pulled a chair out for Maddy. '*Voilà, madame.*'

'*Merci*, kind sir.' Maddy sat down and picked up the menu. 'What's for lunch?'

'I've already ordered,' Leanne informed her. 'Salade Niçoise for me.'

Erik nodded. 'Good choice. But I'll have a croque monsieur. No wine, I hope. We have a long road ahead.'

'Omelette for me,' Maddy said.

'Good.' Erik gave the orders when the waitress arrived at their table.

'Where to next?' Maddy asked. 'I mean, if we're going to Gordes first, perhaps we should spend the night somewhere?'

Leanne picked up a piece of bread. 'Yes, that's what I thought, too. Let's find a nice country inn a couple of hours' drive from here.'

'Gordes?' Erik asked. 'Why do you want to go there?'

'It's Maddy who does,' Leanne explained. 'She's looking for someone. And she has just got a clue that leads to Gordes.'

Erik directed his blue-green gaze at Maddy. 'Someone you lost contact with?'

Maddy fiddled with the cutlery, not sure she wanted to share her story with a total stranger. 'Yes,' she said after a moment's hesitation. 'In a way. Long story. I need to find out why we never—'

He touched her hand. 'It's okay. No need to go into details. I can see this is very hard for you.'

Suddenly tongue-tied, Maddy nodded.

'Closure,' Leanne remarked. 'That's what she needs. And so do I.' She darted a glance at her father. 'But let's not rush it, okay? Or jump to conclusions.'

'Or be quick to judge,' Erik added. 'There are always at least two sides to every story.'

'Anyway,' Leanne remarked in a breezy tone, as if to break the tension. 'We need to crack on after seeing the cathedral. We're really on the wrong side of Paris, so we should continue to Orléans, then cut across and get the A6 to Lyon and then pick up the A7 that goes all the way to Marseille. I'll book us a room at a country inn on the way. What about you, Dad?'

Erik shrugged. 'I hadn't really made any plans. But I'll find somewhere. We can liaise by phone on the way tomorrow.' He glanced at Maddy. 'I'd love to help in your search, if I can.'

'Thank you.' Maddy put her napkin in her lap. 'That's kind of you.'

'Kindness has nothing to do with it,' Leanne said dryly. 'He just can't resist a pretty woman.'

'I'd be grateful if you'd stop sniping, Leanne,' Erik said, looking annoyed. 'It's not very pleasant for Maddy.'

'Okay,' Leanne mumbled. 'Sorry.'

Maddy looked at them and tried not to laugh at how Erik had immediately fallen into the father role. But a child will always be a child in the eyes of a parent, whatever their age, she knew from experience. Their order arrived, and they all fell on the food, eating in silence for a while, Maddy enjoying the light and creamy omelette and the crisp salad that accompanied it. French restaurants managed to make even the simplest meal a treat, she reflected. But the tension between father and daughter was palpable, and Maddy soon found herself wishing Erik would leave them alone. Or that she could travel on her own to Gordes. Why did they have to pick up these awkward travel companions? First Horace and now this Norse god with eyes of steel and a body to die for. He made her feel as if she was walking on a tight wire when he looked at her, and she felt a strange tug towards him she couldn't explain. She swallowed a mouthful and tried to shove aside her feelings for him, instead focusing on her quest to find Ludo.

Chapter Twenty-One

The cathedral of Chartres was mind-blowing to Maddy. Not expecting anything more than an old Gothic church, she nearly stopped breathing when she looked up and saw the vast stained-glass windows, their jewel colours glowing in the dim light, throwing splashes of red, green and blue on the stone floor. She had read in the guidebook that the cathedral was built in 1260 on the foundations of an earlier church that had burnt down in the previous century, but she had had no idea of its magnificence. Awestruck, she stood there, looking up and marvelling at the still vivid hues and beautiful shapes.

Maddy walked around the cathedral, until, in the dim light, she found a little side chapel, where candles flickered in front of a statue of the Virgin. She dug in her handbag, found a euro and put it in the slot under the stand. Then she lit a candle, like she always did when she was in a church, and stood there for a while, deep in thought. Then that familiar sense of loss hit her again. She wished she could talk to her mum, ask her advice, or simply feel her arms around her. 'I made a mess of it, didn't I, Mum?' she whispered into the darkness. 'My life didn't work out the way I planned. What am I going to do?'

Blinking away tears, she looked at the sweet face of the Virgin and felt, like a soft breeze, someone, somewhere telling her that everyone makes mistakes and that all would be well in the end. 'It'll get worse before it gets better,' someone had said when her mother died, and now it seemed to be true. There would be storms but then everything would settle and life would continue down a different, and perhaps smoother path than before. Oddly comforted, Maddy walked away, looking up at the amazing windows again, even more awestruck by their beauty and spirituality.

'Have you seen the rose windows?' a voice mumbled in her ear. 'The north rose is the most beautiful.'

She knew without looking that it was Erik, the faint floral scent from his clothes filling her nostrils. 'No, not yet. I went to light a candle in front of that little statue of the Virgin.'

'For your mother?' he asked, his voice gentle. 'Leanne told me you lost her when you were very young.'

Maddy nodded. 'Yes. I like doing that when I'm in a church. I feel she's there, somewhere watching over me. Then I don't miss her so much.'

'A lovely thought.'

'But where is that window you mentioned? I'd love to see it.'

'It's over there.' He took her elbow, steered her in the right direction and pointed upwards.

She followed his gaze and suddenly felt as if she had been touched by an angel's wings as she looked up at the huge round window and its religious scenes depicted in glowing colours. She shivered. 'Still so vivid. As if it was made yesterday.'

'It was a gift from Queen Blanche of Castile in 1230. And it would have looked exactly like this. Incredible. The Blue Virgin window is even older. 1150, it says in this leaflet.'

'It's almost too much to take in.' Maddy stepped away to one of the pews. She looked up at him. 'I'm going to sit down for a while. I need to… gather my thoughts a little. Things have been a little overwhelming lately.'

He nodded. 'Of course. For me too. I'll leave you alone. See you later.' He disappeared into the shadows and Maddy instantly felt a peace settle on her as she sat looking up at the windows and breathed in the smell of candles and incense. She closed her eyes and thought of what she had been through during the past few days. Arriving in Paris had jolted her back to her youth and her brief love affair. She hoped she would meet Ludo again, but he seemed as elusive as a wisp of smoke from an extinguished candle. She couldn't get a grasp of what had happened to him, but she knew instinctively that he was out there somewhere, waiting to be found. She closed her eyes and prayed that was the case.

Erik chased after her as she was leaving the cathedral. He caught her arm. 'We won't see each other again before we meet up in Provence. I'm going straight to Orange for a meeting. We're setting up a little shop there. You'll be stopping there tomorrow to see the Roman remains, Leanne said.'

She squinted up at him against the bright sun. 'Straight to Orange? That's a long drive.'

'I'm used to long drives.' He steered her around to get her out of the glare. 'There. Better?'

His light touch on her arm unnerved her. 'Yes. Thanks.' She stepped away.

'I just wanted to say that if there's anything I can do to help you find the person you're looking for, let me know. I have friends and contacts in the Gordes area. We get all our lavender for our perfumes from there.'

'I don't know much. Only a name, that's all.' She hesitated. Saying Ludo's name to this man felt like sharing a very intimate secret. But she had to find him, and if he could get some clues, it would be worth it. 'His name is… Ludovic Maximilian de Montrouge,' she said. 'He's about my age, maybe a little older. I'm forty-four, by the way.'

Erik nodded and typed something into his phone. 'I'm putting all this into my notes, so I'll remember.' He smiled. 'Forty-four? So much younger than me.'

'I suppose,' Maddy said flatly.

Erik looked embarrassed. 'Sorry. That was too personal. Anything else you can tell me?'

'No, but—' A thought struck Maddy. 'I have a photo.' She rummaged around in her handbag, and after a little searching, found the old photo-booth picture she had carried with her all those years like a lucky charm. 'Here. An old photo of us. One of those silly ones we used to take.' It felt strange to show it to him. She had never showed it to anyone else. But if it would help to find Ludo…

Erik laughed tenderly as he took the photo and looked at it. 'Two young kids. So sweet. I'll take a shot of it, if you don't mind.' He clicked his phone and handed the photo back. 'Might be a help if he hasn't changed much. You haven't, in any case. Except for—'

'Yeah, I know,' Maddy said with a derisory laugh. 'Wrinkles and bags under the eyes.'

Erik shook his head. 'No. I meant the slightly sad look in your eyes.'

*

Maddy and Leanne continued their journey, staying at a country inn on the way, stopping briefly for lunch the next day and then back on the motorway. They decided against any more sightseeing, despite the lure of mediaeval castles and five-star spa hotels.

'I just want to get as far south as we can before we stop the next time,' Leanne confessed late the next day as they swept through fields of ripening wheat and bright-yellow rape. 'How about you?'

'Oh yes,' Maddy replied, giving Bridget a reassuring pat. 'We're close to Avignon, anyway. We just have to stop to give Bridget a toilet break and water.'

'Of course. And I need a break too. Driving on French motorways is no pleasure.'

'I'll take over after we stop,' Maddy promised.

'Great. There's a petrol station close to here. Two kilometres away, the sign said. I bet it's one of those massive affairs with shops and rest rooms and restaurants. The French do the best pit stops in the world.'

This proved to be true. The huge petrol station could be seen in the distance, with a sign of a petrol pump, coffee cup and crossed knife and fork to signal what was on offer. As they pulled up at the parking area, they saw there was even an enclosure for dogs.

'Look, Bridget,' Leanne cooed. 'An open-air ladies' room especially for you.'

'They thought of everything when they built this place,' Maddy remarked, happy to stretch her legs and stiff back. 'I'll go and get us some sandwiches while you take Bridget for a piddle break.'

Leanne opened the rear door. 'Okay. Come on, Bridge.'

Maddy looked up at the umbrella pines outlined against the blue sky, enjoying the warmth of the sun on her back. The scent of pine made her feel she was already in Provence, even if they hadn't yet got close to the coast. But she could see the snow-covered tops of the Alpes-de-Haute-Provence in the distance and knew they had reached the final part of the journey. *Soon,* she thought, breathing in the warm air, *I'll be in the same town as Ludo. If I manage to find him, how will he react?* Her heart fluttered. It wouldn't be long before she knew. They were near Avignon and, with the stop in Orange, would be in Gordes by early evening. *What then?* she wondered to herself as she queued at the delicatessen counter where they made up sandwiches to order. How would she go about tracking down Ludo or even anyone who knew him? Apart from an old photograph, she had nothing that pointed to him in any way, other than the word of the chef at the restaurant in Paris. Maybe Erik would come up with something. That was the only hope.

As she shuffled forward in the queue, her mind on nothing much except what kind of sandwich she wanted, she scrolled idly through Facebook on her phone while she waited. She saw someone had tagged her to a picture and clicked on the link. The photo that came up made her blink. What was this? A couple dancing, their arms around each other, their eyes closed, their mouths meeting in what looked like an intimate kiss. *The latest squeeze at the golf club*, the caption read. With a sinking heart, Maddy recognised the man. Tom. Kissing some floozy in public. The shock made Maddy's heart flip, and she felt as if a hand was squeezing her throat. Hot tears welled up in her eyes. She blinked them away and looked at the picture again. Who was the woman? Nobody she knew. But who had tagged Maddy to make sure she saw it? She clicked on the Facebook notifications again. Of course. Jacinta. Her sister-in-law. Paying her back for that family row all those years ago, when Tom had stood up against his mother and sister, for the first time in his life. Jacinta had never forgiven Maddy. Now she had got her revenge. And the photo was from the website of the Lahinch local newspaper. Jacinta must have been delighted to find it.

'Madame?' a voice said. 'What would you like?'

As if on autopilot, Maddy ordered sandwiches and two bottles of water and took them outside. She walked slowly to a picnic table in the shade of the umbrella pines, where Leanne was waving at her, Bridget panting at her feet. *It's over,* she thought, feeling numb. *My marriage has finally come to an end.*

'What did you get?' Leanne asked, holding her hand out. 'Hope it wasn't just cheese and ham.'

'No, it's worse than that.' Maddy sank down on the seat beside Leanne. 'Much worse than cheese and ham.'

Leanne stared at Maddy. 'What?'

'Jesus, I've gone completely bonkers.' Maddy put the sandwiches and bottles on the table and clicked on her phone. She held it out to Leanne. 'This is what I just got. Please tell me it's not my husband snogging some tart on the dance floor.'

Leanne peered at the screen. 'Oh God.'

'It is, isn't it?'

'Afraid so.' Leanne put her hand on Maddy's arm. 'I'm so sorry. The bastard. But I already knew. Someone posted the photo in the comments on our blog, too. I just saw it while you were inside. Don't know who put it there.'

'Probably my sister-in-law. The bitch.' Maddy looked at the picture on her screen again. Now that she was seeing it for the second time, it didn't hurt so much. It was more like a confirmation of suspicions she had had but never confronted. Tom's indifference to her was about more than golf. A lot more. 'Younger than me, right?'

Leanne sighed. 'Yes. Looks to be in her late twenties. Do you know her?'

'No. Someone who has a connection to his golf club, I'd say.'

'What are you going to do? Call him and bawl him out? Go back home and sort it all out?'

Maddy shook her head. 'No. I'm going to carry on. But now... well, it's strange, but I suddenly feel...' She paused. 'Free. And not at all guilty. Isn't that mad?'

Leanne grinned. 'No, it's great.' She pointed at the phone. 'Just ask yourself the question – do you want to spend the rest of your life with that eejit? I mean, if he told you he was sorry and it was just a silly fling, would you want to stay with him?'

'No. My marriage is dead,' Maddy said flatly. After the jolt of the initial shock, she felt no overwhelming grief, just sadness that what had started with such happiness and hope all those years ago was now ending in a sordid, clichéd way.

'What about the blog?' Leanne asked. 'You still want to do that?'

Maddy sat up, anger and outrage replaced by a new energy. 'Are you kidding? Now I want to do it even more. He had the nerve to be angry about the blog. What a hypocrite! I want to be outrageous and fun and... wild,' she ended. 'He wants to snog some floozy in the golf club? I'll be doing a lot worse than that. And it'll be a lot less pathetic.'

Leanne laughed. 'Bring it on!'

Maddy unwrapped one of the sandwiches. 'God, I'm hungry.' She took a huge bite.

'What's it like?' Leanne asked. 'The sandwich, I mean.'

'Not bad,' Maddy mumbled through her mouthful. 'Pesto and ham with pickled gherkin. Didn't quite know where I was when I ordered. So I just pointed at stuff.'

Leanne bit into hers. 'Quite tasty. You know what?' she continued as she ate. 'In all the shock about your hubby and his shenanigans, I forgot to tell you we seem to have become influencers. Because of the success of the blog.'

Maddy opened her bottle of water. 'Influencers?'

'Yeah, you know, bloggers with large followings who mention brand names or wear big brands online and then their followers copy them. It's a type of marketing.'

'Oh. Okay.' Maddy drank some water. 'What will this mean for us?'

'We could get sent stuff and be paid for wearing it in our pictures. Do you want to do that?'

Maddy thought for a while. 'No, don't think so. It seems false, somehow. How about you?'

'Could bring in a lot of money. But no, I agree. It wouldn't be true to what we want to do. Those women with boring lives wouldn't be able to afford that stuff, anyway. They're our target audience. But…' Leanne winked. 'I'm sure they'd love the Hovden stuff.'

Maddy laughed and threw her empty water bottle at Leanne. 'That's sneaky.'

Leanne grinned. 'Sneaky is my middle name.'

'I don't even know what the Hovden products are like. I know they sell soaps and make up scents to order as well as making bath and shower gel.'

'Body lotion too.' Leanne held up her arm. 'Here, smell. It's one Dad gave me.'

Maddy sniffed. 'Lovely and fresh.'

'Crushed rose petals with some citrus undertones,' Leanne filled in.

'Gorgeous. Subtle but really nice.'

Leanne nodded. 'That's right. Sweet and sour. Just like me.'

Maddy laughed. 'Spot on, darlin'. Do they make aromatherapy oils? I mean the oils you put in your bath.'

'They do. And that's something you can order to be made up.' Leanne looked thoughtfully at Maddy. 'For you, I'd make a mixture of lavender and orange blossom with a hint of heather. Provence and Ireland mixed up in one.'

'That sounds terrific,' Maddy said and instantly imagined sinking into silky water breathing in that scent. The image of Erik in the bath popped into her mind for a second before she pushed it away. She got up. 'If you're ready, we'll get going, so.'

'Grand.' Leanne gathered the remains of the picnic. 'I'll just throw this in the bin over there and make a quick visit to the loo. Won't be a tic.'

Maddy was just settling Bridget in the back seat when Leanne came rushing back in a panic. 'Quick,' she shouted, her voice filled with panic. 'Get in the car and drive!'

Chapter Twenty-Two

'What's the panic?' Maddy asked, as she revved the engine and took off down the slip road that led to the motorway.

Leanne looked over her shoulder. 'There was a guy, a policeman, in the café when I came out of the loo. He was looking around and asking people about a dog. He said "*chien perdu*". That's lost dog in French, right?'

'Yes. But that doesn't have to be about us.'

'No, but I have a creepy feeling something's going on with Bridget. Maybe Horace has blabbed to the press. I wouldn't put it past him. He loves attention, good or bad.'

'Jesus,' Maddy mumbled, 'that's all we need.'

'I know.' Leanne sat back. 'I didn't see the policeman or his car following. He's probably still in there. But perhaps we should skip the blogging for a day or two.'

'Or pretend we're somewhere else? Maybe they, whoever they are, knew we were coming this way, according to the last post you wrote. So a red herring might be good right now.'

'Brilliant.' Leanne picked up her phone. 'I'll do a Twitter post and then something on Instagram, saying we're taking a detour through the Cevennes. Lots of winding mountain roads. Should keep them busy for a while.'

'Good idea.' Maddy relaxed and started to enjoy driving the smooth car on the motorway. Her thoughts strayed to Tom and the woman in the photo. It didn't have to mean he was having an affair, but the look in his eyes told her that even if they weren't, he would have liked it to happen. That was enough for Maddy. In a way, it was a positive thing, she tried to tell herself. Pretending to be happy all this time had been a strain. They had slowly drifted apart until it was too late to find a way back. Not that it was solely his fault, but she had a feeling he had only thought of how he would amuse himself when the children had left home rather than wanting to spend time with her. And she had let it happen. Now all the cards were in her favour. Let him run around with other women; she would be the injured party. He might have pulled a long face about her going off on a holiday on her own and then the blogging, but his behaviour was far worse.

She sighed and relaxed her shoulders. What lay ahead was in the lap of the gods. This was now and she wanted to enjoy it. An ancient poem her grandmother used to quote popped into her head from nowhere. Something about the present being all there was. What was it she used to say? Oh yes. *Time is… the present moment well employ, Time was… is past… thou canst not it enjoy. Time future… is not and may never be. Time present is the only time for thee.* So true, even centuries later. And time present was truly enjoyable. Maddy felt a sudden rush of joy, like a breeze of warm flower-scented air through her hair. She was still young, still pretty and still looking forward to meeting Ludo again. Even if it turned out to be a disappointment. She had to see his face, look into his eyes and find out the truth.

*

They continued past Avignon and on to Orange, a small Provençal town, renowned, as Erik had told them, for its Roman ruins. They took a break there in the early evening for tea and a quick look at the famous amphitheatre. They were met at the entrance by Erik, who was just leaving. He beamed at them as they approached with Bridget on the lead.

'Hello! I'm glad you decided to stop. The theatre is unique. I believe it's the best preserved Roman theatre in the world.' He handed Maddy a brochure. 'Here, you'll need this. It's the whole story in a nutshell.'

Maddy smiled at him. 'Thank you. I can't wait to see it.'

'Do you want me to mind the dog? It'd be easier to climb all the steps without her.'

Leanne handed him the lead. 'Great. Thanks, Dad. We'll see you in half an hour at the café around the corner.'

'Enjoy the visit.' With a last look at Maddy, Erik left with Bridget.

Leanne and Maddy spent an enjoyable half hour walking up and down the different levels of the amphitheatre, amazed at the ancient site and the history behind it. They finally sat down on one of the seats at the very top, looking down at the half circle that made up the front of the theatre. Up here, they were hit by the magnitude of the edifice, and how the stage down there seemed to echo with voices from the past. The sense of history was so strong, they could nearly see ghostly figures in strange costumes moving around, hear the applause from the people on the packed terraces and smell dusty air, thick with atmosphere.

'Incredible,' Maddy said with awe.

'Yes. I'm so glad we stopped to see it.' Leanne closed her eyes. 'This place smells of decadence and Roman orgies. So different from the holy smell of old churches.'

'I can't get over that nose of yours.'

'It's a bit of a curse, to be honest. I can even smell vibes between people.' Leanne glanced at Maddy. 'Like between you and my dad. Come on, tell me. Is there something going on there I should know about?'

Maddy felt her cheeks flush, more with annoyance than embarrassment. 'You know what? I find him a little smug.'

Leanne looked startled. 'Smug?'

'Yeah. He swans around looking aloof and handsome, fixing me with his ice-green eyes and kind of second-guessing how I feel. Okay, so he's attractive and had we met in different circumstances, we might flirt or something. But at this moment in my life, I don't need some wannabe guru to fix my problems or look into my soul.'

'What do you mean?'

'I mean that he...' She paused, trying to explain the feeling of being drawn into something she couldn't control. 'I don't know. Maybe it's just that I feel vulnerable right now. Like you said, he's just being kind, I suppose. But he's so powerful, somehow. So sure of his charisma.'

Leanne stared at Maddy for a moment. She burst out laughing. 'Yeah, he's a bit of a poseur, my dad. I have a feeling it's his marketing image or something. Like he developed it to sell his scents and soaps. Have you seen his new website? He just set it up. Totally aimed at the middle-aged woman longing for healing or some such crap. But it works somehow.'

Maddy nodded. 'Yes, I've seen it. The target audience is exactly what you said, but there is a core of something there. Something spiritual and wholesome.'

Leanne grinned and nodded. 'See? You're buying it.' She leant forward. 'You're a middle-aged woman, longing for healing,' she whispered.

Maddy bristled, not because it wasn't true, but because it was so close to the bone. 'No, I'm not one of those women,' she snapped.

Leanne raised an eyebrow. 'Oh no?'

Then Maddy couldn't help laughing. 'Yeah, yeah, I know what you're saying. Clever marketing. But he lays it on a bit thick. He should make it more subtle.'

Leanne nodded. 'You're right. Why don't you tell him?'

'Why don't you? You're his daughter.'

'Yeah, but you're…' Leanne paused.

Maddy frowned. 'I'm what?'

'His willing victim.' Leanne laughed and pushed at Maddy with her elbow. 'You big sucker.'

'Oh, shut up.' Maddy returned Leanne's playful push. She got up and started down the steps. 'I'm going for a walk. Enjoy tea with the Norse god. See you at the car in half an hour.'

She stumbled down the steep steps, not quite knowing why she was so unsettled. Was it her confusion every time she was in Erik's presence? The vibes between them were like a collision waiting to happen, something that would be a complete disaster for them both, not to mention Leanne. She had to stay away from him, resist the temptation to get closer and to let him into her sphere, her soul. She didn't want to get close to him, or anyone, in this way yet. Not while she was struggling with a marriage heading for the rocks and trying to find a conclusion to her long-lost romance. But it wasn't Erik's fault that she felt so confused. She realised in a flash of understanding that she was more afraid of her own feelings than his.

The atmosphere in this ancient place felt suddenly like an evil, threatening force. Leanne was right. There was a smell of decadence, something cloying and sweet. She glanced at the statues and effigies, their frozen grins suddenly alive. Maddy ran out through the entrance, into the bright sunlight and breathed the petrol-laden air. She laughed at herself when a car hooted its horn as she ran across the street against a red light. How ridiculous she had been. She suddenly felt silly for having run off like that. Why not join Leanne and Erik at the café? He wasn't some kind of satyr from Roman times or anything. Just a man of flesh and blood and maybe just as confused and lost as she was.

Maddy found Erik and Leanne deep in conversation when she arrived at the café, the terrace of which overlooked the Roman ruins.

Leanne looked up as Maddy reached their table. 'I thought you said you were going to wait in the car.'

'I changed my mind.'

Erik got up and pulled out a chair. 'Sit down. What can I get you?'

Maddy sat down. 'Perrier, please. I'm very thirsty.'

Erik ordered the drink and sat down again. 'It's getting hotter. I suggest you get going as soon as you can. We booked a room in a little hotel in the town of Gordes. Then you can do some research tomorrow and see if you can find that man you're looking for. Maybe even where you'll be staying. I hope you do.'

Maddy met his gaze, expecting laughter, but all she saw was kindness and understanding. 'Thank you.'

He touched her hand briefly before getting up again. 'I'll be off. As soon as I've called into the new shop here to check how it's coming along, I'm driving straight to Nice. We'll catch up there. You're both welcome to stay in my house just outside Vence. Might be better than a hotel. There's a guest cottage, so you'll have some peace.'

'That'd be lovely.' Leanne sighed. 'What do you say, Mads?'

'Peace,' Maddy said, as if to herself. 'That sounds wonderful. I have a feeling I'll need it after whatever happens next. Yes, Erik. I would love to stay. Thank you.'

'Good.' Erik nodded. 'See you then. Good luck, Maddy.'

'Thank you. I hope I'll get some clues at least.'

'You will.' He squeezed her shoulder. 'Stay calm.' He left before she had a chance to ask him what he meant.

Chapter Twenty-Three

Situated on the edge of the plateau of the Vaucluse, Gordes was a village of exceptional beauty, Maddy discovered as they approached in the early evening. The sun sank slowly behind the mountains, illuminating the old buildings in a rosy glow and streaking the sky with pink, red and orange. They opened the roof of the car when they got off the motorway and could fully appreciate the warm breeze laced with herbs, garlic and pine. Swallows swooped around the old buildings, filling the air with their loud chirping.

'What a magic place.' Maddy rolled her stiff shoulders. 'But I'm looking forward to the hotel. Does it have a pool?'

'I think so,' Leanne replied. 'I didn't book it. Dad made all the arrangements. It's outside town, near that famous monastery. You know, the one in the middle of a field of lavender. I'm sure you've seen the photos. Very famous.'

Maddy nodded. 'Of course. L'Abbaye de Sénanque. I have a poster of it in my bedroom. Love it. I'm so excited we'll be seeing it in real life.'

'Me too. But it's getting late and I'm hungry. Let's go and check into the hotel.'

'Show me the way,' Maddy ordered, mentally sinking into the cool water of the pool.

She did just that only half an hour later after checking into what was in reality a charming Provençal villa with only eight bedrooms, a terrace overlooking the Vaucluse valley and the famous nearby abbey, its lavender fields filling the air with their scent. The rooms were bright and airy, all with windows overlooking the garden and the pool, the turquoise water glinting seductively through the screen of shrubs.

Maddy threw her bag on the bed, and changed into her bikini, glancing at herself in the mirror. *Not bad for forty-four*, she reflected, and with Bridget in tow, headed to the pool. She put a towel on a lounger, and Bridget immediately jumped up and settled on it. Maddy padded to the edge of the pool and eased herself into the water, sighing deeply as she floated on her back, looking up at the darkening sky and the stars beginning to appear. She closed her eyes. Nothing seemed real or urgent here, nothing pressed her to do anything or even think. It was as if her very soul was floating into space as the faint rush of wind in the trees and the soft gurgling of the pool filled her ears. Doves cooed and cicadas chirped, a sound forever associated with summer in Provence. Her thoughts drifted to Tom and that photo of him with another woman, then to Ludo, who she might meet soon, then she pushed it all away and emptied her mind. It was lovely to float here and enjoy this moment of peace and leave whatever would happen next to fate – or God.

Maddy heard someone talking softly nearby. She opened her eyes and noticed the outline of a tall man bending over Bridget. The little dog seemed to like him, wagging her tail and licking his hand. Maddy smiled. Bridget could charm an army. The man moved closer to the pool, and she saw he had dark curly hair and a beard. He looked at her and smiled. She met his gaze and froze. Those eyes. It couldn't be. Time suddenly stood still. She felt herself sink, water filling her nose and mouth before everything went black.

'She's coming to,' a voice said.

Maddy coughed. She opened her eyes and discovered Leanne, her face white, holding her hand. Bridget whined and licked her face. Maddy took a rasping breath and pushed the dog off her. She felt sick, her head spun and her chest hurt. She blinked and tried to sit up, but that made the nausea worse, and she threw up over the tiles at the side of the pool.

'Shit,' she mumbled. 'Sorry about that.'

Leanne mopped her face with a towel. 'That's good. You got all the water out.'

Maddy lay back against the folded towel someone had put under her head. 'I'm cold,' she mumbled and tried to get up. 'I have to get dressed. What the hell happened? Did I drown in a pool? How stupid.'

'I don't know what happened,' Leanne said. 'I was on my way to have a swim, when I saw this guy lifting you out.'

Maddy stared at her. 'What guy?' Then it all came back. That face... those eyes. 'It's him,' she said. She looked wildly around. 'Where is he? Did I dream it?'

'I'm here,' a voice said.

And there he was. She hadn't dreamt it. Rigid with shock, she stared at him, and suddenly everything receded: Leanne, Bridget, the cooing doves and the sound of the cicadas disappeared in a distant haze. All she saw was… Ludo.

'*C'est toi*,' she whispered. 'Is it really you?'

'It's me,' he said in English. He crouched beside her and put his arm around her wet shoulders. He looked at her face in silence for a moment. 'But who are you? You look familiar, but I don't seem to remember – have we met before?'

Maddy felt her heart constrict as if squeezed by a cold hand. She had looked forward to this moment for so long. She had expected shock, surprise, even joy. But not this. 'What?' she croaked. 'You don't… remember me?' She tried to focus on his face, but it was too dark. 'I'm Maddy. Madeleine,' she whispered, her lips so stiff she was barely able to get the words out. 'The Irish girl you met in Paris when we were both students.'

'Madeleine?' He frowned, then his face lit up. 'Ah, *oui*. I remember now. *La petite Irlandaise*. Long time since we saw each other.'

'More than twenty years.' Maddy struggled to stand. 'I have to get dressed. Can you wait? We have to talk. Please don't disappear. Please don't be a dream or some kind of hallucination.'

He laughed. 'No, I won't. I can't. I run this little hotel. I'm the owner and manager and the chef, too.'

She stared at him. He hadn't changed much except for the beard and the expression in his eyes – a look of pain and disillusionment. Life had clearly hit him hard at some stage. 'You speak perfect English now. In the old days, you didn't.'

He helped her up. 'Much has happened in the past twenty years. We have a lot of catching up to do.'

'We do.'

'Go and get warm. Have a hot shower.' Ludo put a towel around Maddy's shoulders. 'I'll see you here beside the pool in a little while. I have half an hour before we serve dinner.'

'Okay.' Maddy walked away, her legs trembling, turning to look at him before she rounded the corner – to make sure he was still there, waiting for her.

'Oh my God,' Leanne whispered. 'That man. Gorgeous. Old. But so hot!' She was lounging on Maddy's bed watching her get dressed. 'What are you wearing?'

Maddy turned from the mirror. 'What does one wear for a reunion with a man you haven't seen for twenty years? A man you've never been able to forget?' She twanged her bra strap. 'A Victoria's Secret underwear set? Maybe this time he'll remember me.'

'I can't believe he didn't remember you,' Leanne said incredulously.

'It's true. He didn't,' Maddy replied in a small voice. She stopped and stared blankly into the mirror. 'I can't get over that. He had forgotten all about me and the weeks we spent together.'

'Maybe he lied?' Leanne suggested. 'Maybe he was so shocked he couldn't admit he knew you?'

Maddy shook her head. 'No. I think he told the truth.' She felt a dart of anger. 'But we're here now, so I'll jiggle his memory with the new me. What do you think?'

Leanne laughed raucously. 'Yeah, why not? You still have a great figure, except for a little wobble here and there...'

'Thanks for the vote of confidence.'

'I was teasing you!'

'I know.' Maddy shivered. 'I'm still cold. Or maybe it's nerves. Could you give me a bit of space here? I'm trying to—' She stopped. 'Haven't a clue what I'm trying to do. I can't stop shaking. Can't believe it's happening.' She rummaged in her suitcase and pulled out the summer dress she bought in the outlet store what seemed like several years earlier. 'What about this?'

'Very pretty.'

'No.' Maddy shoved the dress back in the case and shook out her white trousers. 'I'll just wear these and a navy T-shirt. I don't want to look like I'm trying too hard, do I?'

'I suppose not.' Leanne got up and scooped Bridget into her arms. 'I'll mind the baby in my room. I want to change, too. See you on the dining terrace in half an hour. Can't wait for the lowdown on the reunion.'

Maddy looked at her pale face in the mirror after Leanne had left. 'This is it,' she said. 'This is what I have been chasing all these years. The searching is over. I'll hear the truth at last.'

Sitting on a sun lounger by the pool, Ludo was staring out at the view when Maddy approached. He didn't hear her soft step on the tiles and she could look at him surreptitiously for a brief moment. There he was, waiting for her. Not the same Ludo she remembered, but maybe a part of that young man she had loved still remained? He looked the same from the distance of a few feet. Thinner perhaps, a little more hardened by life and whatever he had been through, but his general demeanour was the same. The dark, closely trimmed beard suited him. It gave him a bohemian air, like a hero from an old novel. She stopped for a moment to steady her nerves. Was this really happening? Or was it some kind of surreal dream?

He turned and their eyes met. 'Madeleine.' He rose and held out his hand. 'Come, let's sit on the bench over there and watch the lights come on in the valley.'

'It's so beautiful here,' she said. His hand was warm and strong and the physical contact comforting.

They walked together to a bench at the edge of the terrace, where the view of the valley and the Luberon hills was even more spectacular, especially in the early evening light, when everything seemed wrapped in a soft blue glow and the sun had set but still coloured the few clouds a deep pink. Below them was the outline of the valley and the lights coming on in the houses and along the streets of the little villages. The scent of lavender was even stronger there, making Maddy take deep calming breaths. A single lantern over the bench cast a gentle glow over them.

They sat down. Ludo didn't let go of her hand. 'So we meet again,' he said.

'It seems like a dream. I've tried for so long to find you.' She laughed softly. 'You've hidden yourself well. I could find just about anyone by Googling or doing a Facebook search. But not you.'

'I've been in places that don't encourage an Internet profile. To put it mildly. I've been away for a long time, Maddy.' His flawless English puzzled her, contrasting so much with the Ludo she remembered.

'How come your English is so good these days?' she couldn't help asking.

'I spent a few years in England, Then America. That's where the accident happened. A car crash that left me horribly injured and killed the girl I was with. After that, I shut myself away from the world. I've been on a hard journey most of my adult life. I only emerged a few months ago. It took a long time to heal the wounds.'

She stared at him, her heart aching at his story. 'Wounds? You must tell me what you've been through.'

He squeezed her hand. 'Yes. But first, I have to apologise for not recognising you. Now that I think about it, I remember the time with you as a very sweet interlude back then. That night in the château especially. It was beautiful, no?'

'Yes,' she whispered, tears welling up. He didn't remember their promise to each other or that he had sworn he would follow her to Dublin. She had just been 'a sweet interlude' to be forgotten the next day. 'I gave you my number. You were supposed to call me. I waited and waited. Then I tried to call the number you gave me, but it didn't work.'

'No, it had changed. My uncle became ill and leased the place to—'

'I know that now.' She pulled her hand out of his grip, not because she didn't want his touch but because it distracted her. What a fool she had been to pine for him all this time. 'What happened?' she asked. 'Why didn't you get in touch?'

He shrugged. 'I did call. But all I got was a voice telling me the number didn't exist. Your handwriting on that piece of paper was difficult to make out. I tried a few times and then I gave up. In any case, I thought you might have forgotten all about me by then.'

'I didn't forget, Ludo.'

'That's sweet.'

'But why did you?' Maddy asked in a bare whisper. 'What happened? Did you meet someone else?'

He shrugged. 'No. Yes. I don't really remember. My student days were full of parties and girls.'

'So, I was only one of many?' Maddy asked, bitterness washing over her. So that was it. He had been with so many girls he couldn't remember them all, least of all a little mouse from Dublin.

'I'm sure I thought you were very special. But I was young and not ready to settle down. Maybe, if we had met again a year or two later, things would have been different. It was the wrong time, I think.'

'Possibly,' Maddy said. 'My life changed very quickly after I returned from Paris. I was told my mother had been diagnosed with cancer.'

'How terrible for you.'

'It was an awful shock.' Tears welled up as she remembered that heart-breaking time.

'I did go to Dublin the following year,' he continued. 'In November. I was with a couple of friends for a pub-crawl weekend. I thought of looking you up, but…' He shrugged. 'You had probably moved anyway.'

Maddy put her hand to her hot cheek. She couldn't believe he had been in Ireland, and she hadn't known. 'Oh, God. Yes, we did. My mother died, you see. And I was living in student quarters in Dublin. My dad moved closer to his office and got a little house on the north side. He still lives there.'

Ludo's eyes were full of compassion. 'I see. I'm so sorry about your mother. That must have been a terrible blow.'

'Yes.' Maddy looked out over the dark valley. 'It's still so hard. That kind of grief never leaves you.'

'No.'

He touched her hair, and as he moved, she was aware of his scent that had once been so familiar. 'Life is strange,' he declared. 'Little things can send you on a different path to the one you thought you'd follow. I was so sure I knew exactly where I was going and then –something happened that catapulted me into a kind of hell I've just managed to get out of.'

Maddy was startled by the pain in his voice. 'Do you want to tell me about it?'

'There's not enough time this evening. Maybe later. But in a nutshell, it was about addiction. I started taking painkillers after the accident, which led to more drugs, and then I fell into a downward spiral. I couldn't stop. But I eventually got help and slowly managed to get clean. But an addict is always an addict, even if you never touch the stuff again. I'm a different person to that young man you met twenty years ago, Maddy.' He turned to look at her with his sad brown eyes. 'But what about your life? Has it been – good?'

Maddy sighed. 'Some of it, yes. But not all of it.' She met his eyes. 'A small part of me has always loved you, Ludo. But I had to push it aside. Other people came into my life. My husband, my children. But now my kids have grown up and my husband, well, that's another story.'

'Of course.' He looked at her for a long time. 'How strange that you remember me so well, and for me, you're just a hazy image of a pretty young girl. I'm sorry. This must be hard for you.'

Maddy blinked away tears and tried to swallow the lump in her throat. How could she explain how she had carried the memory of their brief romance in her heart all these years? 'I can't pretend I'm not disappointed,' she said, trying to keep the emotion out of her voice. She dug in the pocket of her trousers. 'I have something here, in my wallet, you might like to see.' She pulled the photo from behind the flap in the wallet and handed it to him.

He looked at the picture of the two of them in the photo booth and laughed. 'I had the same photo. Mine is the one where we kissed. I'm ashamed to say I couldn't remember who you were. A girl I kissed once, who was very sweet to me, that's all.'

'One of many,' she replied, her voice cold, feeling a sudden dislike for what he really was – a flirt – one of those typical Frenchmen Leanne had described. She had been so sure he wasn't one of them.

He shrugged and laughed. 'Yes. I suppose. I didn't take love seriously then.'

'But now you do?'

His gaze drifted to her mouth. He touched it lightly with the tips of his fingers. '*Ma Madeleine*,' he mumbled. Maddy pulled back but he kissed her lightly on the mouth.

His lips were soft but the kiss left her confused. She had waited for this since the day they parted over twenty years ago. It felt so sweet. But did he mean anything by it? It was hard to tell.

'So much to say, so many things to discuss, to find out.' He got up. 'But I have to go and cook dinner. We have only eight tables, but they're always full. Are you dining here tonight?'

'Yes, but if you prefer...'

'No, it's okay. I want to cook for you. Maybe I can make up for my bad memory.'

'You don't have to. Not your fault I'm so forgettable.'

He looked at her and smiled. 'That's not true. I was stupid and arrogant then. You will find I have changed, hopefully for the better. We have a lot of things to talk about. But maybe not tonight? You had a long drive and it might be late when I finish.'

'Tomorrow morning?' Maddy asked.

'We do yoga here at seven. Maybe you'd like to join us?'

'I'll be here.'

'Perfect.' He kissed her on both cheeks. '*A demain.*' His step was light as he walked away. She stayed on the bench for a while, looking out over the dark valley and the stars glinting in the velvet sky. This was it. The end of the long journey that had started ever since they said goodbye all those years ago. They would meet again; he had promised her then. She had believed him, never guessing for a moment he hadn't meant it or that it would take so long to find out.

Chapter Twenty-Four

'How did it go?' Leanne whispered, peeping at Maddy over the menu.

'Fine,' Maddy mumbled, pretending to scan the array of dishes on offer.

'Come on, tell me.'

Maddy lifted her gaze and looked at Leanne. 'Please. Not right now. I'm a little overwhelmed by all this. Could we just enjoy dinner?'

'How could I? I've been on the edge of my seat since you left to talk to your long-lost lover.'

'Keep your voice down.' Maddy looked around the terrace, where the guests chatted softly to each other in the dim light from the candles and lanterns. 'Strange,' she continued. 'There are very few couples. Most of the people here seem to be single or in groups.'

'That's because this is not really a hotel,' Leanne replied. 'It's some kind of healing and yoga centre for people recovering from stress and mental disorders.'

Maddy stared at Leanne. 'How do you know?'

'Dad told me. He managed to find your man—'

'You mean Ludo?'

Leanne nodded. 'Yeah. But he calls himself Max now.'

Maddy blinked. 'Max?'

'Max Ludovic.'

'Your dad found this out?'

'He wanted to help. You'd given him a lot of clues, he said,' Leanne announced. 'So Dad started to look around the Internet but found nothing. He knows Gordes quite well, so he called some people he knew in the area, and they said this was the place. It appears this Max guy – or Ludo – spent a long time in the abbey down there in the valley. And then, a couple of years ago, he left and bought this villa with money he inherited from his uncle. He and his partner – a woman called Céline – opened the hotel and restaurant only last year. It's brand new but going like a bomb. Celebrities queue up to stay here after rehab because it's so simple and relatively unknown. They had' – Leanne looked around and lowered her voice – 'Kate whatshername here only last week.'

'Amazing. I had no idea.' Maddy tried to take it all in: Ludo being in this horrific accident, suffering from addiction and spending years at a monastery. Then opening a secluded spa hotel for the rich and famous recovering from addictions and nervous breakdowns. And all this time she had been bringing up two children and teaching French to teenage girls in a Dublin suburb. 'What a great bloodhound your dad is.'

Leanne beamed. 'Isn't he?'

'It wasn't a compliment,' Maddy said, anger rising in her chest. 'He seems to like poking into other people's business. Is that what he does for fun?'

'Why are you complaining? You found the guy. That's what you wanted, wasn't it?'

Maddy bristled. 'Yes, but I'm beginning to find the whole thing a bit weird. It's as if this is some kind of project for your dad. As if he wants to show off his detective skills and score brownie points.' Maddy stopped. Why was she attacking Erik? Was it the feeling of being drawn to him in a way she couldn't control? She cleared her throat. 'Sorry. Forget I said that. I'm a little overwhelmed by all this.'

Leanne nodded. 'Of course. It's been such a roller coaster for you.'

Maddy sighed. 'Thanks for understanding.' She picked at a piece of bread from the basket on the table. 'Who is this Céline woman, anyway?'

'Don't know.' Leanne looked around. 'But maybe this is her?'

Maddy followed Leanne's gaze and spotted a slim black-haired woman weaving her way with cat-like grace around the tables towards them, carrying two plates.

She stopped at their table. '*Bonsoir.* I'm Céline. Max made something special for you. A selection of Provençal specialities called a *farandole*.' She placed a colourful plate in front of each of them. 'I hope you enjoy it.'

'Thank you,' Maddy said. 'Tell him—' But the woman had left as silently as she had arrived.

'Gosh. That perfume,' Leanne said. 'Oozing sex.'

'What?'

'Shalimar. Didn't you smell it? Like a whole boudoir. But it suited her.'

'I don't smell people like a dog,' Maddy snapped, still jittery after her reunion with Ludo.

'Calm down. Here she is again,' Leanne warned as Céline reappeared with a carafe and two glasses.

'Sorry,' she said in her heavily accented English. 'I forgot to give you water.'

'How about a glass of wine as well?' Leanne asked.

Céline frowned. 'We don't serve alcohol. Our guests come here to, how do you say—'

'To detox?' Leanne suggested.

'*Voilà*,' Céline said. '*Exactement. Bon appétit, mesdames.*' She glided off into the darkness.

They ate in silence for a while, both hungry after a long day on the road. Maddy found herself enjoying the array of food on her plate; duck pâté, stuffed peppers, deep-fried courgette flowers, tomatoes filled with spicy mince and other things she didn't recognise with delicate flavours of herbs and spices. Céline appeared once more with two pots of crème brûlée for dessert. Maddy smiled wistfully as the taste of the dessert brought her back to that time with Ludo. Maybe he remembered too?

'Heavenly food,' Leanne declared when they were savouring the dessert. 'Five-star stuff, really.'

Maddy nodded. 'Oh yes. Ludo was supposed to become one of those world-famous chefs. His uncle told me that day we went to see his restaurant. But it never happened.'

'And you didn't meet again. Why? Did he tell you?'

'Yes. As I told you, he forgot about me. Completely.'

'Whaddyamean?' Leanne asked through a mouthful of crème brûlée.

'I was just one of a number of girls he dated at the time. Dated being a polite word for—'

'Screwed? Oh, God, what a stinking bastard,' Leanne exclaimed.

Maddy sighed. 'You can say that again. But to give him his due, he did try to call me, but I scribbled down my number so badly he couldn't read it.'

'Funny how a small thing can change your life forever. My parents wouldn't have met if my mam hadn't forgotten her notes in the lecture hall at UCD. Dad found them and tracked her down. Saved her from failing her exams. He was her hero then. I wouldn't be here if she'd been more organised.'

'And we wouldn't be here if I hadn't been so stupid,' Maddy said bitterly. 'If I'd realised our so-called true love was nothing more than a quick fling to him, we could have done something better.' She put her napkin on the table and got up, feeling thoroughly drained. 'I'm really tired. I think I'll go to bed and try to sleep.'

Leanne looked surprised. 'Oh? But I thought you might have planned some kind of rendezvous with—'

'Tomorrow morning, he said. Yoga at seven.'

'Count me out. I think I'll sleep in.' Leanne pushed away her plate. 'I'll have some herbal tea before I turn in. You go on to bed. You look wrecked.'

'I am. Goodnight. See you in the morning.'

'Night, love. Sleep tight,' Leanne said.

Maddy walked across the dark terrace, around the corner behind the restaurant towards the reception area and the bedrooms. When she was about to step inside, a small shape bumped into her. She bent down and discovered a little boy of about three. He rubbed his eyes and looked up at her. '*Où est Maman?*' he asked.

'*Viens, chéri.*' Maddy took him by the hand and was about to lead him to the restaurant to ask if someone there knew him, when Céline came rushing towards them.

She scooped the little boy into her arms. 'I'm sorry,' she said. 'I thought he was asleep. Don't worry, madame, I'll get him back to his bed.' She kissed the boy and walked away, cooing softly into his ear.

Paralysed with shock, Maddy looked at Céline's receding form. That child – those dark eyes...

She suddenly knew what she had to do.

Chapter Twenty-Five

Leanne yawned. 'What's the rush all of a sudden?'

Maddy gripped the steering wheel and accelerated down the slipway to the motorway. 'I just wanted to get away.'

'At six-thirty in the morning?' Leanne yawned again.

'Yes.' Maddy clenched her jaw.

'Why?'

'Because.' Maddy glanced at Leanne. 'No need to look so cross. We'll be in Nice sooner than planned. That's where you wanted to go, wasn't it?'

'Yeah, but not this early.' Leanne leant her head back. 'I know what's going on. Your lover boy wasn't as hot as you thought?'

'No. He's as hot as I remembered.'

'Weren't you supposed to meet up after the yoga?'

'Yes. No… We were, but—' Maddy hit the steering wheel. 'Shit! I told you. He didn't remember me.'

Leanne sat up. 'So you said. But I thought it would all come back to him when you talked. How could he be such a gobshite? Maybe he didn't mean it.'

'He meant it. He explained it all in detail during our talk. He hadn't a clue who I was until I reminded him. And even then I was just a fleeting memory.' Maddy blinked away her tears. 'And here I've been pining for him all these years, imagining it was the love story of the century, while all this time he hadn't even spared me a thought – or even remembered me. What a fecking waste of time.'

'You've been pining for him? But you married someone else.'

Maddy sighed. 'I know. But… I've been thinking about it lately and I see it clearly now. It was such a dark time in my life.' Maddy fought back tears as the sorrow threatened to well up. 'Everything seemed to happen at once. It was unbearable.'

'Of course. That guy never showed up after promising he would, and then your mam…'

Maddy nodded, changed gears and slipped into the right lane. 'Yes. After losing my mother, I was so alone. I needed someone to love me, to hold me. And there Tom was at that stupid student ball, looking so handsome, dancing with me, flirting, telling me I was beautiful. It saved my life in a way. Made me feel like life was worth living again. Everything happened so fast after that. I got pregnant, we got married in a rush. We had two babies very quickly. It was amazing and fun and totally mad. And of course, I loved Tom and we were happy. For a while. Then we had the daily slog of childcare, two jobs, paying bills and all that stuff. And every time things felt dreary and boring, I had this fantasy of the perfect man, the perfect love story that I lost. You know, something to cheer you up in all the drudge.'

'And you thought that maybe, one day, you'd meet again and fall into each other's arms and live happily ever after?'

'Stupid, huh?'

'Nah,' Leanne drawled. 'Fantasies? We all have them. I don't blame you. But I have to tell you I feel a little disappointed. It seemed lately as if everything would fall into place for you. The lottery win, your hubby smooching that floozy in public and the marriage on the rocks. You could throw it all in his face, keep the cash and move in with Mr Smooth in lovely south of France. Final kiss and fade out. Fabulous. That's a movie I'd love to watch in front of the fire on a cold night.'

'You're laughing at me.'

'Aw, come on, Mads, it's a bit of a farce, isn't it? All of it, I mean. You, me, the poodle, the car, Horace, my dad and now your hottie French boyfriend with amnesia.'

Maddy shook her head and managed a wry smile. 'I suppose it is when I think about it.'

'Great that you see it my way. Then you'll love the latest blog post. I did a little ditty about the fancy rest home back there. Not mentioning any celebrities, of course. Just a hint here and there. Took some photos, including that faran-thingy we ate last night. And your boyfriend as he was cooking up a storm in the kitchen. Too good not to post. The result was terrific. A kaleidoscope of impressions.'

Maddy laughed. 'You're so mad.'

'Aren't we both? So why did we run out of there like that? Was it getting to be too much?'

'Yes. I felt humiliated somehow. As if I was begging him to remember me and maybe fall for me again. As if that was going to happen. And then the little boy I found crying in the reception area. Turned out to be Céline's son.'

'And the dad? You think it's whatshisname?'

'Must be.' Maddy sighed. 'Whatever. He seemed to have forgotten to mention a wife and child during our talk. And then he had the nerve to kiss me.'

'Jesus,' Leanne muttered.

'Yeah,' Maddy said. 'The final nail in the coffin of my beautiful romance. He hasn't changed at all. I think that the best thing to do right now is to get away from him and all the memories that were built on false hopes. Now I want to go somewhere lovely and have a good long rest before we start the journey back.'

'I think my dad's house in the hills above Nice is just the place for that. Stunning views, big pool, comfy beds and champagne on tap.'

'Bring it on,' Maddy said and floored the accelerator.

After stopping for a long lunch in the pretty town of Aix-en-Provence, they reached Nice in the afternoon and drove through the heavy traffic on the Promenade des Anglais, not minding the slow progress along the beach front. That way, they had a chance to admire the view of the deep blue sea, the coastline, the shiny white yachts at anchor in the bay and the sailing boats on the glittering horizon. The palm trees swayed in the gentle breeze and petrol fumes mingled with the smell of coffee and fresh bread.

'Oh Nice, I love you,' Leanne declared and stretched her arms against the blue sky when they stopped at a traffic light. 'This is way better than Paris. It's so warm and blue and… sinful,' she added, glancing at a handsome young man coming out of a restaurant. He waved at her and blew her a kiss. Leanne blew him one back.

The lights changed and they surged forward into the roaring traffic. Leanne giggled and hugged Bridget. 'I feel reborn.'

Maddy shook her head and laughed, feeling better now that the meeting with Ludo was behind her. 'Yes, I know what you mean. This place is intoxicating. So great to have a convertible on a day like today.'

'Not just any convertible.' Leanne ran her hand over the shiny red door. 'I love this car. I think I might buy it.'

'Can you afford it? What about the flat?'

'Screw the flat. I'll just live in the car.'

'Sounds like a good solution. Turn on the GPS, will you, and stop spoofing. I need to find the road to Vence.'

'I want to put on some French music. We don't need the GPS. We're picking Dad up at his shop in the old town. He'll direct us. All we have to do is to find the store. It's near an area called the Cours Saleya or something, he said.'

'In that case, I think we should park and continue on foot,' Maddy suggested. 'Impossible to drive through those narrow streets.'

'You've been here before?'

'Only once, a few years ago. Tom took me with him on a business trip,' Maddy said with a dart of nostalgia. Those were the happy days – all gone now. 'He was at a conference, so I had plenty of time to walk around the city. The old town is lovely, but I wouldn't want to drive through it.'

They found a parking place in an underground car park and carefully locked up after taking all their valuables with them.

'Have your phone ready,' Maddy ordered. 'The old town is full of beautiful vistas and quirky shops and bars. Great material for the next blog post.'

Leanne took Bridget in her arms. 'Brilliant. Great contrast to our last one from Gordes.'

'Gordes,' Maddy said, her heart constricting. 'It's like a dream. Did it really happen?'

'Sure did. That old hunk was not just a hologram.' Leanne winked and walked ahead out of the car park. 'Hey, you know what?' she said over her shoulder. 'You're too good for that kind of guy. You'd be better off forgetting him. He isn't worth your tears.'

'You're right.' Maddy trailed after Leanne, her mind full of the night before. It had been surreal to come face to face with the man she had fantasised about all her adult life. He had been like a mirage at the end of a hot dusty road, an image floating in front of her, tempting, teasing, full of promises. A parallel universe she could have lived in. If only they had met up again, she had thought. How silly to think Ludo had pined for her ever since they parted. She had just been a brief flirt to him, a girl he slept with once and then disappeared, only to be replaced by another girl, then another and another. The image she harboured of a beautiful young man with a pure heart was replaced by the real, not-so-noble Frenchman to whom women were easily discarded commodities. He had obviously been through some kind of hell, and she felt for him, but his journey through life had nothing to do with her. She played no part in it, and he had been in no way instrumental to her own troubles. They had led parallel lives and her imagined connection between them was but a fantasy. Leanne was right. It was time to forget and carry on. Life was too short to let this destroy her.

They emerged into a sunlit street that led to a large square, lined with little restaurants and boutiques selling clothes, shoes, handmade leather goods, arts and crafts. Leanne consulted her phone and came to a stop in front of a sage-green door with art-deco style stained glass panes. 'This is it. The Hovden hub. This is where the magic happens, where people come to buy bespoke soaps, scents, lotions and potions.' She pushed the door open. 'Abandon all hope,' she said darkly.

Maddy rolled her eyes and laughed. 'You're such a drama queen.'

Just as in the Paris shop, bells tinkled as they walked in. This shop was twice the size of the one in the capital city and the décor more elaborate and expensive. The packaging and displays were exquisite and a delicate scent of orange blossom and lavender hung in the air. Customers queued at the counter waiting to collect orders or place new ones. The pretty girls who worked in the shop were all in floaty Provençal print dresses. The boutique had a dreamlike atmosphere, like something from an impressionist painting.

'Lovely place,' Maddy remarked.

Leanne put Bridget down on the floor, looking proudly around. 'Yes. It's a bit girly, but I love it. I expected something more minimalist and Scandinavian. But it suits this area and the general idea of perfumes from Provence.'

The door opened behind them, and Erik, cool and elegant in a white linen shirt and beige trousers, walked in. 'Ah, you're here. Great. We could head up to my house when—'

'How about right now?' Leanne checked her phone. 'It's coming up to five. I don't want to get stuck in the evening traffic. I'll drive if you like, Mads.'

'That'd be great,' Maddy replied.

'No,' Erik interrupted. 'The rush hour doesn't really start until around six-thirty. In any case, there's someone who wants to see you, Maddy. He called into the shop about twenty minutes ago. He's waiting at the café around the corner.'

'Who?' Maddy asked. *Ludo*, she thought. *He's realised we need to be together. He has finally remembered what happened between us, and he wants to apologise for causing me so much pain.* Her heart racing, she ran out of the shop and around the corner.

Chapter Twenty-Six

But the man waiting for her at a table outside the small café wasn't Ludo.

'So here we are,' Tom said.

'Looks like it,' Maddy agreed and sank down on a chair opposite him. 'But what on earth are you doing here?'

'I came because I thought we needed to discuss... well, everything.'

'Terrific timing,' Maddy remarked, making no effort to be pleasant.

'What do you mean?'

She shrugged. 'I just meant I'm in the middle of a lovely holiday, and then you arrive wanting to "talk".' She leant forward. 'But whatever. Let's talk, then, beginning with that woman you're obviously involved with.'

Tom frowned. 'Woman? What woman?'

Maddy pulled her phone from her bag and clicked until she found the picture. She stuck it under his nose. 'This woman. Your sister posted this charming image in the comments section of our blog.'

Tom sat back, glaring at her, ignoring the picture. 'Yeah, and what about you parading around Kildare Village buying sexy underwear? And flaunting yourself with that tart you call a friend in a series of blogposts, where you go all around Europe doing God knows what with I don't know who. That's pretty cheap, if you ask me. How do you think that looks to my friends and colleagues?'

'Not to mention the members of your golf club,' Maddy filled in. 'One of whom must be that woman in the picture Jacinta so kindly provided. I think we might start with your explanation of that one.'

Tom squirmed, momentarily reprieved by the arrival of a waitress. 'What do you want?' he asked.

'*Deux cafés*,' Maddy ordered.

'It's too late for coffee,' Tom protested when the waitress had left.

'It's too late for a lot of things,' Maddy retorted. 'Can we get started on this? I don't have all day.'

'Neither do I,' Tom said. 'I'm only here until late tonight. I'm catching the Ryanair flight back at eleven.'

Maddy blinked. 'What? You're only here for a couple of hours? What on earth is so important it couldn't wait? That golf tournament?'

'No. That was the other day. Our club won, by the way. The photo you saw was from the dinner at the golf club.'

'Oh. Hip, hip hooray, hang out the flags.' Maddy stirred some sugar into the coffee the waitress had just served. 'And that woman is?'

Tom coloured slightly. 'Claire Murphy. Secretary of the Lahinch club.'

'And your relationship with her is something you want to tell me about?'

Tom sighed and pushed away his cup. 'I don't know what to say. There's no relationship to speak of. But okay, she's attractive. We danced and flirted a bit. I don't see that's a crime considering—' He stopped and took a deep breath. 'Feck it, Maddy, this is not going the way I planned. I didn't know Jacinta posted that picture. She didn't tell me when she called the other day. All she said was that she'd found out.'

Maddy stared at him. 'Found out? About what?'

'The money.' Tom stuck out his chin. 'You won all that money and never told me. Two hundred thousand.'

Maddy's stomach sank. 'How did Jacinta find out?'

'One of the other teachers told her. They're in the same bridge group.'

Maddy sighed, admitting defeat. 'Okay. I knew it had to come out one day.'

Tom's gaze hardened. 'Jesus, Maddy. Don't sit there pretending it's nothing. You lied and said you'd won two thousand on a scratch card. But you won so much more than that. A huge amount of money. How could you keep such a thing from me and cover it up with lies?'

'It wasn't that hard,' Maddy mumbled. 'What you didn't know wouldn't hurt you, I thought.'

'Yeah, well, now I know.'

Maddy raised an eyebrow. 'And?'

'Shouldn't that be our money to share? Why should you keep it all?' Tom demanded.

'Why shouldn't I? It's mine. I can do what I bloody well like with it. All these years I've never done anything remotely irresponsible or selfish. It's always been about you or the kids. I feel I deserve a bit of fun before I die.'

Tom gave a snort. 'Don't be melodramatic. We've had lots of fun. What about that holiday in Majorca?'

'Yeah, I remember. Our room was broken into and then the kids got a tummy bug. I had to look after them while you were ogling women on the beach. The only one with a tan was you.'

Tom looked a little sheepish. 'I suppose that was a bad example.'

'You bet it was.' Maddy studied Tom more closely, noticing he wasn't his usual jaunty self. He hadn't checked his appearance in the window of the café once or smoothed his hair. Dressed in chinos and a polo shirt, he looked as if he had stepped straight from a golf game onto a plane, which was probably very close to the truth. Something suddenly dawned on her. 'You need money for something?' she asked. 'Is that why you're here on this flying visit?'

'Well, uh…' Tom fiddled with his teaspoon. Then he looked at her. 'Okay, yes. I've been invited to represent our club at an amateur tournament in Florida in August. But it's pretty expensive, what with flights and hotels and all that.'

'I see.' Maddy looked at him, not knowing how to reply.

So that's why he was here. Typical. He didn't deserve anything from her. Flirting with another woman in public was such a low thing to do, but wasn't what she had done just as bad? Their marriage had been heading for the rocks with increasing speed even before the lottery win. His indifference to her, his selfishness, his obsession with golf had all contributed to the slow death of their marriage. But maybe it had been her fault too? 'It takes two to tango,' she mumbled.

'What are you talking about?'

She leant on her elbows and looked at him. 'I'm talking about us – our marriage. There doesn't seem to be much left of it. What do you think?'

Tom sighed. 'No. Don't know what to say. But yeah, it's feeling a little dead all right.' He looked at Maddy with sad eyes. 'I'm sorry. I haven't made you happy, have I?'

'You did. In the beginning. We had such good times then.'

He nodded and smiled. 'Yeah, those were the days. But now...' He paused. 'I was thinking during the flight over how nice it would be if we were friends. Because I do like you, Maddy. And I care for you. A lot. So if we could part right now, with no hard feelings, and celebrate the good times and try not to get into bitter arguments and drawn-out fights that would only hurt the kids, wouldn't that be—' He stopped. 'God, that wasn't at all what I meant to say. I only came to ask if you could see your way around sharing some of the cash with me. Then all this came out instead.'

'I'm glad you've said it.' Maddy reached out and took his hand. 'And yes, I agree. We should part in a friendly manner and stay friends. I like you, too, Tom. I'll always care for you. We have so much history.'

He looked relieved and squeezed her hand. 'That's nice to hear.'

Maddy suddenly felt she couldn't let him off the hook that easily. She realised how much she had to get off her chest. She let go of him. 'Of course, I could start a whole string of complaints,' she continued. 'Starting with how you always made me feel you did something noble when we got married because I was pregnant. And how you never honoured your end of the deal we made about sharing housework and childcare, not to mention the valet service I was supposed to provide, even though we both worked full-time, and how golf became your religion and made you forget about me and all the things we planned to do when the kids left home.' She drew breath. 'But maybe that was my fault. I wasn't fascinating enough, was I?'

Tom flinched at the sarcasm in her voice. 'That wasn't why—'

Maddy flicked her hand. 'Oh, whatever. Let's not go into that. I want to stay friends and keep in touch with you. Meet up at Christmas with the kids and do other stuff together. As friends. And...' She paused. 'I'd like to share some of the money with you. Go on that golf trip. Have fun, fall in love, whatever. Neither of us should waste the rest of our middle age trying to breathe life into the corpse that is our marriage. Life's too short for that.'

Startled, he stared back at her. 'Wow. You are some woman, Maddy.' Then a happy smile spread all over his face, and he leant over and kissed her. 'I can't believe it. Thank you. You deserve all that money. How much are you willing to share?'

'How about twenty thousand?'

His eyes lit up. 'Are you sure? That's very generous. I'll accept without protest.'

All her anger gone, Maddy beamed at him, his selfishness not bothering her any more. 'Isn't this fun? I mean, yeah, divorce is a pretty sad affair. But isn't being unhappy with someone even sadder?'

'That's true. But it seems a little weird to feel this happy, sitting here with you planning a divorce. How do you feel?'

'Free,' Maddy said without thinking.

'What are you going to do now?' Tom asked. 'I mean with the rest of your life?'

Maddy shrugged. 'Haven't a clue.' She lifted her cup in a toast. 'To an amicable divorce. Go forth and fornicate or whatever. You have my blessing.'

Tom clinked his cup against Maddy's. 'Cheers, Maddy.'

She rose from the chair. 'I have to go. My friends are expecting me.'

He shot up. 'Oh, yes, me too. I'm going to wander around town for a bit. Do some shopping, and then I have to get back to the airport.'

'Give Jacintha my love,' Maddy said with a wicked glint in her eyes. 'Such a shame I won't be seeing her much from now on.'

Tom laughed. 'I'm looking forward to seeing her face when she learns we're splitting up but staying friends. Now she'll have nothing to bitch about.' He held out his arms. 'How about a hug?'

Maddy melted into Tom's arms, feeling a pang of nostalgia. She had truly loved him once, and maybe part of her always would. She pressed her cheek against his and breathed in the smell of his aftershave for the last time. Then he let her go and they pulled back, looking into each other's eyes.

'It'll be okay.' Tom wiped away a tear from Maddy's cheek with his finger. 'Be happy, sweetheart.'

She nodded. 'I will,' she whispered. 'And so will you.'

'I'll do my best. I'll be in touch. Have a great holiday.'

As he walked away, she watched him disappear around the corner. A chapter in her life had closed forever.

Like a giant spaceship suspended in the air, the house hovered over the landscape. The brilliant white façade was nearly blinding against the blue sky.

'Your house is the epitome of discreet,' Leanne remarked as she pulled up in front of the tall iron gates. 'Such a modest little place.'

Erik laughed and took his phone from his pocket. He tapped in a number and the gates slid open silently. 'The architect is Finnish. I said "simple" and this is what I got.' He glanced at Maddy in the back seat. 'Are you feeling all right? You've been very quiet.'

'I'm fine. Just a little sleepy.' Maddy patted Bridget absentmindedly. Erik had been forced to take the front seat because of his long legs, but she didn't mind. Sitting at the back gave her a break from Leanne's chatter, and she had a chance to mull over what had happened at the café. It was weird to think the two men in her life were now history. First Ludo, then Tom. Just like that her life had changed overnight. It was difficult to imagine she was now technically single. Not divorced, but separated. And, in a way, she had lost a husband but gained a friend. 'Sorry if I've been boring. Much to think about, you see.'

Erik smiled. 'Of course.'

'We'll soon be in the pool,' Leanne said. 'And Dad has promised us a dinner party. Just a few guests and us.' She smirked at Erik. 'I bet you're trying to set Maddy up with some French hunk.'

Erik laughed. 'You're too suspicious, darlin'.'

Leanne drove up the steep hill onto a plateau and then through a garden that took their breath away. Bougainvillea and oleander bushes in full bloom were set off against the green background of palms and olive trees planted in perfect symmetry to form a beautifully landscaped park. They came to a stop outside a massive iron-studded oak door that flew open as they approached. Two smiling young men in white jeans and T-shirts greeted them as they alighted from the car.

'Pierre and Marcel,' Erik said. 'Meet my daughter, Leanne, and her friend, Mrs—' He stopped, looking embarrassed. 'I'm sorry. I can't seem to remember your last name.'

Maddy laughed. 'Probably because nobody told you. Just call me Maddy,' she said to the young men and shook each of their hands. 'My last name's Quinn,' she said to Erik as an afterthought. 'But I might change it after, well, you know,' she ended, not wanting to say the word 'divorce' out loud. Not yet, anyway.

'We don't know,' Leanne said. 'But I'm guessing something happened back there. No need to talk about it right now, though. Let's just have fun.'

Maddy sighed. 'That sounds good. I'm looking forward to seeing the house.'

Erik nodded. 'Let's get you settled in. The lads will take your bags, so come with me and I'll show you around.'

Maddy let Bridget out, and she trotted beside them as if she knew this was her perfect environment. They entered a bright hall with a wooden floor and white walls hung with seascapes by well-known Scandinavian painters. The living room was furnished with a white seating arrangement, a big marble coffee table littered with magazines and books in front of the picture window overlooking the enormous blue pool that seemed to hover over stunning views of the mountains and the azure Mediterranean in the distance. A big carpet with an exquisite pattern of flowers and leaves lay on the floor.

'Holy shit, Dad,' Leanne whispered as she stood by the window. 'I had no idea you lived like this.' She turned to stare at him in awe. 'How did you make all this money?'

He smiled and put his finger to his perfectly straight nose. 'This,' he said. 'I was born with a sense of smell that has led me around the world and made me a lot of money.'

Leanne nodded. 'I have it, too. That sense of smell. But it hasn't made me rich. I just thought it was a bit weird.'

Erik's eyes lit up. 'You do? I remember thinking you might when you were a little girl, but I didn't know if it would develop.' He put his arm around Leanne. 'You're a chip off the old block, sweetheart.'

Leanne gave him a hug. 'I'll be proud of my nose forever now.' She stepped back and looked at him with awe. 'But how did you do it? How did you make a fortune with this weird sense of smell?'

'It all started after I left Ireland to work for a cosmetics company in Grasse,' Erik replied. 'I had a science degree from UCD and was bored with my job in a pharmacy. And I always wanted to live in Provence. Then they discovered my sense of smell, which kick-started my new career. I was what you call a "nose" for many years with Fragonard and other companies in Grasse. We made a lot of very well-known perfumes over the years. Then I wanted to create my own fragrances. My ideas didn't go down well with the big guys, so I thought I'd stick my neck out and go it alone.' He spread out his arms to encompass the house, the pool and the view. 'And this is what it brought me.'

'What about Mam?' Leanne asked. 'Why didn't she want to share this adventure with you?'

Erik looked glum. 'She was afraid to leave everything and take a risk. I had no money, just my degree and ambition. But by that time, we'd already fallen out. She said she wanted to give you a safe environment. "You don't bring a child into the chaos and uncertainty," she said.' He shrugged. 'The rest you know. I tried to keep in touch, but—'

'I know.' Leanne put her arms around Erik's waist and hugged him. 'Not your fault.' She stepped away. 'But Mam had me for most of my life. Now it's your turn. Not that I want to live in your pocket, I've had enough of an overbearing mother, but I want to be in your life.'

Erik kissed Leanne on top of her head. 'There has always been a space for you in my heart and my life.'

She looked up at him. 'What about your love life? Any women I should know about?'

Erik's eyes met Maddy's over Leanne's head. 'Not at the moment.' He stepped away. 'But now you should go and inspect the guest cottage. You'll want to have swim before dinner, I think.'

Maddy turned away from Erik's gaze. 'A swim sounds like heaven.'

The guest cottage was decorated in the same Scandinavian style as the main house. Simple but comfortable wicker chairs and sofas with white cushions were scattered on the little patio overlooking the pool, and both of the large bedrooms had king-size beds. The bathrooms were stocked with Hovden products and light blue-and-white towels.

'Fabulous,' Leanne sighed and lay back on the bed in her room. Bridget jumped up on the bed and snuggled down beside her. Leanne waved at Maddy and Erik. 'I'll have a snooze here with Bridget for a little while. See you later, gang.' She closed her eyes and appeared to have fallen asleep in an instant.

Erik gently closed the door. 'She's exhausted.' He fixed Maddy with his green eyes. 'What about you? Do you need to sleep?'

Maddy stepped away. 'No. I'd love a swim.'

'Of course. Me too. Did you bring a swimsuit?'

'Yes.' Maddy opened the door to the adjoining bedroom. 'I'll see you at the pool in a minute.'

'I'll be outside the little pool house on the other side. I'll get you a drink and a snack if you feel like something to eat.'

'Great.' Maddy slipped into her room and closed the door.

She stood there for a while, enjoying being alone. She understood Leanne's sudden fatigue. It had been a long journey; first the emotional upheaval of the reunion with her dad and then ending up in a place that looked more like a film set than a home. This place was somehow too rich, too overwhelming, even for Maddy, with its cool elegance and comfort. It was like landing on a cloud in a kind of heaven, where everything was provided, even a handsome man who seemed attracted to her in a way she found oddly disturbing. *Is this real?* she wondered as she went to the window overlooking that incredible garden. *Maybe this is a dream, and I'll wake up in my bed in Dublin on a wet Monday morning, Tom beside me, asking if I've remembered to iron his shirts for some business trip.*

She laughed at herself and went to find her bikini in the bag one of the staff had put on the bed. She could hear the cicadas' loud chirping, the screeching of a jay and a plane preparing to land at Nice airport through the open window. Real sounds that told her she wasn't dreaming. Maddy caught sight of herself in the tall mirror of the wardrobe. The red bikini she had bought in the Victoria's Secret shop was truly flattering. With her slightly tousled hair and a band of freckles across her nose, she looked young and happy.

She grabbed a towel and ran out the door to the pool, where she could see chairs and a table with drinks and snacks set up under the striped awning. There was no sign of Erik, which was more of a relief than a disappointment. She needed a bit of a space, a moment to breathe and catch up with herself. She dived into the cool blue water, surfacing moments later and swam to the edge, where she rested for a while, looking at the breath-taking view. What a perfect place. But dangerously addictive. Maddy smiled and mentally shook herself. Why not enjoy all this luxury while it lasted? Go with the flow and take all it had to offer. Life was too short to be miserable. And definitively too short not to enjoy the admiration of a very attractive man...

Chapter Twenty-Seven

Leanne still hadn't appeared when Erik arrived at the poolside. 'I'm sorry,' he said. 'I had to deal with a business call.'

Maddy opened her eyes and sat up in the lounge chair where she had been dozing. 'Oh. That's okay. I was quite happy on my own, to be honest. I had a little wine and some of the delicious snacks you served. You must have a very good cook here.'

Erik sat down in the lounger beside her. 'No. I do all the cooking. It's one of my hobbies. I'll be cooking tonight as well. Just a simple barbeque.'

'Sounds good.' Maddy sighed and stretched out in the sun lounger. She didn't feel like talking but he seemed to understand, and the ensuing long silence felt comfortable. She lay there, enjoying the cool breeze, the gurgling sound from the pool and the cooing of doves, letting her mind drift, thinking of nothing in particular.

'May I ask you a question?' Erik asked after a long silence.

'Okay,' Maddy mumbled.

'Where did that dog come from?'

Suddenly wide awake, Maddy opened her eyes. 'Why do you ask?'

There was a concerned look in his eyes. 'That business call I was talking about earlier wasn't about business. It was from the police in Nice. Someone from Scotland Yard called them and said a dog belonging to a member of the British royal family was stolen a little over a week ago from a country house in Gloucestershire and has been traced to you and Leanne through your blog.'

'What?!' Maddy shrieked. 'Are you serious?'

'Very serious.'

'Jesus!' Maddy jumped up from her lounger. 'What are we going to do? Are they going to arrest us?'

'So it's true then?'

Maddy paced around on the tiles. 'No... yes, I mean, we didn't steal her. She was smuggled from the house, after that mad party, into our car by that sneaky creep Horace. One of your most loyal customers, I might add. *Sir* Horace if you don't mind.'

Erik nodded. 'Yes. I know who you mean. He even helps with a little marketing in the UK. He gets free products in return for his recommendation to all those celebrities his wife entertains in their house.'

'Marketing by stealth,' Maddy remarked. 'How weird that you know him. Is he a friend of yours? You might have been to one of those celebrity parties?'

Erik's mouth curled. 'No. I'm not a huge fan of that kind of scene. But to get back to the dog...'

'So he squealed then? The dirty little gobshite.'

'I'm not sure. I don't know who reported it. They didn't say.'

'Oh, shit. Whoever it was, we're in trouble.' Maddy wrung her hands. 'What are we going to do? Can we hide Bridget somewhere? Did you say anything?'

'Not much, no. What could I say?'

'But... but we have to – I don't know, explain this somehow.'
She glared at Erik. 'Don't just sit there, you eejit! Do something!'

'Like what?' Erik poured himself a glass of white wine from the
bottle in the cooler.

Maddy suddenly noticed he was enjoying himself. 'You're
laughing at me.'

'Not at all.' Erik sipped some wine. 'This could be serious. You
could end up in a French prison or worse, be deported to a British
jail. Not so nice for an Irish girl.'

'But your daughter is implicated in this affair, too. Don't you
care?'

Erik smirked, a twinkle in his eyes. 'That might be very educa-
tional. Maybe she could start another blog? "My life in prison" or
something?'

Maddy looked at him and then realised what was going on.
'You're having me on, aren't you?'

He laughed. 'I was wondering how long it would take you to
figure that out.'

'So there was no French police or Scotland Yard?'

'There was. But while I was talking to the police in Nice, they
got a message from the British police to say the dog has been found
and returned to its owner. They were forced to apologise to me.'

Maddy stared at him. 'What? The dog has been—?' Then it
dawned on her. 'Oh my God, she bought a look-alike dog. Edwina,
I mean. Is that what happened?'

Erik laughed. 'You guessed it. Just as I hung up, I got a call from
Horace. He wanted to let you know. He also said he hoped there
were no hard feelings and he's very sorry about blackmailing you.'

'Why didn't he call me directly?'

'He's scared of you, he said. You can be very fierce when you're angry, apparently.'

Maddy started to laugh. 'How utterly ridiculous.'

Erik shook his head and grinned. 'Hilarious.' He put his glass on the table. 'I'm sorry I strung you along like that.'

Maddy giggled. 'Must have been great fun, though.'

He touched her cheek. 'I couldn't resist making you all hot and bothered.'

She sighed. 'Thank God it was only a joke.'

'So now, no more problems. You can just relax and enjoy this place.'

'I certainly will. And the company,' Maddy added, returning his smile.

He raised his glass. 'I drink to that. I like your company, Maddy.'

'And I yours,' she said, realising how true it was. They might not have agreed about everything, but she liked his calm, his kindness and total lack of vanity, so rare in a successful man. What had irritated her initially she now found attractive, especially his Scandinavian good looks and sensitivity. Not her type at all, but there was a warmth in his eyes despite the cool air, something that stirred her senses like no man had for a very long time.

They stayed there for over an hour, Maddy doing most of the talking. All her inhibitions gone, she lay on the lounger under the awning and told him about her marriage, how it had hit the rocks and that now they had finally agreed to part as friends. It was good to talk about it with someone who was so sympathetic. 'I feel we have finally made peace and can go on to be friends.'

He looked at her with that steady blue-green gaze and listened while she spoke. 'Peace,' he said, when she had finished. 'That sounds good. I'm sure a lot of couples would love to have been as sensible as the two of you. Including me,' he added wistfully.

She turned her head and looked at him and noticed he looked suddenly sad. 'You parted on a bad note?'

He looked out over the view of the sea. 'Yes. We ended up hating each other and that wasn't good. Not for us or Leanne. I tried to make peace but she wouldn't listen. We're still in that hateful cold space.'

'It must be hard to live with.'

He looked back at her with a touch of sadness in his eyes. 'Yes. It was. Still is.'

'Maybe you could make peace too?'

'I don't think that's possible.'

'And…' She hesitated. 'Have you had other relationships since then?'

'Yes, of course. Dates with some lovely women, brief affairs and one or two that might have worked. But I was too caught up with my business. That was my first love and I'm sure it was quite obvious. Not fair to a woman. But now things have slowed down…' He glanced at her. 'I find myself at a loose end, somehow.'

They were interrupted by Leanne skipping onto the tiles of the pool. 'Hey there, why didn't you wake me up? I must have been asleep for hours. What time is it?'

'I don't know,' Maddy said. 'And I don't think I want to know. That's what this place does. It makes you feel suspended in time.'

Erik got up. 'My stomach says it's time for dinner. I'll go and light the barbeque.'

Leanne made a thumbs-up sign and dived into the pool, her slim body breaking the blue water with a tiny splash. She swam under the water to the edge, where she rested for a while, looking out over the incredible view. 'This is heaven, isn't it?' she said in a low voice.

Maddy looked at her sleek head. 'In a way. But it doesn't seem real.'

Leanne turned to look at her. 'No, it doesn't. I'm not sure I'd like to live here forever. What about you?'

'Right, now, yes. But forever? No. It's kind of—' Maddy tried to find a word to describe the house and its surroundings. 'Sterile.'

Leanne heaved herself out of the pool. 'Exactly.' She found her bag and took out her phone. 'But our fans will love this scenery.'

'Yes. It's like something from a movie.'

'Exactly.' Having taken the shot, Leanne padded to the patio and helped herself to olives and stuffed tomatoes. 'Everything at your service at all hours. It's too fecking perfect, isn't it?'

'That's for sure,' Maddy agreed, getting out of the lounger. 'Not that it isn't fabulous. But I like a bit of a struggle from time to time.'

'Yeah. Me too.' Leanne took a towel from the back of a chair and draped it around her shoulders. 'Funny how we think alike, isn't it? I feel as if you're reading my thoughts sometimes.'

Maddy laughed. 'But I do. Didn't you know I'm psychic?'

Leanne backed away in mock fright. 'Wahoo, that's scary. So what do we do now, my psychic friend? Get out your crystal ball and tell me. Is this where we end our travels? Will we just sit out the holidays here and go mad with boredom?'

'I don't know. My crystal ball is on the blink.' Maddy paused. 'I thought you might want to stay and spend some time with your dad.'

'Oh yes. I do. But not for that long.'

'We could stay for a week and then drive on,' Maddy suggested. 'To Italy maybe? Go to Florence then drive across to Venice. Then maybe take a ferry to Croatia. I'd love to see Dubrovnik. Or down to the Amalfi coast?'

Leanne smiled and nodded, her mouth full of stuffed tomato. 'Both of those sound great. We'll discuss that over dinner. I gave Bridget to one of those cute lads who work for Dad. He offered to walk her. I told him to keep a low profile. You don't know if the cops are after her still. Wouldn't be so great to end up in jail just when I've found my dad.'

'Oh, I meant to say! Bridget is okay,' Maddy filled her in. 'Horace called Erik and said she has been found. The missing dog, I mean.'

Leanne giggled. 'Ah, they found a body double? How sneaky. But that's the toffs for you. Nobody's as sneaky as them.'

'But that means Bridget is ours from now on.'

Leanne beamed. 'Really? That's terrific. Another perfect thing in all this perfection. Jesus, all we need now is for you and Dad to fall for each other and I'd have the perfect parents. "Careful what you wish for", seems like a very true saying.'

'Maybe our followers will love the perfection?' Maddy said, avoiding Leanne's eyes. She seemed to have some kind of antenna for people's feelings. Or were the vibes between her and Erik that obvious?

Leanne picked up an olive. 'No, they'd hate it. It would mean a Cinderella-happily-ever-after ending. And they don't want our adventure to end. They'll want us to go on and do fun stuff. If the blog were gone, they'd have nothing to dream about.'

Maddy laughed. 'You're right. What a huge task we've set ourselves. It'll never end.'

'Ah, it will. Someone else will think of something even better soon.' Her eyes focused on Maddy. 'Are we dressing up tonight? Dad has invited some guests, he said. I wonder who?'

'I have no idea.' Maddy sniffed the air. 'We'd better get ready. The barbeque seems to be all lit and ready to go.'

Leanne rubbed her hair with the towel. 'You go on. I'll see you…' She paused. 'Where's this party taking place?'

'Erik said right here, beside the pool. The guys will set everything up, and he'll cook the food on the barbeque.'

Leanne nodded, looking impressed. 'Oh, a poolside party. Let's go and get dolled up, then.'

They walked back to the guest cottage together, Leanne chatting about their upcoming trip, Maddy deep in thought. It seemed her life was falling into place after having rapidly fallen apart only hours earlier. Making peace with Tom, accepting Ludo was a dream, solving the problem with the dog and Leanne's plans for the rest of the summer had all fitted into the plan. But there was one piece of the jigsaw she couldn't find a place for.

Her budding attraction to a very interesting man.

Chapter Twenty-Eight

The guests invited to Erik's impromptu barbeque were not the glitterati of Nice society. They were the people who had worked for him, both in the business and on the house project. Mostly French with some from other countries, they were all dressed up for the occasion: the introduction of Erik's long-lost daughter. Leanne, surprised but delighted to be the star attraction, soon got involved in chatter and laughter, flirting with the men and making friends with the women, especially those involved with the production of the perfumes.

'Look at her,' Erik said proudly, his eyes shining. 'She's a natural. She'll be a great help to me in the future. I can't tell you how happy I am to have her back. And to find that she's so like me in many ways. I never knew she had the nose until she told me today.' They were standing at the other end of the pool, watching the party from a distance, Erik having pulled Maddy aside after dinner.

Maddy laughed. 'She's been entertaining me with it all through the trip.'

Erik frowned. 'You make it sound like a party trick. It's going to be a great asset for the firm. My sense of smell will wane with age. Hers has another thirty years at least.'

'Assuming she wants to stay,' Maddy remarked, taking a sip of champagne from the glass Erik had offered her. 'Have you asked her?'

'No, but... I thought...' Erik suddenly looked crestfallen. 'You're right. I should ask her. How stupid of me to take that for granted.'

'Leanne is a very free spirit,' Maddy said softly. 'That's why I like her so much. And isn't that a quality you have as well? I thought that was the reason you came here to do what you did. You followed your star. You must allow Leanne to follow hers.'

'But what about—' Erik made a wide gesture with his champagne glass to encompass the house, the garden and the stunning view. 'All this? It will be hers one day. If she stays.'

'Only if she stays?' Maddy sat down on a stone bench and turned to look out over the hills rolling down to the sea far below them. It was getting dark, and she could see the lights along the Promenade des Anglais and on the yachts anchored in the bay. A soft lavender-laden breeze caressed her face and bare arms.

Erik sat down beside her. 'No. You're right. She is all I have. Whatever she does, she will inherit my life's work.' He turned to Maddy. 'What about you? Are you following your star too?'

'I will when I find it. I came out here chasing a dream that proved to be just a silly fantasy. Then my marriage ended. I'm trying to get used to all of that, and to being single. I feel both confused and a little sad right now.'

'That's understandable.'

She took a deep breath of the soft air. 'Lavender. I will never be able to smell it without thinking of Ludo.'

'Your student boyfriend?'

'Yes. Funny, I thought we were made for each other. I thought that our love would never end and that one day we'd find each other again and—'

'You'd live happily ever after?' Erik asked in a voice so gentle she barely heard him.

She laughed. 'Yeah. Something like that.'

'It didn't strike you that if he really loved you, he'd have turned every stone to find you?'

'No,' Maddy replied. 'I thought that something had gone wrong somehow and that he'd lost the piece of paper I gave him. But I suppose you're right. Had he searched long enough, he would have found me.'

'I can't imagine it would have been that hard.'

'No, of course not, now that I look at it in hindsight. But I suppose I didn't want to think rationally. I had this silly dream, always running in the background, especially when things got rough. It was like a bright light, a bit like that Neverland star, and it kept me going through the dark times.'

Erik put his arm lightly around her shoulder, looking at her face. 'And then, when you met again, the light went out. How did you feel about that?'

'Disappointed. But mostly stupid. And relieved in a way.' She shrugged. 'I'm not sure I've sorted out my feelings yet.'

They were interrupted by loud laughter and shouting from the patio. Leanne ran around the side of the pool towards them. 'Hey, we're all going down to Vence. There's a club there with a great DJ. Do you want to come?'

Erik looked at Maddy in the dim light of the lanterns around the pool. 'I don't, but you go, Maddy.'

'No thanks,' Maddy said. 'I prefer the peace up here. Have a great time, Leanne.'

Leanne glanced at the two of them, a glimmer of a smile in her eyes. 'Okay. I get it. See you in the morning, Mads. We'll plan the rest of the trip at breakfast, okay?'

'We will.' Maddy smiled. Leanne's youthful energy was contagious. 'Have fun, sweetheart.'

Leanne winked. 'You too, darlings.' She ran back to the group, who were shouting their farewells and thanks to Erik.

'I love the silence here,' Maddy said when they were gone. 'Or maybe I should say peace?' She pointed at the lights of Nice in the far distance. 'It's truly far from the madding crowd.'

Erik gently took her face and turned it towards him. 'I've been waiting for this moment. I wanted to be alone with you.' He bent closer, his lips nearly touching hers.

Maddy's heart beat faster as she felt his warm breath on her face. 'Me too,' she mumbled, aching for the touch of his mouth.

'Please don't tell me you're leaving tomorrow.'

'I won't.' Maddy closed her eyes, breathing in his scent: clean linen and smoke from the barbeque. His breath smelt of champagne and peaches. She was about to say something else, but his lips silenced her. The kiss was light at first, then deeper, and she instinctively returned his embrace, pressing herself against him. She felt safe in his arms in a way she had never experienced before, not even with Tom. Erik was as solid as a rock, honest and true. The feel of his body and his hands on her bare skin made her head spin and her heart race.

He pulled back and took her hand. 'I don't know how to say this without sounding like a dirty old man, but do you want to see my bedroom?'

'A dirty old man at fifty-four?' She laughed and stood up. 'Take me to your room.'

'Are you sure?'

'I can't think of anything I'd like more right now.'

'Thank God for that.' He grabbed her hand, and they ran across the grass to the house, up the steps to the terrace, in through the open glass doors of the living room and up the wide stairs, finally coming to a stop in a big dimly lit bedroom.

Maddy stood still to catch her breath and looked around. 'Oh wow, what a room!'

'It's a bit different from the rest of the house.'

'A bit?' Maddy walked slowly across the deep pile of the carpet in blue, white and sea-green, admiring the paintings on the deep-red walls. There were a few portraits, but the rest were mostly landscapes mixed with some abstract paintings and a few small tapestries in hues of purple, orange and red. The room vibrated with colour; even the king-size bed with its patchwork quilt and piles of cushions was a mass of rich soft patterns and shades. The room was a startling contrast to the Spartan look of the rest of the house. And the smell... Maddy sniffed, trying to make out what it was. 'Patchouli?' she asked. 'And something musky and sensual.'

'Excellent. Do you like it?' Erik asked.

'The room? Or the smell?' Maddy sighed and sank down on the bed. 'I love all of it. I don't think I've ever been in such a seductive, sensual room. It's like – the boudoir of the Queen of Sheba, or...'

He walked across to the bed and silenced her with his mouth on hers. 'I'm so glad you like it,' he mumbled. 'It's my very secret personal space.'

Maddy grabbed the front of his shirt and pulled him down on the bed beside her. 'Okay,' she whispered, her body on fire. 'I get it. You're trying to seduce me, aren't you? And you've succeeded with flying colours. So let's just—'

He laughed. 'Your will is my command.' With the skill of a practised lover, he proceeded to undress her while she removed his clothes.

This was it, she thought, that passion she had felt with Ludo, but never with Tom. With him it had been sweet, comfortable and – dull. Erik's touch lit senses that had been dormant for so long.

Naked, they lay back on the soft quilt and did what Maddy knew they had both wanted to do since their first encounter. She knew this was different from any of her other relationships: not like her short, intense affair with Ludo and certainly not like her lovemaking over the years with Tom. But it didn't matter. This was now and the past was the past. She was entering a new phase in her life, when she would live for the moment and not fret about how it would affect the future. The thought filled her with joy.

Erik was, as she had suspected, an experienced lover but also considerate and gentle. He didn't notice her stretch marks and cellulite, and her pleasure seemed to be as important to him as his own, which surprised and delighted her. His slow rhythm and gentle touch turned her skin to fire, and they finished in a heated frenzy, their breathing laboured, skin to skin: hot, sweaty and, finally, relaxed.

Maddy lay back, her eyes closed and a blissful smile on her face. 'Oh, wow,' she whispered. 'That was hot.'

'In more ways than one,' Erik said, wiping her face with a towel. 'How about a midnight swim?'

'Is it midnight?' Maddy said, alarmed. 'Leanne isn't back yet, is she?'

Erik walked to the open window and looked out. 'No. There's nobody out there. Only the moon and the stars will see us.'

Maddy got out of bed and stood beside him at the window. She took his hand. 'Let's go then,' she whispered.

'Where are you taking me?'

'Wherever you want to go.'

Chapter Twenty-Nine

Hand in hand, still naked, they retraced their steps through the house and garden until they were at the pool, glinting in the moonlight. Maddy climbed down the ladder and sank into the cool water with a sigh, floating, her head back, looking up at Erik, who was still standing on the edge. She couldn't believe the turn of events and she was revelling in soaking it all in.

'Come on in,' she said, splashing her feet. 'The water's lovely.'

He sat on the edge and eased himself in, swimming alongside her until they were at the end, looking out over the still, moonlit landscape.

'Where do we go from here?' he asked, his voice echoing in the silence.

'Who knows?' she replied. 'Do you?'

'No,' he said, taking her hand. 'But maybe that's a good thing. Not knowing but trusting that somehow all will be well. Eventually.'

'Whatever happens, we have tonight,' she said. 'Nothing can change that.'

Much later, they were still at the pool wearing identical bathrobes and reclining in the deck chairs, drinking champagne.

'I have a dream,' Erik said.

'You sound like Martin Luther King.'

He laughed. 'Not that kind of dream. Although it would be much nobler. No, my dream is of a more selfish nature. It's about what I want to do next.'

Maddy sipped her champagne, enjoying the crisp flavour and the bubbles dancing on her tongue. 'Do next? But I thought you'd achieved your dream. Isn't all this everything you ever wanted?'

'Yes. And no.' He sighed. 'It was my ambition to build my own company. It was a huge challenge, but with all such challenges, when you reach the summit, you miss the struggle. When you get what you want, you find you don't want it any more. The saying that it's better to travel hopefully than to arrive is so true. I'm proud of what I've achieved, but I don't want to grow old here. I want to get back to real life, to nature, to—' He paused, looking at her meaningfully. 'To a simpler life.'

'I see what you mean.' Maddy looked at him through the darkness. 'You want something closer to earth, maybe? Where you get your hands dirty and grow your own food?'

He sat bolt upright. 'That's it,' he exclaimed, his voice laced with excitement. 'I've just bought an old farm in Haute Provence. An ancient olive grove with buildings in ruins. Old stones waiting to be built up again. I want to rebuild the house with my own hands, grow olives, fruit and vegetables, keep goats and a few sheep.' He put his glass on the table beside him. 'Please don't laugh.'

'I'm not laughing,' Maddy assured him, touched by the longing in his voice. 'I understand what you're saying. But what about this place? Your company? Who's going to run that?'

'I was hoping Leanne—'

'Ask her,' Maddy said. 'I don't know how she'll react. I mean, she always thought you'd deserted her but now she knows the truth. Being asked to take over your life's work is a huge legacy. And remember, only a short time ago, she only knew you as the father who walked out on his wife and child.'

'But I didn't—' Erik started to protest.

'I know you didn't,' Maddy soothed. 'And so does she. But that was what she had to live with for the past twenty years. She knows what happened now, which must have been a shock. Then you throw all this at her. That's a lot to deal with in a very short time.'

'I suppose. So you think she'll say no?'

Maddy shrugged. 'I have no idea. She might jump at the chance. And if she doesn't, she might in time. You could always appoint a manager for now and then see what Leanne wants later? I wouldn't push her, though.'

He lay back. 'No. You're right.' He touched her hand. 'Thank you. You're a font of wisdom.'

'I don't feel wise,' Maddy protested. 'Look at my own life. Not what you'd call impressive.'

'You were dealt some dud cards. You did the best you could. What do you want to do next, then? Now that you're free to choose.'

'Me? Funny, that's the first time anyone has asked me what I want.' Maddy mused while she stared into the darkness. 'There's a lot to do before I can live my own life. The divorce, sorting out our assets, selling the house. Telling our kids and helping them cope with the situation. I don't think it'll affect them much. They both have their own lives to live. My daughter's in Australia but will come home eventually. My son has just started a career in the hotel business. Then my job… the school. I want to go back and see those girls through to their finals next year. After that—' She stopped. 'I don't know what'll happen.'

'That's a year away,' Erik remarked. 'What about the rest of the summer? Will you stay here with me? I'd love that.'

Maddy didn't reply for a long time. She was taken aback, not knowing what to say. It was such early days. She wasn't quite sure of her feelings for him, apart from a sizzling sexual attraction and perhaps a mutual understanding that might, much later, turn to love. It was too soon to go further, to even contemplate a relationship. Especially after everything she had been through with Ludo and Tom. 'Erik…' she started. 'I can't—'

He took her hand. 'I know. You don't want to rush into anything. I have to be patient. Sorry. That was just wishful thinking. I thought I should say it, just in case.'

Maddy took a deep breath, realising what she needed to do. 'You have to let me go before I can come back.'

'Yes. And I need to sort myself out and get going on the new project before I can make a life with anyone else.'

A car door slammed in the distance. Leanne was back. Time to get back to reality. Maddy got out of the deck chair and drained her glass. 'I have to go.'

He didn't stir. 'Yes. I'll stay here for a bit. To think.'

'Don't be sad. It'll be okay.'

'Eventually,' he said with a touch of sadness in his voice. 'But I won't wait forever, Maddy.'

'Neither will I,' she whispered before walking away.

*

'I think I'm in love,' Leanne said in Maddy's ear the next morning.

Maddy turned in the bed and squinted at Leanne. 'What time is it?'

'Nearly eleven. You slept around the clock. Dad's already up and gone to the office. What time did you go to bed last night?'

'What time did you come home?' Maddy countered.

Leanne sat down on the edge of the bed. 'Uh, around two or so. I found Dad at the pool fast asleep in a deck chair. What did you two get up to last night, eh?'

Maddy sat up, her mind still on what had happened the night before. 'Nothing much. What was that about being in love? With whom?'

Leanne sighed. 'Carlo. You know, that gorgeous Italian guy. He was at the party last night.'

'You mean the tall one with black hair and green eyes? Very handsome, I have to admit. I thought he was a male model or something.'

'I think he did some modelling a while back when he was living in New York. But now he's in marketing. He has started this company with Lucilla. You know, the curvy brunette in the red top and short skirt. Not to mention the Louboutins.'

Maddy stretched and yawned. 'Oh yes. I remember her. Very beautiful. And the shoes – to die for. But she also seemed glued to your man all evening. I thought they were married.'

'No, they're just business partners, he said. They do the marketing for Hovden.'

'He said? What did she say?'

Leanne shrugged. 'I didn't ask her. But whatever. He was very romantic and smoochy last night. We danced under the stars outside this amazing club and drank champagne – and talked for hours.'

'And where was the lovely Lucilla during all this?'

Leanne frowned. 'I don't know. I think she left early. I kind of lost touch with reality there. I mean, the warm night, the stars, this hot guy and me…'

'Sounds fabulous,' Maddy said, the memory of her own evening giving her a burst of pure joy. 'No wonder some of those stars are still in your eyes.' She got out of bed and pulled on a silk kimono she found hanging in the wardrobe. She tied the belt and looked squarely at Leanne. 'So where are we in all of this? Are we going on down to Italy as planned or…? I want to see Naples and drive down that amazing Amalfi coast.'

'How about staying here for another few days?' Leanne suggested.

'I'm not sure,' Maddy said. 'Maybe it's better to leave before…'

'Before what?' There was a suspicious look in Leanne's eyes as she met Maddy's gaze.

Maddy turned and picked up a hairbrush from the bedside table. 'I don't know what I meant really. Before we – I mean you – get involved in something that could end in tears, perhaps.'

Leanne shot up from the bed and grabbed Maddy's hairbrush. 'What are you really saying? It sounds as if you're thinking of yourself here. Is there something going on between you and Dad?'

Suddenly exhausted, Maddy let her arms fall. Words started to pour out of her mouth in a torrent, like turning on a tap. 'Yes. And no. I don't know. I feel drawn to him in a weird way, as if he has been there waiting for me all my life. And the road to him has been long and full of bends and dead ends. But at the same time, I feel scared. I've just left my husband. My lifelong fantasy turned out to be a foolish dream. I can't jump into something new just like that.'

'I know. That would be mad.' Leanne handed the brush to Maddy. 'Here. Sorry.'

'It's okay. I know it must be weird to you – your dad getting involved with one of your friends.'

Leanne smiled. 'Nah, that doesn't matter. Yeah, if it had been someone my age, maybe. But you're twelve years older than me, so you bridge a gap in some way. I think it would be great if the two of you got it together. But you're right. It's too soon for you – and me. I need to get used to the idea and you need to take a break and be on your own for a while.'

'That's true. Thank you for understanding.' Maddy gave Leanne brief hug, feeling relieved that she had got it off her chest. 'But you want to stay around to see if you and Carlo could work?'

Leanne nodded and pressed her face against Maddy's shoulder. 'Yes. I do. I haven't had much luck in love really. I don't think I've ever had a guy look at me like Carlo did last night.'

Maddy let go of Leanne. 'God, I had no idea. I've been going on about me all this time and never stopped to ask or listen to you. What a self-centred bitch I've been.'

Leanne laughed. 'No, please. Don't beat yourself up about it. You helped me when I found Dad. That was my mission on this trip. My love life was a minor matter. Until now.'

'Do you want to talk about it?'

'I dunno. Maybe. A bit, just so you have an idea. There's only you and me here today. So let's eat, swim and relax. We can spend all day sorting out our emotions. And take pictures of us having the time of our lives. That should make the bitches green with envy.'

Chapter Thirty

'Bitches? What bitches?' Maddy asked when they were sitting under a huge umbrella on the main terrace having a late breakfast of crusty bread and strawberry jam.

Leanne's eyes flashed. 'All those bitches with huge, sparkling engagement rings on their fingers. Showing off on social media, filling up our newsfeeds. Those who've been going on and on about their wedding plans and honeymoons in Ibiza and sofa cushions and kitchen islands in their new semi-detached little boxes in the suburbs. Do you know that I am the only one in my class not to be married or engaged?'

'But you left school more than ten years ago. You mean you're still in touch with them?'

'Some of them, yeah. We meet every Friday for drinks in Temple Bar. Used to be a hoot. Now it's just like a show-off club.'

Maddy slipped on her sunglasses. 'Oh. I see. So getting married is the new black?'

Leanne sighed and tore a bread roll apart. 'Yeah. Something like that. But it seems so false somehow. It's all about the ring, then the wedding in some fancy hotel and the wedding dress and what the bridesmaids are wearing, blah, blah. They all merge into one. Some of them have had babies and are pregnant now with their second child. So it's beginning to be more about breastfeeding and potty training and how to cope with a job and family and a career. It's getting to be really boring. And I can't stand the constant needling about me being still single. They can't seem to get their heads around the fact I haven't met a suitable guy yet.'

'So why do you still meet them?'

Leanne stuffed a piece of flaky, buttery croissant into her mouth. 'Don't know. Just habit, I suppose.' She leaned forward with a wicked smile. 'But you know what? A lot of them follow our blog. I bet the semi-detached dream is beginning to fade.'

Maddy had to laugh. 'Revenge at last. Even if the blog is not about that, it's about inspiring women, not showing off. But to those girls in your class, it could be justified. You're having fun while they have to face the reality of marriage. Funny how girls these days think the wedding is the most important thing about getting married. They never seem to spare a thought for their future life or the man they married. But…' She paused. 'Is that what you want? Getting married? I don't see you walking up the aisle in one of those meringue dresses, somehow.'

'Me – the blushing bride?' Leanne let out a raucous laugh. 'Nah, I'm not into marriage and weddings and all that crap. But I still don't want to live alone for the rest of my life either. And children—' She shrugged and looked away. 'Maybe. One day.' She looked back at Maddy, her eyes suddenly full of tears. 'Yeah, I'd like kids, I really would.' She sighed deeply. 'It's all my own fault. I've put blokes off by looking the way I did and my prickly attitude. All that was to stick it to my mam, but I managed to stick it to everyone else as well.'

'Maybe you just picked the wrong men? You've never told me about your love life,' Maddy remarked. 'I don't even know if you've ever been in love.'

Leanne shrugged and picked up her glass of orange juice. 'Sure I have. But it always ended in disaster. I sometimes broke it off myself before he could, when I suspected the relationship was about to end in the toilet. But let's not go there right now, okay?'

'Of course. But if you ever want to tell me, I'm here.'

Leanne put her hand on Maddy's and gave it a squeeze. 'You're a brick, Mads. I do love you, you know. I've never had a friend like you. I've built up a defensive wall and pretended to be tough, but you know I'm all marshmallow on the inside. I built that hard shell so I couldn't be hurt.'

'I suppose you did. Except I thought you were such fun from the moment I met you. And those girls you teach, they all love you. Isn't that why you got an extension on your contract?'

Leanne brightened. 'Oh, I never thought of that. You're a pet for saying that.'

Maddy leant forward and fixed Leanne with a steady gaze. 'You're a terrific person, you know. And you're attractive, fun, intelligent and charming. Don't ever forget that.'

Leanne squirmed and blushed. 'Aww…'

'And look at you now,' Maddy continued. 'All glowing and happy after a night out with a handsome man who seems to fancy you. Aren't things truly turning out for the better?'

Leanne grinned. 'You're right. I'm a right auld misery guts, aren't I? What a total bore. And it's such a grand day and all.' She peered up at the cloudless sky. 'Does it ever rain here?'

'I'm sure it does, from time to time.' Maddy finished her orange juice and got up. 'Come on, enough of this. Let's go for a swim. We need to top up our tans and take some more of those selfies.'

Leanne grinned. 'Work, work, work. What a slog this is.'

'It's a killer. But we do it for our fellow man – I mean woman.' Maddy picked up Bridget, who had been asleep under the table. 'I'll take her for a little walk and pee. You go on. I'll catch up with you later.'

'Okay, darlin'. See you at the pool.' Leanne skipped down the gravel path. Her phone rang as she ran and she stopped to answer. Maddy could hear her say: 'Hi Carlo. How sweet of you to—' The rest faded as Leanne walked away.

Maddy sighed, hoping Leanne wasn't heading for another heartbreak. What she had seen of Carlo did not inspire trust. And an Italian ex-model with those kinds of looks was hardly husband or father material. But Leanne was an adult and must make her own choices. Hopefully they would be the right ones. When Bridget had finished her business, Maddy, deep in thought, walked her on the lead toward the guest cottage to change into the red bikini. As she rounded the corner, she narrowly missed bumping into a tall figure, sending her heart racing.

'Oh!' She backed away and squinted up at Erik against the bright sunlight. 'I thought you had left for the office.'

'Yes. But I'm back.'

'So I see.' Their eyes locked for a loaded minute. Being so close to him after their night together was unnerving. In the warm, velvety darkness, they had whispered things to each other that now seemed too intimate in the bright light of day. The memory of his hands on her naked flesh was suddenly too much for Maddy. 'I'm – going for a swim,' she managed, starting to walk away, her heart beating.

But he wouldn't let her escape. He took her gently by the arm. 'Maddy? It's okay. We're okay, I mean. All is well. Last night meant a lot to me. But we can take it slow and easy for now if that's what you wish.'

Overwhelmed by his smell and touch, she could only nod, even though she wanted to press herself against him and feel his hands on her again. 'Yes,' she mumbled. 'I think that would be best. Let's not—'

He smiled. 'I know. You feel a little embarrassed about what we did, perhaps? Not really your usual mode with men you've just met, I guess.'

'That's putting it mildly,' Maddy said, letting out a nervous giggle.

'But never mind. I came to ask you if you'd like to come for a drive with me. I want to show you the farm I was talking about last night. You know, the one I bought. Do you think that'd be okay? If you're not too busy, of course.'

'I remember.' She noticed a wistful look in his eyes, as if he needed to share this new dream with her, but was afraid she'd think it was foolish. She smiled and shook her head. 'Busy? Oh yes, I was going for a swim and then taking selfies with Leanne. That kind of busy.'

He laughed and squeezed her hand. 'You go on and do that. I'll go and get a picnic together and then we'll meet at the front of the house in, say, an hour?'

'Perfect.' They looked at each other again before Maddy walked away with a swagger that mirrored her mood.

*

Leanne was floating on her back staring up at the sky with a blissful expression when Maddy joined her. The heat was intense as the midday sun stood high in the pale-blue sky and the air was full of the smell of lavender and wild thyme, which Maddy would forever associate with Provence in summer. She slipped into the cool water and swam across to the edge, looking out over the peaceful landscape.

'Don't move,' Leanne shouted. 'That's a gorgeous shot, with you at the edge of infinity.'

Maddy stayed where she was. 'Infinity?' she mumbled. 'That's a dizzying thought.'

'I meant the infinity pool, ya twit,' Leanne laughed. 'Come on. Let's do some selfies.'

Maddy looked up at Leanne's long, tanned legs, the slim body in a blue bikini and the happy smile on her pretty face. 'Give me the phone. I want to take a shot of you from here. You look gorgeous.'

Leanne handed her the phone. 'Careful. If you drop it, you're dead.'

'I won't.' Standing on tiptoes, Maddy took the shot and handed the phone back. 'There you go.' She turned and did a few laps, then got out of the pool, feeling refreshed.

Leanne was uploading the pictures onto the blog page. She glanced up when Maddy climbed out of the water. 'Why are you getting out? I thought we'd float around and talk for a bit. Carlo had some great ideas for the next leg of our trip.'

Maddy stopped drying herself. 'What kind of ideas? Don't tell me he wants to come with us.'

'Not quite, but…'

Maddy faked a yawn. 'You can tell me later. I think I'll go and have a nap. I need to catch up on some sleep.'

Leanne looked back to her phone that had just pinged. 'Okay. I might do the same. See you later. Drinks on the terrace at six, I think Dad said.'

'Perfect,' Maddy said, echoing what she had said to Erik earlier. She glanced at Leanne, wondering if she should tell her the truth; that she had a date with Erik for a drive up the hills and a picnic lunch. But no, she decided. Why stir things up before anything happened? Feeling only slightly guilty at telling a lie, Maddy left the pool and walked into the shadows of the oleander bushes. Her future was hers to make or break on her own.

Chapter Thirty-One

The road wound around boulders and outcrops, high in the hills above the town of Vence and its surrounding villages. Maddy felt as if she was in the middle of one of the *Manon des Sources* movies about the village in Provence, as she looked at the scorched reddish soil and sparse vegetation. As the sunlight bounced off rocks and sandy soil, there was a wild beauty to this landscape, not unlike the Rocky Mountains or the Grand Canyon.

'Gosh, it's wild around here,' she remarked, holding on to the dashboard of Erik's SUV. 'I'm glad we're doing this in a four-by-four. The roads would wreck any car.'

'Yes,' he said, his eyes on the road. 'It's a little rough up here. But still, not too far from civilisation.' He glanced at her. 'You okay?'

'I'm grand. Not getting seasick yet.'

'Good. We're nearly there. Then you'll see it was worth the pain.'

They turned into a narrow track and trundled up a short slope until Erik drew up outside an old house, part of which was in ruins. 'Here we are,' he announced with pride. 'My future home.'

Maddy looked at the crumbling pile and laughed. 'That's a bit of a contrast to your present one, I have to say.'

'I know. But it has more character, don't you think? And wait till I show you the period features.'

'What period would that be, the stone age?' Maddy quipped, wondering if Erik had a screw loose. But as she got out of the car and walked around the house, she started to see the charm of it. At the back, wild roses climbed up the ancient walls and the remnants of a terrace had stunning views of the valley and rolling hills all the way to the deep blue sea in the far distance. Up here the peace had a spiritual quality with the sound of the wind and the distant squawk of a raven high in the cloudless sky. The breeze cooled her hot cheeks and she could hear water gushing nearby. 'You have a stream?' she asked.

'Yes.' Erik pointed down the unkempt garden which was a mass of olive trees and cork oaks. 'In the clearing behind the trees. The water comes from an underground well in the mountains.'

'Just like in *Manon*,' Maddy exclaimed and started to run down the slope to the trees. She found the stream and sank down on the grass to take off her sneakers. Barefoot, she got into the water and stood, her eyes closed, enjoying the feel of cool water washing over her feet and legs.

Erik followed with the bag of food he had brought and put a bottle of white wine to cool between two rocks in the stream. 'It's really what makes this place so perfect,' he remarked as he followed Maddy's lead and took off his trainers, standing beside her in the water.

'It really does.' Maddy squinted up at him in the dappled sunlight and smiled. 'It's a little piece of heaven really.'

He looked at her with such affection it made her blush. 'It is when you're here with me,' he said, as if to himself. He took her hand and held it to his cheek for a moment. 'Pity I promised to be good.'

She looked up at him and moved closer, feeling reckless. 'Maybe you could be released from your promise…'

His smile broadened. 'That sounds good. You're sure?'

She put her arms around him and pressed her breasts against his chest. 'Yes,' she whispered.

In one smooth movement, he picked her up in his arms, carried her to the bank and laid her on the damp, soft grass. It didn't take long for her to whip off her T-shirt and shorts, her cotton bra and knickers joining them among the pebbles on the edge of the stream. He was beside her as soon as he had removed every stich of his own clothing. She found herself admiring his toned physique, not feeling the slightest bit embarrassed in this green, shady space, where the gushing water accompanied the sound of their voices as they made love on the grass under the canopy of old olive trees. It seemed somehow primeval – and so natural – this lovemaking in the old garden, where the crumbling house stood in the distance, watching, waiting for them.

They lay still for a while, eyes locked, smiling. Erik touched Maddy's face. 'Thank you.'

'Please,' she whispered. 'Don't thank me. I didn't do this for you, I did it for me – us.' She sat up and eased herself into the water to wash.

He watched her for a while and then joined her, trickling water over her shoulders and breasts. 'You're more than beautiful. You're – a real woman.'

She kissed him and got out of the water. 'I'm a hungry woman,' she said, laughing. 'Where's the food?'

'In the bag I carried down. There are sandwiches and fruit. Nothing fancy, just bread, cheese and tomatoes.'

'Terrific.' She found the bag and when she had dressed, laid out the food on the grass while he opened the wine. They ate and drank, satisfying both thirst and hunger. Then they talked. The conversation was friendly at first, even loving. But as Erik laid out his plans for the old farm, his future there and how she might join him, Maddy felt a little chill run down her spine. What was going on? He seemed so sure of her and how she would share his dream. He never once asked how she felt about it or if she really wanted to move here.

He stopped talking. 'What's the matter? You look annoyed.'

Maddy stiffened. 'Annoyed? No. But I'm a little puzzled. How can you sit there and be so sure I'll want to join you in this remote place? Didn't I tell you yesterday that I want to go back on the road and see a bit more of Europe before I return to Ireland? That I want to teach for the whole of the school year, remember? And my divorce and my children… Didn't you hear when I opened up about all of that?'

'Uh, yes, but…'

Maddy got up from the boulder she had been sitting on. 'But what?' She hurled the core of her apple into the stream. 'But once you got me here and seduced me with this gorgeous place and the sunshine and the stream and the olive trees, you thought I'd forget all about my own life and live with you?'

Erik's eyes darkened. 'Yes. That's what I was hoping. Who wouldn't love this place? And imagine the life we'd have. It would be a simple life, growing our own food, going to the market, keeping goats, producing our own olive oil…' His voice trailed off.

'Holy shit, you're delusional,' Maddy exclaimed. 'Or just a man, really. I'd be the little woman, is that it? Where do you think we are?

In the nineteen fifties? You didn't even ask if I like goats!' Without another word, she marched up the slope to the house and the jeep, where she came to a stop and burst into tears.

She stood there for a while in the hot sunshine, sobbing, trying to wipe her face until Erik caught up with her. He took her hands and prised them away from her face. 'I'm sorry. Oh, God how stupid I've been. Of course you're upset and confused and angry. Jesus, what an idiot you must think I am. You've just broken up from a long marriage and we only just met, and here I am talking about the rest of your life, as if it's something I have any right to plan. Please forget everything I said. Let's start again. Let's...' He sighed and held her close. 'I don't know what else to say.'

'Just take me back.' She looked up at him, not bothering to wipe away her tears. 'It's okay. I understand,' she said, softening. 'You were in the middle of a dream, thinking it was real. I've been there before,' she added regretfully.

Erik let her go. 'I suppose that's what I was doing.'

'Nice dream. Except—'

'What?'

'I hate fecking goats.'

Chapter Thirty-Two

'We have to get away,' Leanne said the next morning. They were on the terrace outside the main house, where breakfast had been laid out for them under a huge white umbrella.

Maddy put on her sunglasses and sipped cold orange juice. 'Why?' she asked, even though she knew. The night before, she had heard Erik and Leanne shouting at each other in the garden during a flaming row that ended with Leanne running into her room in the guest cottage and slamming the door behind her. Not wanting to interfere or pry, Maddy had gone for a walk with Bridget up the hill behind the house, only returning at dusk. The house and garden had been silent and she was grateful to spend the evening in peace beside the pool, reading and eating a light supper brought to her by one of the young servants before she went to bed. But she hadn't slept, her thoughts about Erik keeping her awake until the early hours. She knew her temper tantrum had shocked him, but she had suddenly felt cornered as he talked about his future plans that he was so sure would include her.

She knew she was falling for him, but it was too soon to go further. She had rushed into marriage when she was very young for the wrong reasons. She had got carried away with her fantasy of Ludo. She didn't want it to happen again. She wanted to try her new-found wings and fly solo for a bit before she committed herself to a new relationship.

She had lain in bed, thinking about it from Erik's point of view for a while, and then it had come to her. He wanted a woman to share his new life, and any attractive woman would do. She had simply happened to arrive at the right moment. Yes, there was a strong physical attraction and they truly liked each other, but it was just a start. She needed to get away and grow as a free, single woman, and he needed to truly want her – Maddy – with all her flaws and difficult sides, and not just any woman who fitted his needs. Time alone, away from each other, was what they both needed – a chance to think and let their feelings grow. Maybe they even needed to miss each other too? Having resolved all this, she had finally relaxed and fallen asleep, dreaming about a little farm in Provence with olive trees and sunshine – but no goats.

'I have a plan,' Leanne announced, cutting in to Maddy's thoughts about her dream the night before.

Maddy blinked. 'For what?'

'For the rest of the summer, silly.'

'Okay.' Maddy spread apricot jam on a croissant, glancing at the open French windows to the living room. No sign of Erik. 'Let me hear it.'

'Dalmatia,' Leanne said, gulping coffee out of a huge bowl. 'The islands. A sailing boat. Let's do that.'

Maddy blinked. 'What? Could you say all that slowly and add in some more words, please?'

Leanne swallowed. 'Okay. Carlo just called me to say that he and a group of friends are hiring a sailing boat to sail around the

Dalmatian islands in about a week. He asked if we'd like to join them. If we chip in, we can hire a big comfortable boat instead of the small cramped ones. He told me all about the Dalmatian islands and how beautiful they are. They sound incredible. What do you say?'

'Will the delectable Lucilla come too?'

'Yes, but that's not a problem.'

Maddy raised an eyebrow. 'Really?'

Leanne squirmed. 'I have no idea what their relationship is, but I have a feeling it's not something serious. Maybe friends with benefits or something, who knows?'

'But maybe you should stay away from him if there's something going on between them? I don't think I'd dare come between an Italian woman and her man. Could end in a lot worse than tears.'

Leanne shrugged. 'Nah, I'm sure she'll be fine. She was very happy to invite us on the trip. And Carlo said she likes us. I don't want to stay here in any case. Dad and I had a row last night. He's trying to push me into joining the firm.'

'And you don't want to?' Maddy asked, wondering if Erik wasn't a tad too pushy about what he wanted from them both.

Leanne sighed. 'Not now. Not yet. It's too soon. We've only just reconnected, after all. Maybe sometime in the future, when I'm a bit older. I don't know. It's just all too much right now. He's such a control freak. Always managing people's lives. I'm sure that was why he and Mam split up. Partly anyway. Obviously Mam played a big part too.' She looked pleadingly at Maddy. 'Ah, come on. It'll be great craic.'

Maddy looked at Leanne's glowing face. The Dalmatian islands? She had never been there. Never even contemplated sailing in the Adriatic. What a mad idea. But she suddenly felt a need to get away too. This could be the perfect way to break away from Erik and give herself the space she craved. It fitted perfectly with what she had been trying to resolve during the night. 'Yes. That'd be fabulous,' she heard herself say.

Leanne grinned. 'Really? Gosh, that was easy. I thought I'd have to beg. I even asked Lucilla and Carlo to come over so they could help me persuade you. Brilliant. We'll set it up so. We'll drive across Italy to the Marche region and take the ferry to Split, where we pick up the boat.' Leanne picked up her phone and tapped in a number. 'Lucilla? She said yes. We're on!'

Maddy could hear Lucilla laughing and chatting at the other end. It would probably be fine.

Leanne hung up. 'So that's all sorted. Wow, how fabulous. I'm really excited now.'

Maddy sobered up. 'But what about the car? And Bridget? Can we take her on a boat?'

Leanne put her phone on the table. 'Why not? Loads of people take their dogs on a boat.' She nudged Bridget with her foot. 'You want to come on a boat trip with us?' Leanne peeped under the table. 'She's wagging her tail. That means yes. And the car will be parked in a garage in Italy until we get back. Easy-peasy. And just imagine what it'll do for the blog. Our fans will love this new adventure.' She leant forward and stared at Maddy over the rim of her sunglasses. 'What's the problem? Cold feet already?'

'No,' Maddy said. 'But I have to get used to this new idea. Everything seems to be happening so fast these days.'

Leanne nodded. 'I know. It's the new era of the quick fix, the immediate and instant gratification. But you have to go with the flow, or you'll be left behind.'

'Scary,' Maddy mumbled, looking out over the garden. Suddenly she heard footsteps on the tiles and felt Erik standing behind them.

'Good morning,' he said and pulled out a chair. 'I heard you saying something about sailing?'

Leanne nodded. 'Yeah. Sailing in Croatia. Our next venue. We're taking off later today to go to Italy and then across to the Adriatic and the ferry ports. Lucilla and Carlo have invited us to share a yacht with them.'

'Oh,' Erik said flatly and poured himself coffee from the jug on the hotplate. He drank slowly from the cup, glancing at Maddy. 'So you're off then.'

She met his eyes. 'Yes.'

Leanne patted his arm, clearly defrosting a little from the tension last night. 'But we'll be back later in the summer. We might stay a bit longer then, before we head back to Ireland.'

Erik nodded. 'Good. I want to talk to you when you come back, Leanne. We need to discuss that matter further.'

Leanne got up. 'Okay, Dad. I'm going for a quick swim. Then we'll pack and get going.'

'I'll finish breakfast,' Maddy said.

'Fine. See ya,' Leanne shouted, running to the pool, Bridget behind her, ears flying.

Erik looked at Maddy, concern in his eyes. 'You sure about this?'

She met his gaze. 'Yes. I think it's a good idea. Great for the blog and great for me, too. It'll give me a little time to breathe and adjust.'

'You're right. Not sure I like it, though. Could I ask you to do something for me?'

'Of course.'

He put down his cup .'Could you talk to Leanne about me and the firm? About her running the company? We had an argument about it last night. She says she doesn't want to go into it right now. Then she refused to talk about it any more. You were right, it's too soon. But when she comes back, I'm hoping she'll be ready to discuss it again.'

'What can I do?'

'You could prepare the ground for me, so to speak. Maybe make her open up about her feelings. Is that too much to ask?'

'No, not at all. I can't guarantee she'll listen, though. It's a huge undertaking. I'd leave her alone for a bit if I were you. You have to let people make their own decisions, Erik.' She looked at him, hoping he'd get her drift.

He looked contrite. 'I know. I can be overbearing at times.' He took her hand across the table. 'Take off those sunglasses. I want to see your eyes.'

Maddy took them off. 'Why?'

'I want to see if…' He paused. 'If yesterday was just a fling to you. Or—'

She squeezed his hand. 'No, it wasn't. Not at all. I felt it was the beginning of something new and exciting. I'm sorry about my outburst. I overreacted. I love your dream. But I'm not sure I can share it with you yet.' She paused. 'Erik, I know you think I should stay and build this new life with you. And it sounds truly wonderful. But I'm not sure it's really about *me*, you see, but just a woman you're attracted to who happens to fit the bill.'

'Of course it's you,' he protested.

'I'm not sure.'

'Don't you trust me?'

She looked at him and met his honest blue-green eyes. 'I'm not sure I trust myself. I feel like you could be right for me and that we could be happy together. But think about it. Do you really believe you can decide the rest of your life based on a few days? I thought it was possible when I was very young, but now I know it's not. Can't you see that?'

Erik looked at her thoughtfully for a while. 'Yes. You're right. It would be foolish.'

Maddy let out a long sigh. 'I knew you'd understand. You're the most complete man I've ever met.'

He touched her cheek. 'Thank you. And now it's time to part. For a while.'

'That feels right to me.'

'Me too, now that you've made me see clearly.'

'I'm glad you feel that way.' Relieved, Maddy stood up. 'We'll say goodbye later. I think we'll be ready to leave in about an hour or so.'

'I'll be there.'

Maddy packed her bag with more than a pang of regret. Should she have stayed and spent a little more time with Erik? No. It would have been the easy option and one she knew would be wrong. It was harder to leave like this, so soon after their wonderful moments together, but she felt a need to be away from him, or she'd rush into something she couldn't control.

She took her bikini from the rail in the bathroom where it had been drying, put it on top of her clothes in the suitcase, glancing out of the window at the hills and the winding road that led to the little farm in the mountains. What an enchanting place. A haven away from everything that was hard and stressful. But could she really see herself there, cut away from the world, living like a hermit? She wasn't sure. It would take a lot of soul-searching before she knew.

There was a soft knock on the door. Maddy went to open it, knowing who it was.

He stood there for a moment. 'I know I should just have waited until you were ready to leave, but I want to give you something.'

'Come in,' she said and opened the door wide. 'I'm all packed. What was it you wanted to give me?'

'This.' He stepped inside holding out a small package wrapped in light-blue tissue paper.

Maddy unwrapped it and found a small green bottle with a stopper. 'It's a bottle of perfume.' She looked at him with awe. 'Did you make this for me?'

He nodded. 'Yes. I mixed the components together in my little lab here and emailed the formula to our main laboratory in Grasse last night. They just delivered it by courier.'

'Oh. Amazing.' Fascinated, Maddy pulled out the stopper and sniffed.

Erik laughed and took the bottle from her. 'Apply it to your skin, sweetheart. You won't get all the notes by just sniffing at it.' He dabbed a little of the perfume on his finger and touched it behind her ears and her temples. 'Like this. On the pulse points.' He lifted each of her hands and touched the inside of her wrists with his finger, briefly brushing her cleavage before he put the stopper back in the bottle.

Maddy shivered at the feather-light touch of his finger. She lifted her wrist to her nose and breathed in the scent. 'It's gorgeous. I can't really smell everything that's in it, but I get a little hint of lavender, lemons and something deeper…'

'Violets,' he said. 'Like your eyes. They're blue with violet flecks. Unique and beautiful.'

'Thank you.' She smelled her wrists again. 'It's divine.' She looked up at his handsome face and touched his cheek. 'The perfect present. Are you going to market this?'

'No. This one is only for you.'

'That's so sweet.' Maddy put the stopper back in the bottle and wrapped it in the tissue paper. 'I'll only ever wear this perfume. And each time I wear it, I'll think of you.'

'That's the idea.' He took her hand and pressed it to his cheek. 'Goodbyes are so hard.'

Maddy smiled tenderly. 'I know. This one is especially hard. But you know what? I'm more and more convinced that we have to be apart for a while. And please don't take this the wrong way, but I'm looking forward to the trip. This has been such an adventure. It has set me free from so much. I'm not ready to settle down yet. I want to fly a bit more, test my wings and get strong again. Can you accept that?'

He nodded and stepped back. 'Yes. I can. I don't want to hold you down. I want you to go and enjoy the rest of the trip, see more of the world and come back when you feel ready.'

'Thank you.'

He shrugged. 'No need for thankyous. It's the way I feel. And now I'll let you get sorted. I'll see you when you're ready to go.'

Maddy was going to step forward and kiss him, but he left before she had a chance to stop him. But it was better this way. No drawn-out farewells or kisses. Plenty of time for that when she came back.

Their bags in the boot, Bridget secured on the back seat, their phones charged and maps ready, Leanne opened the door, ready to get into the car parked at the front steps. 'Where is he?' she grumbled. 'I want to go! I can't wait to get on that boat!'

'Me neither,' Maddy exclaimed. 'Now that we've decided to go I'm so excited.' Her talk with Erik earlier had resolved their problems and now she was eager to start the next chapter of their adventure. A quick goodbye would be best. She looked around the deserted garden. 'He said he'd be here to say goodbye.'

'Maybe he had some business stuff to attend to?' Leanne suggested. 'Will we just go? We can call him later.'

'No, hang on. I'm sure he'll be here.'

Leanne reached in and pressed the horn, the piercing sound making Bridget jump up and bark. 'Come on, Dad,' she yelled. 'We're taking off!'

'Calm down,' Erik ordered as he came out of the house. 'I'm here.' He walked to the car and took Leanne in his arms. 'Bye for now, my wild, wonderful daughter. Have fun and don't forget to write.'

Leanne hugged him back. 'Bye, Dad. Take care. If you follow the blog, you'll see what we're up to. But I'll email you other stuff too. And text and call. You'll be sick of me.'

Erik laughed and let go of Leanne. 'I'm looking forward to that.' His gaze drifted to Maddy. 'Bye, Maddy. Good luck. Come back soon.'

Maddy smiled and walked around to his side. 'We will.' She stood on tiptoe and kissed him on the cheek, her lips lingering for a sweet moment. 'Thank you,' she said.

'For what?'

'For my perfume. And for waiting.' Maddy pulled away and got in beside Leanne.

'That's the hard part.' He leant in touched her cheek. 'Fly carefully.'

She blinked away tears. 'I will.'

'Okay, let's go,' Leanne urged and started the engine. 'I hate long goodbyes.'

Maddy nodded. 'Me too. But this time it's more of an *au revoir*.'

'That's a happy thought.' Without further discussion, Leanne put the car in gear and took off down the drive. 'Don't look back,' she urged. 'Look forward!'

But as they drove away, Maddy turned to look at the tall, handsome figure standing by the door. He lifted his hand and she waved back, knowing that whatever happened next, they would meet again.

When the time was right.

A Letter from Susanne

Thank you so much for reading *The Road Trip*. I hope you enjoyed this mad trip just as much as I did writing it.

If you want to keep up to date with my new releases, please click on the link below to sign up for my newsletter. I will only contact you with news of a new book and never share your e-mail address with anyone else.

www.bookouture.com/susanne-oleary

I love hearing from my readers and would be very interested to hear your reactions to the story. Did it make you smile or even cry at times? Did something in the life stories of Maddy and Leanne feel familiar? And did you love the settings as much as I did when I went there in real life? I would love to hear your reactions to the book in a short review. Getting feedback from readers is hugely helpful to authors, as it might help new readers want to pick up one of my books.

While you're waiting for my next book, you might like to try one of my earlier releases, which you will find on my website: http://www.susanne-oleary.com

Best wishes,
Susanne

 authoroleary

 @susl

Acknowledgements

To my wonderful editor, Christina Demosthenous, thank you for your support and never-ending enthusiasm. Huge thanks also to the team at Bookouture, who have all made me feel so welcome. Hugs and kisses to my friend and star beta-reader Cathy Speight, who read this book in its first rough form before I dared show it to the world. I would also like to thank my family, especially my husband for the cups of tea, TLC and all the words of encouragement during this particular writing journey. Last but not least, my author friends, especially the members of The Writers' Pub, who have given me so much support through the years. I don't know what I'd do without you all.

Made in the USA
Las Vegas, NV
08 March 2023